Oblivious

Stories

By

Howard J. Seigel

Chapbook Press

Schuler Books
2660 28th Street SE
Grand Rapids, MI 49512
(616) 942-7330
www.schulerbooks.com

oblivioustales.com

Oblivious – Stories

ISBN 13: 9781957169934

Library of Congress Control Number: 2024918743

Contents

*Dedicated to Polly, Deborah, and Mark Z.
for their inspiration and encouragement.*

Marty's
Second Chance

Marty's Second Chance

Marty Epstein offered his guests cool lemonade and iced tea. Living room shades were drawn blocking out summer light. Marty sat down on a musty sofa, its springs worn and creaking. His bushy dark eyebrows arched while he spoke.

"Thanks for coming. I assure you it's not a prank. My offer is serious."

Marty Epstein had placed a personal ad in the local weekly seeking men who resembled him: slender, dark dreamy eyes, thick wavy hair, and bonus points for perplexed expression. He tried to be honest in his brief description. Marty isolated himself from people and the foreboding world beyond his modest house. Lonely and wanting outside contact, he decided to shake things up. The proposal: Earn good money for being his double.

"Experience life's enticing events and adventures!" Marty's quirky ad read. He hadn't meant to sound like a sales agent fishing for clients, and was pleased that anyone had responded.

"Earn extra income while you have *fun*. Must be outgoing and at *ease with* people." Marty was none of these things, but wished he could tolerate the company of others more often, even a pet.

On sleepless nights, he lay awake conjuring up soothing images of distant tropical islands, but grew anxious knowing that daylight was soon on its way. His nighttime school custodian job had provided solace and medical benefits (plus a pension), but the position was outsourced due to budget cuts. He was replaced by cheap labor. Marty's unemployment eventually ran out but he remained calm, pretending he was retired at fifty-five, and could now do what he wanted. He told himself that at heart he was a lazy sloth.

Then the inheritance arrived, a tidy sum left by a deceased uncle, which brought financial relief. Marty had money and time, but he needed stimulation. Flustered by his self -imposed isolation, he imagined starring in a late night B-movie, his character lost at high sea, drifting. In the part, he'd be rescued and led ashore by a buxom brunette in a sailboat. Secure on land, she'd put him aboard a luxury train and blow kisses through the window as the train departed. Winding through mountain passes and then wild prairie, he'd finally arrive home to a roaring throng and to an honorary parade down Main Street. He, the lost and returning hero, would describe how the dapper conductor in blue had punched his ticket and soothed him with light banter and good cheer.

"Good morning Sir. Hope you enjoyed the journey. Next stop, Marty's town!"

"You OK Marty?" asked one of the invited guests. Marty snapped from his deep reverie, rubbing his eyes. He wondered how long he'd drifted off.

"Yeah, thanks. Just daydreaming about a train ride, but I got sidetracked. I invited you here and intend to pay well for going on adventures. Ones that I'd like to go on but can't." His voice trailed off. "You'll take risks that I'm afraid of taking."

The promise of a generous advance lured the four of them. Marty handed each an envelope containing cash and a written request detailing what was expected. He became light headed from lack of sleep. Images from the distant past flooded Marty's brain, causing muscle fatigue.

He was only ten, dutifully helping his father stack women's apparel on metal shelves. Young Marty hoisted cardboard boxes of blouses, bras, and nylon stockings.

The sign on the storefront window proclaimed: Epsteins' Clearance Sale! Wholesale Apparel. Marty's exhausted Dad labored and struggled, and wanted his son to become more than a clothes merchant on the Lower Bowery. Marty helped out on weekends and during the sweltering summer months. A young thief once grabbed merchandise and dashed toward the store exit. Marty saw this and reached under the counter for a baseball. He hurled it at the shoplifter and struck him hard in the back. The stolen boxes crashed to the floor, and he let out a grunt. The teen turned toward Marty and cursed, threatening to return and do it again. Dad thanked Marty for being alert but advised him not to take risks like this. Marty kept a special baseball behind the store counter to remind him that he'd someday play with friends when he wasn't needed at the shop. He'd be ready and willing.

Dad cut corners during hard times and postponed fixing a leaky bathroom toilet to save money. For two months, when he or Marty needed relief, they scurried next door to Max's sporting goods. Or in dire emergency peed into a juice carton or jar surreptitiously, behind the counter toward the back. Marty pretended he was counting receipts while relieving himself so as not to attract attention. On break he'd step outside into the gutter to spill the waste from the container. Squeegee men stood nearby cleaning motorists' windshields for spare change. Young Marty wasn't sure if he felt sorrier for these abandoned souls or for himself. He vowed to one day surpass his father and create meaning and fun in his life.

Marty sipped pink lemonade, and cleared his throat. He was nervous. Seated nearby were four strangers, the respondents to his ad. Three were younger, in their mid to late twenties. Marty had a special assignment planned for the one closest in age. It was critical that each was willing to pursue his wishes. Marty studied the faces before him and made quick decisions.

"Let's get down to business. Don't open your envelopes just yet." Marty thrust out his palm as if stopping traffic. "I'll first respond to all your questions. You must have some." Marty began perspiring and was tempted to dash off and hide in a nearby closet. He imagined what it would be like to conduct conversation from inside there.

A hand rose. "I hope these bills aren't counterfeit."

Marty ignored the comment and pressed on with his orientation talk.

"Okay. You're wondering why *I* don't pursue what I'm asking of you. Unfortunately, I don't leave the house. I'm an eccentric." Marty paused, glancing up at the ceiling. "There are experiences I'd *love* to have, but because I cannot or will not leave the house I'm unable to seek them out. I fear going outside and being in public."

"He's agoraphobic," someone said.

Marty eyeballed the group, catching his breath. They stared back, one nodding in sympathy. Marty's shoulders slumped forward as if carrying a barbell on his neck. Then the man Marty's age whispered consolingly. He had an angular face and dark eyes, like Marty.

"Listen. I don't want your money. I happen to know a good therapist who might help you overcome your fear."

"Uh, Phil?"

"Yes, that's right. My nametag isn't showing, is it?"

"I don't go outside, not even for chocolate sundaes or walks in the park. I'm here for good. I have my groceries delivered and I cut my own hair."

Marty swatted at a fly that landed on his arm but it got away.

"What if you have a toothache or need a dental cleaning?" Phil asked.

"Good question. I never said this was easy."

"Listen. Maybe a therapist can come to *you*. I'm sure there's medication for your condition. How long has this been occurring, if I'm not intruding."

Marty nodded appreciatively for his concern.

"It's hard to tell when it all started. I lose track of time." Marty's eyes drifted again toward the ceiling. "When I got laid off I went into a funk and fell into bad habits. I think it's called depression." As he spoke, Marty was determined to go through with the original plan.

"If any of you want to back out, I have no problem with that. But if you choose to accept the advance, then you must go through with it."

"Are we robbing a bank?" Rudy said, half joking, smiling to break the tension.

"No. This is all legal, above board. No one is obligated without their consent." Marty started to apologize as he faced the group.

"By the way, sorry there's no cold beer to offer. But we're not here to watch football on T.V. and bullshit. When done with your adventure, I'd like you to report back to me so *I* can experience what you encountered."

Then Marty swallowed, his throat parched. "I'll trust you to see this through. Please don't disappoint me."

It got dead quiet in the room. Marty leaned over, giving specific instructions to Rudy, who shifted his torso forward. Rudy's job: to attend the funeral of a dear old friend of Marty's from college, whom he'd lost contact with. Marty handed over cash for flowers and for an expensive new suit. Rudy was to tell the family that he was a former piano student of the deceased and was composing a lovely song about the teacher's life and accomplishments. The funeral home was located in the neighborhood and the service would take place in two days. The piano teacher was Jewish and if Rudy desired, he would offer to sit Shiva with the widow. This was optional, and Marty would compensate Rudy for extra time invested. Marty provided general details about the teacher's life so Rudy would be prepared. He had clipped out the obituary from the local paper and gave it to his understudy.

"Remember, it's not necessary to say much. Show compassion through your eyes and demeanor. Like this." Marty leaned forward placing his hand on Rudy's shoulder. "Go ahead, practice on me."

Rudy complied by leaning forward.

"And," Marty continued, "don't disclose anything about me. Much time has passed, and I feel negligent about having lost touch. Do you understand?"

"Yes, Marty. No problem," said Rudy. "I'm your goodwill ambassador and roving diplomat. I'll represent you in dignified manner."

Marty knew Rudy was good for the role. His submitted application had listed work experience in health care and hospice. Rudy nurtured, and enjoyed healing others in need. Marty had noted this on the submitted form that lay on the coffee table.

"Then off you go. Thank you." Marty gave a soldier's salute.

Rudy stood, his lanky frame towering above Marty. He wore a bright Aloha shirt covered in palm trees. Rudy's hand overlapped Marty's moist one, shaking it vigorously, and then gave a thumbs- up gesture while exiting the front door.

Marty refilled the remaining glasses with iced tea. It was a hot July day but tolerable in the darkened house. The living and dining room walls were bare, giving no clues to Marty's past life. Furniture was sparse. The winding staircase led upstairs to Marty's bedroom. One wall had picture postcards from popular places like Reno and Disneyland. Teachers from his former building had donated these for his private collection. His room looked out over a tree lined block of ranch houses. Neighbors had children and small backyards with wading pools and swing sets. He knew no one on the block, sealing himself off from contact.

Then Marty turned toward Justin. Marty guessed his lean physique helped him compete in swimming or gymnastics. Justin's wavy blond hair and surfer good looks placed him on a vintage Beach Boys album, perched atop a shiny sports car with an admiring honey nearby. Here was an unabashed extrovert with no self-doubts. Marty had gleaned from Justin's submitted inquiry that he was between jobs. A software tech slave in a cubicle thought Marty. Justin had disclosed that his funds were depleted by a volatile and edgy stock market. Marty witnessed no strain on his unblemished face. Justin had nonchalantly shared personal information during their initial phone interview.

"You'll like your assignment," said Marty sounding like the recruiter on Mission Impossible, and this made him self-conscious.

"Do I attend a funeral too? Or a wedding with great food!"

Marty stared at Justin, who sat on the far end of the slumping couch.

"This is better than a wedding. I'm sending you on a cruise ship adventure. I've always wanted to go on a cruise, let alone leave my fucking house. Excuse the language."

Justin forced a smile. Phil and Frank, the other two applicants, listened intently.

"I always wanted to learn to dance: Fox trot, Tango, Cha Cha." Marty clasped his hands. "Is this something you can do?"

"Yes! I love to dance. Especially with beautiful women," replied Justin.

"I bet you do."

Marty recalled his high school prom night and what occurred. He would've dropped dead before asking anyone to the prom and had spent prom evening reading the uplifting classic, Grapes of Wrath. He hid and read all night in his small room; and was spared from ridicule and derision if caught on the dance floor.

"You'll enjoy dancing with many attractive women," Marty continued.

Justin turned pale. "You're not asking that I sign on as a male escort and dance with seniors awash in overbearing sweet perfume. Does it?"

Justin lost his cocky edge for a moment and this pleased Marty.

"Don't be ridiculous," Marty countered. "And stop assuming. There are appealing women of all ages."

"How would you know? You never leave..."

"...my house?" Marty glared at Justin.

"Look, you're not applying as an escort. Dress down and relax. Pretend you're the goddamn captain if you desire. *You* choose the dance partners. I don't give a rip which ones or how many, but I insist they receive your best effort."

Marty slammed a fist into his palm and was on a roll. "Tus ojos brillan como la luna. Now repeat that back to me!"

"Huh? What's that?" Justin stammered.

Then Marty's eyes brightened. "You'll make her feel sexy, radiant, goddamn special. Get it?" Marty was getting worked up. His underarms perspired and his shirt grew damp.

Justin rubbed his bleary eyes. "And you're paying for the whole cruise ticket, Marty? You know this isn't cheap. Why aren't you going since you're the expert. Huh?"

Marty sighed. "You're not saving the world from disaster. Bring light and spark into someone's life, even if it's temporary. That's your job."

Marty placed the travel ticket, itinerary, and extra cash in Justin's hand. A travel agent had mailed him the necessary documents. He also conducted business on line when needed.

"I want a postcard from the Caribbean describing your adventures. Include all important details. I'm enclosing a journal too so be sure to note the sumptuous food in your daily entries. No shortcut blogs or texting allowed. I'm handing you a real journal with a pencil."

"Anything else?" asked Marty's surrogate. Marty could see that Justin liked a challenge and was determined to prove himself. He was a risk taker.

"And be careful," Marty warned. "Watch your back."

"Why?"

"Don't upset a jealous husband or boyfriend. You might get tossed overboard to the sharks."

Justin grinned. Then Marty wished him luck and apologized for overdoing the lecture. Justin opened the door and a blast of hot air shot through. Marty turned on a floor fan and clutched instruction papers so they wouldn't blow about.

There were two left: Frank and Phil. But before Marty could continue, he needed to calm down. His pep talk to Justin roused both nostalgic and disturbing memories. While in college he'd fallen in love and grew infatuated with a classmate. He'd known her only a few months, but was drawn to her quirky humor and spontaneity.

They had bonded, and enjoyed being together. Marty asked his sweetheart to take a short summer road trip to Nova Scotia. He had no car and intended to rent for a week. At the rental agency he'd asked if his companion could be added as an additional driver. He was informed that only spouses could be added free of charge, and otherwise, a steep daily surcharge would apply. Then Marty unexpectedly asked Lisa to marry him and briefly delay the trip. Marty could tell Lisa thought he was joking. He suggested they marry and then travel up to Canada to celebrate. His spontaneity stunned and electrified him, and Lisa agreed to the proposal.

The road trip, or honeymoon, had gone well until day four. Marty brought along a AAA guide to help navigate. He feared getting lost by altering the plan and venturing off the beaten path. One clear morning, Lisa veered off the main route and took a side road that meandered around a sparkling glacial lake. Marty awoke from his nap and fumbled for the AAA trip-map.

"What are you doing!" he had barked. "How can you do this?"

Marty noted that Lisa asked herself the same question and he saw his ugly self reflected on her frightened face. He apologized for acting like an immature, rigid stick in the mud. But it was too late. He had ruined a good thing and knew it. They separated and divorced not long after other ridiculous outbursts on their getaway. He had to be in control and do things his way, and wasn't always pleasant to be around.

Marty snapped from his lengthy trance and fidgeted to regain composure. He began sweating and felt as though he'd been lit on fire. He gulped more iced tea to rehydrate.

Marty saw that Frank, a graduate student on summer break, needed an assignment. An avid nature lover, he was pursuing a Geology degree, and had shared this information. Frank had asked Marty to send him into the wild, and far from the city. Marty obliged his request. Frank would embark on a backpack adventure along the Pacific Crest Trail, and snap photos of wildflowers and exotic mushrooms. He'd also identify interesting birdlife and record sightings in a special journal. Marty looked forward to Frank's eventual return and anticipated discussing his findings and observations.

Marty could only imagine the vast wilderness from behind his sealed front door.   As the late shift custodian, waxing and buffing classroom and hallway floors at midnight, he'd wondered: Does a Yellow Bellied Sap-Sucker owe its survival to inhaling tree sap? He envisioned Pileated Woodpeckers at Douglas Fir stands hammering away for hours. He'd taken work breaks scouring National Geographic one teacher kept on her bookshelf. While cleaning the school bathrooms, as Marty gathered toilet paper and soggy paper towels strewn about by careless students, some too immature to flush toilets, he asked himself why he disappointed his parents by never completing a masters degree.

Why don't you have your masters by now, Marty? Why did you stop in the middle? Lazy shit. Some better life you made for yourself!

The voices had haunted him in the silent school halls. And Marty gamely answered back: "I know I could've done better. Sorry I screwed up, but I hate academic pressure. And failure." He'd laugh aloud in the hallways to keep from going nuts. And soon the voices were gone and he was alone with himself, his thoughts, his shortcomings, and fuckups.

"Marty?" Phil's hand tapped Marty's tense shoulder. "I'm the last one. Do you have something for me? I'd love to go on a cruise too."

Marty could see from Phil's expression that he identified with his longings, and understood his lethargy. Divorced twice, Phil once relied on alcohol to get through turbulent evenings that brought on fitful dreams. Weekly AA meetings and male retreats kept him afloat and functioning. He'd worked for state government in Human Services, but budget cuts recently eliminated his position. Phil was landing on his feet and collecting unemployment when he saw Marty's personal ad. He had completed the application figuring he had nothing to lose.

"Sorry, you're not going on a cruise. I'm handing you an outrageous, risky assignment and if you turn it down, I'll understand." Marty broke into a sheepish grin. "If *I* could do this, believe me I would."

Phil inched closer.

"If you're wondering, assisted suicide isn't my plan. If that were true, I'd have you play a full round of golf in the scorching summer heat of Tempe, Arizona. You'd chase down little white balls on the fairway with no caddie or cart. Now that's punishing! Golf is a death sentence for many of us shut-ins." Marty let out a genuine chuckle.

"Well, let's not get desperate," said Phil. He fidgeted with the buttons of his plaid rayon shirt. Phil's black trouser cuffs rolled up exposing pale flesh. His brown eyes and tousled hair matched Marty's appearance and they could've been brothers.

"We anesthetize ourselves from heartache daily," Phil continued, hands spread for emphasis. "Video poker, game shows, daytime soaps. How 'bout those narcissistic show-offs baring their souls on daytime shows. It's competition to see who reveals the most pain. All reasonable escapes I suppose." Phil stretched his monologue further. "How 'bout a trip to the horse track and pick a winner. Are we missing out on the fun?"

Marty listened, showing no expression.

"For big time escape," offered Phil, "I'll take us to the casino. It's only an hour drive. You'll like it, Marty. There's blackjack, the slots, and even an entertaining nightclub act. Dinner's my treat."

Marty listened to Phil's sardonic suggestions and then interrupted.

"Calm down. This is what I need you to do."

He handed over a multipage script with dialogue. Phil studied the script, turned the pages and noted parts written for him and parts for the woman he was to make love to. Phil shook his head.

"Why don't *you* contact an escort agency and have someone make a steamy house-call? You won't have to go anywhere Marty, and receive carnal pleasure. Why have *me* do it? Do you intend to watch?"

"You're missing the point." Marty twirled his hair. "I need you to do what I don't have the gumption to do. I won't watch. You won't have to take notes or describe it like the other adventures I paid others to take. I'll just imagine what's happening. Crazy, huh?"

"Passive," said Phil. "Kind of sad. But it makes sense considering your affliction."

Marty slipped Phil an envelope containing a thousand dollar cashiers' check. Phil needed the money but this didn't feel right.

"So I hire someone," said Phil, "to come to my place and say what you've written." Phil tapped the script with his knuckle. Then he reread sections sub-vocally, rolling his eyes. "There's nothing kinky," complained Phil. "You don't take me for a fool. No whips, chains, or any vile cursing."

Phil's tone grew sarcastic. "Yeah, she'll go for it. She'll think I'm a nutcase with this romantic claptrap about emotional intimacy and spiritual connection. I don't even consummate the act. What good is that?"

"That's right, Phil. Stay clothed if you prefer, while you woo her." Marty could see by Phil's expression that he thought the dialogue was loony. And Marty knew it too, even downright self-effacing. The woman would pretend to experience a loving bond, a deep and tender connection. She would stroke Phil's hair and whisper in broken Spanish or Italian, as scripted by Marty, and caress his body. She'd profess her deep love for Phil despite his fatal medical condition. He'd pretend that prostate cancer would soon kill him and ask to cry on her shoulder. He'd beg to be loved, authentically. Candlelight, incense, wine, and soothing background jazz was optional, but encouraged. Phil would be offered a final chance to experience true emotional intimacy, the grand prize.

Phil placed the script in his lap and sighed. "This is total bullshit and you know it. A farce."

"It's made up and contrived. You'll both be acting," said Marty.

"How can you act out intimacy, Marty? It's something that comes from your heart!"

"Make it come from your heart. Believe it. For the moment anyway." Marty hoped he hadn't alienated Phil with his quirky request.

The script dropped from Phil's lap. He scratched his scalp and dislodged dandruff flakes. Silence ensued while the floor fan blew stale air onto their cheeks.

"Marty, pardon me, but you're one angry, frustrated man. Is this how you let it out?"

"What do you mean? What are you saying?" Marty sat up, attentive.

"Hiring us to pursue your dreams, your concocted fantasies."

"Yes, Phil. Is this a bad arrangement? There's no harm, is there?"

 "Why not pay *me* to get angry for you? I promise to throw tantrums and fits of rage if you'd like."

Marty rocked forward as sweat rolled from his temples and cheeks. "What can you do, Phil? Smash a plate against the wall. Pound a pillow? Or pray at sunrise, shake a fist at the heavens and scream 'why, it's not fair'! I've tried *all* that nonsense." But Marty lied. He tried none of it.

Just then, a hardball came crashing through Marty's living room window, knocking down a lamp. Marty and Phil sprang up and approached the broken window.   Glass shards were strewn about. Next, Marty peeked through drawn curtains, while straddling fallen debris. He covered his eyes to block the sunlight and squinted. A kid about ten with a baseball mitt approached Marty.

Marty and the boy stared at each other through the shattered window- pane, their faces inches apart. He resembled Marty at that age: Skinny arms and slender, crooked front teeth, and an oversized baseball cap covering his forehead. This kid *was* Marty when he escaped the confines of his father's shop and could sneak in fun.

"Sorry Mister. I'll pay for it. We were playing catch and I threw it hard and wild. I wanted to run away but didn't."

Marty peered out through the cracked hole, and sniffed the humid air. His nostrils and eyes opened wide. He saw kids playing ball down the block. Marty assumed that most kids were consumed with inane video games, or texting friends with instant updates. But he was wrong. Being a hermit, what did he know?

These suburban boys were engaged in stickball, a game Marty loved when he wasn't bound to his dad's shop. One kid clutched a broomstick for a bat, with thick black tape snaking up its handle. Marty watched a pink rubber ball sail over two manholes. This was fungo- style: hitting without a pitcher and running imaginary bases, the way he played long before depression and hopelessness set in. Marty grazed Phil's hand and appeared wild-eyed, like a madman sprung from a dungeon.

"You okay, Marty? Don't be upset at the petrified kid. The smashed window was an accident for Pete's sake."

"Toss the intimacy script Phil, ditch it. You're going on a new mission. Lace your sneakers and put on your sunglasses. I hope I'm ready for this."

Marty galloped up the staircase to the bedroom, leaving Phil below. His heart raced, and he almost fell on his face while jumping into Bermuda shorts and polo shirt. Next, he rummaged through the closet for the tattered mitt given as a birthday present by his favorite uncle years ago; the same kind uncle who'd left him an inheritance, and who occasionally took him new places. He was the only person to spoil him, the only one to show Marty a good time.

"What in hell are we doing, Marty?"

Marty scampered back down, his face visibly relieved yet resolute.

"I'm not absolutely sure my friend, but I have a hunch we're embarking on a new adventure of our own making. Please don't disappoint me."

A Lucky Find

A Lucky Find

Natalie stepped onto the Amtrak platform. It'd been chilly and overcast, a Saturday morning in mid-February. The New London rail station was familiar and friendly. She was home, and, it was Natalie's birthday. She carried a backpack across the outdoor platform under the stylish canopy, her mind cluttered with details of her recent messy breakup with Andy. Natalie needed to see her father so she could calm down. She watched out for her dad, anticipating their reunion at noon.

It'd been a soothing and distracting ride down from Amherst, mostly flat terrain, some of it paralleling the partially frozen Connecticut River. Natalie had tried reading a trashy magazine, but mostly pressed her nose against the frosty window, absorbing the barren scene. Tree limbs dangled, rocking with the breeze, exposed to the stark elements. Winter landscape had whizzed by, forcing her inward, grateful to be on the inside peering out. Snow tumbled from the roof of a small farmhouse perched up on a hill. A distant bird soared across the gray sky and disappeared. She couldn't fathom driving this distance in winter, especially in traffic and on roads caked with snow or ice.

Her regular work commute from Amherst to Montague, a sleepy town north of the university, was pleasant and low key. Natalie taught third grade at the lone public school in Montague, and recently joined the staff. She'd done a ten week practicum at the school the previous year and liked it there. While other staff ventured off skiing or snowshoeing in the mountains over the long weekend, Natalie needed to visit her dad, a retired high school biology teacher. She missed spending time together, and exchanging e mail was barely enough to sustain their bond.

She saw him approaching, taking long strides and waving. Soon, Natalie felt dad's comforting arms, her pack strap dangling from the shoulder. The quaint clock tower atop the station roof rang twelve chimes.

"Greetings, birthday girl! How was your ride down?"

"It was okay," said Natalie. "Numbing, but relaxing."

Natalie hugged Dad again, blocking out the train whistle and shuffling nearby. It'd been a few months since her last visit. They sauntered through the station lobby, seeking chewing gum, mints, and a restroom. High ceiling fans turned slowly. The marble walls featured vintage black and white photos of New London's town center and train station from the 1940's. The building displayed an arched entrance, a multi-faceted roof, and elegant brickwork. At the newsstand, a silly postcard caught her eye. It showed an oversized dairy cow devouring an ice cream cone outside a Vermont creamery. Above the cow's head the caption read, 'New England's Finest.'

They exited the station and walked to the parking area on Water Street. It was chilly and breezy, the frigid air penetrating Natalie's clothes and skin. She wore a plaid flannel shirt and wool sweater, a down vest and jeans, and red high top sneakers. A blue longshoreman stocking cap covered her head and thick dark hair.

"Hey dad, you could've bicycled down here. It's only twenty miles and would've got your blood moving. Then I'd hop on the handlebars and make you do the hard work getting us home." Natalie grinned while her nose turned red from the stiff wind.

"Yes, I considered this. But it's thirty outside so I left the single gear Schwinn at home. Now, five degrees warmer, I'd have reconsidered. Don't think you have a wimp for a father."

Natalie breathed frigid air while clearing her dry throat. She then shouted over the wind. "Don't let me down next time. In Amsterdam, they bike through fog, rain, and hail. They're tough cookies those Dutch." Natalie sounded upbeat even though she was sullen over recent events. Seeing her dad helped smooth the rough edges.

They got into the Subaru and drove along the main thoroughfare. Downtown was free of big box outlets while smaller stone and brick buildings dominated. During summer and autumn, tourists shopped on the waterfront and rented pleasure boats on the harbor. Today, sidewalks were almost deserted due to foul weather. Encroaching storms were descending from the Arctic and North Atlantic.

They drove south, near the harbor's choppy waters leading to the Sound. Seagulls flew overhead, and began diving along the shore. The fishing pier was deserted. A ferry boat had just departed, disappearing into the mist.

"Are you hungry, Natalie?"

The heat in the car was turned full blast.

"I'll have a light snack when we get home. Don't want to ruin my appetite for the birthday dinner we're making."

Dad's brown eyes and slender bone structure matched hers. Cooking had been Mom's passion, but now that she was gone, Natalie's dad prepared meals and cleaned the house himself.

Suddenly, Natalie sobbed as sleet pounded the windshield. The wipers picked up speed as the car slowed down. She reached for a tissue while they navigated meandering curves on slick narrow country roads.

"This is nasty stuff, Natalie. When we get home..." Dad placed his hand on her shoulder. "What's up?"

Natalie regained her composure and whispered. "I

know we've been a little out of touch but there's been a lot going on."

"Is teaching going okay?"

"Yes, fine. I'm enjoying school but it's draining by week's end."

Dad nodded. "I know. Thirty years of those rascals and I'm done. Whew." He feigned rubbing a hand across his brow.

They passed a pottery studio and an old cemetery with gravestones from the 1800's. "So, what's up?" Dad fixed his eyes on the road and looked every so often in Natalie's direction.

"Where to begin," Natalie sighed. "It's Andy. I think he's gone berserk."

"He seemed nice, down to earth, when we all had dinner a while back."

"He's changed, completely different now," Natalie said. "How?"

"Well, over winter break, we drove through the Berkshires thinking we'd go skiing. He'd gotten some time off from the software company he works at. Then we came upon this meditation/yoga retreat nestled in the woods and stopped for the day."

They drove past an antique shop and were ten minutes from the house. Natalie glanced out at mist covered rolling hills and at bare branched oak and birch trees. A charcoal sky loomed overhead as black storm clouds hovered above.

"Then what happened?"

Natalie bit her lower lip, shaking her head. "He got smitten with the place and stayed."

"What do you mean?"

"He loved it so much he soon quit his job, packed his bags and moved onto the retreat grounds."

Dad arched his bushy eyebrows. "You're kidding."

"Nope. In fact, when I visited him in mid-January he already found a new girlfriend. Her real name is Linda but she goes by Meadowlark."

Natalie observed Dad's puzzled expression.

"Sounds like a late night B-movie, a bad one. Did you ever see 'Invaders from Mars?' Regular folks have their minds taken over by...."

"Just listen, Dad. No joking around. Thanks." Natalie paused. "I didn't know he had a suppressed yearning for spiritual stuff. I knew he'd grown disenchanted with his job and complained about being stuck in a rut. I listened to his mounting frustrations and suggested we take a week's vacation together, somewhere far away. I just didn't see IT coming." Natalie closed her eyes, tilting her head back, numb inside.

They began climbing the small hill leading up to their gravel driveway. Hand painted birds adorned the mailboxes out front. A local newspaper wrapped in plastic protruded from the opening, and the red handle on top was raised. From the curb, Dad reached inside the mailbox and retrieved bills. He inched up the driveway and shut off the engine. Natalie wanted to stay inside the car. She liked the sound of ice pellets striking the windshield and hood. Natalie glanced up at the two story Cape Cod structure. This was the only home she'd known, never having moved until college. Natalie loved this stability and abhorred upheaval, any loss she had no control over, including Mom's fatal auto accident a year ago.

"I don't want to go in yet, Dad." She placed a cold clammy hand on his arm.

"Okay. No problem." They sat for a minute or two.

"Is Andy still there, at the retreat?"

Natalie nodded. "Yep. When I visited him in January

we had breakfast together in the dining hall. He began eating his oatmeal and I inquired about us, and why he had a change of heart. Then he shushed me!"

"What?" Dad's jaw dropped.

"He put a finger over his mouth and said we weren't allowed to talk, that it's a silent breakfast."

Dad arched his eyebrows. "What's a silent breakfast?"

"At this place you're not allowed to converse during the morning meal."

"What happens if you do? Are you thrown out or fined?"

"I got thrown out. Asked to leave."

"You're kidding."

"I won't shut up. I give Andy the business and tell him I won't wait until after breakfast to clarify things. I insist he break the goddamn rules and talk to me right then and there." Natalie began hyperventilating. "So we leave the dining hall, his bowl of oatmeal sitting half eaten, and guests at the tables are stunned into further silence. Then, I lose it. I yell, whine, and pout, disturbing everyone's meal. That's when staff asks me to leave, but I had it coming." Natalie grew more animated, moving her hands in circles. "And get this, Dad. The retreat director, the head guru, is sleeping with younger women left and right. Can you believe this?"

Dad inhaled through the nose, narrowing his eyes. "How do you know? Was it just a rumor?"

"Andy told me. Others asked the horny guru to leave, and I think he fled somewhere down south, maybe Tennessee, then landed another job at a retreat working his magic charm."

Dad raised an index finger as if making a proclamation. "As they say, 'power corrupts absolutely,' or something like that."

Natalie regretted losing her cool at Andy, and surmised she inherited her occasional temper and sarcastic outbursts from Dad.

Soon, they scampered into the house, dripping wet. Natalie's bedroom was upstairs, still waiting.   It overlooked the modest backyard vegetable garden Dad once tended. Her parents had spent weekends together planting tomatoes, radishes, and lettuce. Mom sectioned off an area for perennials and enclosed the flower beds with cottage stones. Since her death last year, the flower and vegetable garden lay fallow, an empty reminder of her obsessive energy nurturing herbs and plants. Dad had lost interest in the garden.

In summer, deer came through and ate what they wanted until a fence eventually went up. Natalie peered through the white curtain at the surrounding hillside, grateful that her private sanctuary was preserved. Many familiar neighbors still lived down the road. Their kids were now grown and scattered about the area.

Natalie rested on her bed sipping hot tea, unwinding. She reached into her backpack and removed a pair of sweatpants to change into. Then, something fell from inside the nearby closet. The loud noise rattled Natalie and she sat up. This closet once emitted spooky sounds on dark stormy nights when her folks left for a movie or dinner. She'd been alone, curled up in bed with a book. In her mind, the closet held an intruder, a stranger, waiting to pounce. Natalie had clutched a frying pan, or a bat,   too petrified to surface from the covers and investigate. That was then, Natalie reassured herself, taking shallow breaths.

Natalie opened the closet door and searched. It smelled a bit musty, like mothballs. She ran long thin fingers over the cotton fabric of some blouses and shirts.

Dad's voice from below startled her. "Are you okay? I'll steam some broccoli and beets for dinner and I'll bake chicken. You can throw together a salad when you're ready."

Natalie's head was buried inside the closet inhaling familiar scents. When five, she'd cleared the dinner plate by discreetly stuffing the beets under the couch cushion. The repository evolved into a compost pile, and was soon discovered. Her irate mom had thrown a fit and punished her. Natalie grew to appreciate broccoli and beets though.

She poked her head further into the closet, looking for the source of the crash. Then Natalie discovered what had made the noise. A cardboard shoebox had fallen from the top shelf and burst open, spilling its contents. Splattered on the closet floor were assorted photos, postcards, and letters. She bent down to inspect. At her feet was a music box, a high school graduation present from a nearby cousin she'd grown up with. They were like sisters. What a find, Natalie thought. She wondered what had become of this misplaced music box. It was lacquered, with swirly designs painted on top.

Natalie held the artifact in her hand and blew off dust. She brought the box over to the bed and opened the lid and turned the attached key. The romantic and maudlin Doctor Zhivago theme played. She and this cousin had watched the entire movie twice, including the perilous fall of the White army and czar. Natalie had hummed the plaintive tune repeatedly while recalling the film's doomed love and misery. The hypnotic music box melody had cushioned lonely Saturday nights when bored. She placed the box on the nightstand for safekeeping.

Next, she returned to the closet and bent down to gather photos and old letters. Amidst the pile was a worn paperback dictionary, its pages loose and protruding. She remembered her favorite high school English teacher, Mr. Frank, the eccentric man who wore a bow tie and short sleeves through the frigid winter months, marching to school without a coat like a soldier on a mission. He'd stuff a textbook down his pants, for posture he said, and to alleviate back pain. Natalie had once jokingly asked if grammar textbooks worked as well as history books and got a blank stare. Mr. Frank was intoxicated with vocabulary words, forcing students to memorize twenty five definitions each week, and she became obsessed. She had risen at all hours to look up new word meanings and applications, having taken the pocket dictionary to the toilet. She'd worn that faded book to a pulp by taping the pages, and refusing to replace it.

Under the dictionary lay grainy prints of her and a friend clowning in a Woolworth photo booth. Natalie examined the black and white collage strip costing a dollar. It had taken forever for the distorted photos to emerge from the clumsy machine after the red light flashed. She had imagined a mischievous gnome doctoring print images from within the lens, and winking at those mugging for the camera while posing inside drawn curtains.

Natalie combed through an assortment of artifacts, carefully placing the loose contents into the torn box. She'd kept high school letters that bore no relevance but resisted tossing them.

Finally, Natalie glanced at a worn newspaper clipping depicting a mangled sedan lying in an embankment, its smashed windshield covered with tree branches and fallen debris. She shook in revulsion while stuffing the grainy photo into a nearby drawer. Chills and nausea made her dizzy and she stumbled to the bed. By leaving the news article buried in the drawer, she wouldn't have to envision

Mom's grisly auto accident. Natalie had had no desire to view Mom's disfigured body at the funeral home before cremation. That ugly episode had all been a blur.

The storm outside grew nasty as snow and ice pelted the windows and roof. Dad climbed the stairs, stopping halfway up.

"Are you okay, Natalie? Are you resting?"

"Yes, Dad. I'm going in for a hot bath. Be down shortly." Natalie pretended to be calm.

An hour later, Natalie found Dad half asleep on the couch with an unfinished crossword puzzle in his lap. She bent down to peek at a word clue and couldn't resist waking him. She rubbed his shoulder and he roused.

"Where was I?" Dad put on his glasses. "Six down. What's the name of a former Soviet republic, ends in 'stan' and borders Iran?"

Natalie scratched her head and guessed. "It could start with 'Kaj' or 'Turk'. I'm displaying gaps in geography knowledge. Sorry."

"No problem. I don't usually finish these anyway."

She watched him place the puzzle on the cushion, remove his bifocals and secure them in his cardigan side pocket. Natalie stepped over to the window and witnessed new, wet snow. A fierce wind picked up, knocking down tree branches. Dad ran a hand through thick wavy hair, and stared out the window. It was approaching five and becoming dark. Natalie moved from the window and sat on a floor cushion nearby him.

"So Raymond, tell me what you've been up to recently."

She addressed him that way as an endearment, a respectful way to level the playing field between father and daughter.

"Not much. Not much at all." His voice dropped.

"I've had this desire to not leave the house." Raymond leaned forward.

"Why's that? I hope you're not becoming a loner, a hermit. We can always procure a companion pet but those allergies will flare. Can you part with your own stimulating company?"

Raymond forced a smile. Natalie acknowledged his reluctance to open up, but also knew he trusted her.

"It's hard to explain. Since I retired a year ago, around the same time Mom died, I haven't felt the urge or need to get out. Not that I was ever the man about town to begin with." Raymond paused. "The only friends we had were a few other couples. I don't want to bother them."

"Do old friends contact you?"

"Now and then. But I make excuses not to get together."

"You're just stubborn. How can you stay sane when you lock yourself away and not share your quirky ways."

Natalie could see that Raymond was down and tried lifting his spirits. She wanted to nurture *him*, for a change. Natalie could relate to foul moods, suppressing sour feelings at work so she could function effectively. But come weekends, she wept and ruminated over her recent breakup with someone she very much cared for. Or the person she envisioned but who'd change.

"You need to find a hot date, Raymond. You're still not bad looking, and, available women want to meet an offbeat character like yourself." She winked at him while delivering her pep talk.

Raymond nodded and chuckled. Light from the antique table lamp reflected off his angular jaw. She worried about him but didn't want to show it. Natalie had once tried antidepressant medication but didn't like lingering side effects, and stopped. And she wasn't going to recommend this approach to Dad, who'd refuse to consider taking anything other than a vitamin or aspirin.

"To be honest, I don't miss people or conversation. Most of the blabber is boring drivel, background noise." He reached over for a sucking candy. "I'm not turning into an old curmudgeon I hope, but have you listened to the inane nonsense blaring from cell phones? You can't hear yourself think!" Raymond stroked his chin, elbow planted firmly on knee, still hunched forward. "No patience for small talk, a waste of time. Is anyone really connecting in any meaningful way? I doubt that. Perhaps I'm a stubborn fool who's content being a loner."

Natalie agreed with his assessment regarding inane banter. She thought about her last phone conversation with Andy, who'd returned her call from the yoga retreat center. They had exchanged mild chitchat before Natalie confronted him, again, long distance. She replayed the banal, silly conversation over in her mind while Raymond stared ahead, now upright on the sofa. Natalie recalled asking Andy about his plan and new goals, and if they as a couple might reconcile. Andy described his desire to market travel underwear, ones that would dry overnight. This way he explained, you'd only need one or two pair on extended overseas adventures. She thought his idea both whimsical and practical, and then wished him luck trying not to sound too hurt or sarcastic.

"You okay, Natalie? I guess we both zoned out. Let's get that salad going, shall we?"

She shook her head as if woozy. Natalie recoiled from major change and surprise. Andy's recent actions triggered fears of abandonment and she didn't like that.

"How long were you and Mom together? Close to thirty years?"

"Yep. And she's *never* coming through that front door again. Guess I need to move on."

"I liked how you amused her with silly pranks. She ate it up."

Natalie recalled how he'd poke fun at himself, at his own perceived futility fixing things, once climbing the roof and pretending to swing a hammer while Mom did the actual repair below. Natalie had stood next to Mom and watched her giggle at his false bravado. He often assisted at home upkeep, but wanted her to take the lead and get the credit.

"How long did you and Andy know each other?"

Natalie winced. "A friend introduced us over a year ago. We had discussed marriage before he went off the deep end. He's a good guy I suppose, with a goofy sense of humor. He loosened me up, but we're off in different directions. Kaput. I'm upset at him for surprising me out of nowhere. Perhaps I'm too rigid and not flexible."

Natalie exhaled. She wanted to know more about Raymond's current situation. "If you're bored as widower, you can join the Peace Corps and teach conservation or biology in rural areas. You need an adrenalin rush, and to reinvent yourself." Natalie didn't like adrenalin rushes herself, preferring consistent and predictable routine.

Raymond's hand rose. "Let's be realistic. I could volunteer around here leading botany and birding trips. But I've led outdoor school for years. A little more time and it'll all fall into place. I'll find my stride again." Raymond slouched forward, eyes cast downward.

"Check out this thick mane." Natalie ran fingers through his scalp. "Men *your* age would kill for that. Don't sell yourself short, buddy. You're not up all hours of the night dousing your hair in replacement formula. Just call 1-800 for a free trial..."

"No," Raymond broke in. "I'm awake at night battling insomnia. I keep the werewolves and bats company when I can't sleep."

"Then invite me to the party next time. Your nocturnal friends could use a little company. I'll bring the brie cheese and wine."

Raymond began a reply but was cut short when the lights flickered and went out. They sat in the dark for a minute or two as the storm raged on, rattling the blinds.

"I've got candles by the sink," Raymond said. "I'll get a few from the kitchen."

"Save some for my grand birthday celebration."

Raymond returned with a long thin candle. He set it on the coffee table while wax dripped into a small glass holder. "A power outage means no heat, so let's get a cozy fire going," he said. "Sound good?"

They moved to the fireplace, and after a failed attempt, got a fire started with old newspapers and a split log. Freezing rain and sleet pounded the roof. Raymond secured a down comforter for warmth.

"This outage is a bit eerie," said Natalie. "It reminds me of holing up under the bedcovers during a raucous summer thunderstorm."

"Ever wish you had an annoying sister or brother to pester?"

Natalie chuckled at the suggestion. "I enjoyed the lone spotlight and the attention and control. You know that." Natalie's face grew solemn. "Mom was quite reserved and distant. I wonder what made her so driven at times." Natalie sighed. "I wish we'd gotten on a bit better, laughed together occasionally."

"Don't say that. Mom is liable to hear you and whip up this ice storm worse than it already is."

"I bet she'd give us a hard time if she could hear us,"

said Natalie. "She'd say we weren't getting enough done by sitting around and chatting."

Natalie reached into her sweatpants pocket and removed the small wooden music box she'd found earlier. She held onto it. "Guess what I discovered in my closet this afternoon?"

"Something was happening. I heard a bumping sound from below. You weren't throwing a temper tantrum over Andy?" Raymond winked. "And it's time to move on and find someone flawless, like me."

Natalie suppressed a laugh. She held the music box at eye level and opened it. A plaintive lullaby filled the room. It replayed a few times as they listened by the crackling fire. Natalie placed the box in Raymond's hand. She noted his long thin fingers, rounded at the tips.

"I bequeath this artifact." Natalie continued with her speech, overdramatizing. "May it heal and release you from turbulent restless nights. Sustain thee through loneliness and fatigue."

Natalie could tell Raymond enjoyed the attention and levity.

"I can use a lucky charm. A great find, thanks."

"Let it provide comfort and solace on chilly winter nights."

Raymond nodded, and glanced up at the clock which had stopped. "I've a surprise for *you*. So I don't misplace it, hold onto your offering. Be right back."

Raymond dashed off to the kitchen. He soon returned with a lopsided chocolate cake, an earnest first attempt. It appeared smashed in and concave and contained crooked candles.

"For you, even if it's deformed."

Natalie sat cross legged with eyes shut, and made a

wish. In her reverie, she romped through a field of towering sunflowers on a breezy summer morning in southern France. Everything was in perfect order, just right. She lay down on the spongy ground, absorbing the sun's glow. A castle came into view and she stood and decided to explore. As she approached the tall stone structure, a slender young man could be seen through an open window, eating porridge at a plain wooden table. It was Andy. He wore his special overnight drying travel shirt and pants, the wash n' wear underwear folded on the kitchen radiator. Ravenous, he devoured his oatmeal. Andy spotted her and waved, imploring her to enter. She smiled and reached into her back pocket for the hemlock poison she'd slip into his hot chocolate while embracing him. She'd bury Andy, his body forever preserved like a mummy wrapped tightly in his lightweight durable travel clothes.

Natalie felt chilled and opened her eyes, and blew on the candles. She liked the darkness and the power outage. It was cozy inside with her dad present. She suppressed thoughts about soon returning to work or about Andy. Perhaps he'd drop a line from somewhere tropical and exotic, spewing mystical revelations.

She told herself she didn't care and vowed to initiate a fresh start. Her precious visit with Dad was brief, and wouldn't let random distractions sully their reunion. These blemished fragments of Andy had become a nagging burden and she craved a release. And Natalie found one. She would create new images, fresh ones.

"I've got a nutty idea."

"You dozed off. Your eyes were shut like you were meditating, or obsessing."

"Obsess? I'm done with that." Natalie grinned, her eyes opened wide. "Let's plunge into the storm and take photos."

Raymond shook his head. Natalie expected him to dissuade her, but she was determined.

"Then go ahead. I'll sample the cake and stay dry and cozy." He touched her shoulder. "Return soon or dessert will be gone. Dress warm and stay way clear from downed power lines, okay?"

"Yes. I'll be careful."

Natalie grabbed Raymond's poncho and flashlight from the hallway closet, and ran upstairs for her digital camera. She pushed out into the chilly night, her poncho flapping in the breeze, and wishing she'd grabbed a warm parka instead. No stars were visible and Natalie saw her breath. She discerned a faint outline of Raymond through the frosty window, watching him stare in her general direction. Falling wet pellets soaked her hair and as she moved to the backyard, moisture seeped up through her soles and wool socks. Her nose turned red and cold.

She snapped photos of twisted branches and white rooftops now covered with snow. She noticed a cluster of stones next to the house and under the eaves, and moved toward it. A plastic zip-lock bag protruded from under one of the stones. Natalie bent down to inspect, ready to take another picture.

With chilled hands she retrieved the bag, and shone light at the photograph preserved inside. She balanced the flashlight between her knees and examined the print. It showed her parents digging in the dirt, side by side, planting tomatoes or radishes on a summer day. Natalie had taken the photo months before Mom's death, her parents unaware that she'd sneaked up on them. Natalie recalled giving the memento to her dad for the family scrapbook, but it ended up here.

The wind picked up. She tucked the print into the zip

lock, placing it securely under the same stone. Natalie glanced up at the sky and wiped away a tear. She glimpsed the outline of a crescent moon that emerged from dense cloud cover. When her dad wasn't looking, she'd furtively slip the music box into his cardigan pocket for safekeeping.

Natalie went back inside the house forcing the front door shut. Wind gusts toppled tree branches and roared. Power to the neighborhood was still cut off but candles lit the cozy living room. Raymond lay back on the sofa, asleep. An open bottle of gin stood on the coffee table. Natalie heard him snore. She walked over and tapped his shoulder. Raymond roused from his slumber rubbing his eyes. He shook as if emerging from disturbed sleep.

"You're back safe and sound. It's nasty out there."

Natalie picked up the gin bottle and shot glass.

"Bottoms up," said Raymond. "We'll toast."

"I thought you'd bring out champagne, not hard liquor."

"Huh?" said Raymond, scratching his chin. "I happen to have an unopened bottle of champagne in the fridge. I'll get it."

Natalie touched his shoulder, gently guiding him back onto the sofa.

"It's okay. Pour me a shot of whatever you're having." Natalie noticed a newspaper article on the coffee table. She picked it up to read, but the candlelight was dim. Raymond tried to snatch it from her.

"Don't read that, Natalie. It'll upset you."

Natalie noticed the local headline dated a year ago. It was the same article, but in better condition, than the one she'd stuffed in her bedroom drawer that afternoon. An enlarged photo showed a wrecked vehicle toppled on its side in an embankment. Natalie began to whisper-read, forgetting that she'd skimmed this story shortly after the accident. Now she needed to read it aloud from start to finish, detailing the crash and the ensuing sections depicting Mom's community involvements and volunteer work. It had been a blur, but Natalie recalled close friends gathering at the house to celebrate Mom's life and generous spirit. Her urn had been placed on top of the fireplace. A friend or two had sung and performed a musical tribute.

Raymond asked Natalie to stop reading.

"Why is this out here? Is there something you need to tell me?"

Raymond sighed. "The story is about how mom died."

"I know what happened," said Natalie. "I rode the train home after your frantic phone call describing the accident. She suffered head trauma and died instantly. The roads were slick and you skidded and crashed into a tree. You were returning from a holiday gathering, right?"

Raymond poured them each a gin shot, and added tonic water to Natalie's drink. He fidgeted, and to Natalie, his face appeared ashen.

"Yes, the pavement was slick as we rode a dark stretch, a few miles from the house, around midnight. I used the white line to the right as a guide. The article doesn't mention why I skidded."

Natalie locked eyes with Raymond. She didn't touch her drink but still clutched the article. "You skidded because the road was icy and lost control."

Raymond downed his shot and promptly poured another. Natalie held up her hand, surprised that he was drinking so much.

"Dad, put the drink down. There's a logical reason why you crashed, considering the weather conditions. I know all this. And it's not entirely your fault."

Raymond relit the candle on the table. Then he moved closer to his daughter, who always adored him. In Natalie's eyes, Dad could do no wrong. She realized this prevented her from accepting flaws in a romantic partner. Few could measure up to Dad, who she saw as predictable and steady. And she hated surprises.

"Sweetie, I have a surprise and it's not a pleasant one."

Natalie flinched. Sometimes when upset, she'd scratch her skin until it became red and splotchy, and raw.

"What surprise?"

"The article omits some details: What the police don't know, and what the insurance company doesn't know is that I fell asleep at the wheel. Because I dozed off momentarily and conked out, I skidded and overcorrected, and drove us smack into a tree."

Natalie saw the blood drain from Raymond's face. The light from the candle cast an uneven shadow on his pale cheek.

"I killed mom. I screwed up and killed her."

"Shit. You're not serious."

Natalie's heart palpitated. Her stomach knotted. She didn't know what to say or how to comfort Raymond, who downed his gin shot. Natalie reached into her pocket and placed the music box on the coffee table. She opened the lid and the lullaby played. The burning log in the fireplace died out.

Raymond reached over, touching Natalie's arm. "Sorry. I couldn't bear to tell you. I've kept it a secret. I'm so sorry." Raymond lowered his head.

Natalie tapped his moist hand. "You've carried an awful burden." She cleared her throat. "May I ask if you were drinking at the holiday party before returning home? Did you consider asking mom to drive?"

"Good questions. No, we weren't drinking, except for a

little rum in the eggnog earlier in the evening. I felt lucid, fine, just a tad sleepy, but I wasn't going to drift off like I did."

Raymond continued in a whisper. "I didn't feel the need to ask mom to drive. I was fine when we set off. I even volunteered for a sobriety test at the crash scene and passed easily."

"So I forgive you, dad. I really do. I don't blame you."

Natalie grasped his hand. "But how will you ever forgive yourself? Answer me, please."

Natalie was surprised at the authority in her voice.

Raymond sat erect, and took shallow breaths. "I don't know. I don't know."

"Have you considered getting help?"

"What kind of help? I wasn't hurt in the accident, just a few scrapes and bruises."

"Counseling," Natalie whispered. "Someone to listen and assist you work through the trauma."

"No, I've never gone to anyone for this kind of help. Your mom was always there." Raymond paused. "I'm just stubborn and defiant."

Natalie wanted this nightmare over. "You better relieve your burden, or you'll die broken and miserable. Mom would forgive you for the accident, but she'd give you hell for making yourself suffer like this."

Raymond tilted his head to the side, his eyes narrowing and turning misty. "Why didn't the side air bag deploy like it was supposed to? Doesn't it activate in a roll over? Her neck was broken from the blunt force." Then Raymond snapped his fingers. "I can't believe she's gone."

"I can't either. And you hid details from me!"

Natalie realized that ruminating over Andy was petty and foolhardy, and almost laughed in derision. She chided herself but had needed comfort. Meeting someone new lost its urgency and the idea of a boyfriend seemed downright silly. And she wouldn't expect the moon and the stars or perfection from anyone. She'd wait long and hard before prying open her heart.

Raymond stroked his hair in a daze. "I got a phone call from an old teaching colleague last week. Do you remember my friend Dennis? I think you took his American History class before graduating high school."

"Yes, I do. He's a great teacher, like you. Is he retired?"

"We retired the same year. I do see him occasionally."

"What's he up to?"

"He stays busy. We have lunch and a couple of beers now and then. Well, he phoned last week wanting to reconnect but I turned him down. I said I couldn't right now."

"Why?"

"I'm returning his call next week to accept his offer. After all, the phone's not ringing off the hook. I could use an excuse to get out and spend a little time with an old friend. Maybe, just maybe, I'll get a thing or two off my chest. Dennis and I go way back. He'll understand."

Natalie didn't know if he'd ever forgive himself, but *she* would. And remind him again that his job was to survive and grieve, and distract himself to remain sane. Natalie opened the music box before placing it in his cardigan pocket. Then she hugged him and wept. Raymond caressed and patted her on the back.

A few lights flickered in the living room and kitchen, but as the power was about to be restored, everything went dark again.

The Doogan Man

The Doogan Man

Sara Shapiro was settling into her new rented apartment in the East Flatbush section of Brooklyn when she made an unusual discovery. She found it tucked in the corner of her bedroom closet. Sara had been removing clothes from boxes and folding a sweater when she spotted the small spiral notepad. She bent down to inspect, blowing dust from the cover. The notepad resembled a student's homework ledger. Sara had retired from teaching high school English and required freshmen to record assignments in notepads like this one.

The writing contained unintelligible scribbles and smudged pencil marks that might have once made sense. These may have been anecdotes or journal entries. While flipping pages, Sara noted various lists containing food items and delivery dates. She brought the notepad over to the dining room table and put on reading glasses. Sara sipped instant coffee, having all day to decipher the scribbled code. She had all the time in the world. Children shouted below her third floor window, chanting rhymes while jumping rope on the front stoop. Her renovated brownstone sat on the corner of a busy street. Flowerpots decorated neighbors' windowsills. The area was safe, even at night, but Sara loved staying put. She fell asleep to the television, her antidote to insomnia after reading for hours.

While in her twenties Sara attempted a novella with a morose ending, but never submitted or mentioned her project. Writing the piece had depressed her. She vowed to revise and create an uplifting outcome, but it never happened. Her old manuscript lay buried in a trunk, wedged between musty texts accumulating dust.

Sara studied the notepad contents and its numerous lists, concluding they were baked goods items or food inventories. Toward the middle section the writing became legible and Sara confirmed that this was a diary. Perhaps the previous tenant had mistakenly left it behind. On the surface, fragments told a mundane story of an ordinary person. But Sara read more into it. She flipped to the inside back cover, and noted the scrawled name of Charlie Doogan. In parenthesis he'd written 'Doogan Man'. Sara reread Charlie's entries and grew intrigued with his routine. Parts were crossed out, and Sara decided to restore this artifact by filling in the blanks. Sara wanted to begin anew and write an uplifting ending. No jilted lover, tragic mishap, or filed bankruptcy.

Sara hoped that he wouldn't mind her taking liberties to embellish a few sections. She'd safeguard both their privacy by storing the manuscript in a locked trunk. She'd leave notes along with Mr. Doogan's original entries for a new tenant's eyes and imagination, if she moved or left this world for good.

I'm squeezed for time, Charlie Doogan muttered during his regular morning delivery. He maneuvered his lumbering white truck down narrow streets, watching for potholes and sinkholes. The truck was rickety and if he wasn't careful, he'd blow a gasket again or throw out the clutch. Charlie stood as he drove, his head barely touching the metal roofing. Gears squealed and ground while he manipulated the tall stick shift. Charlie inherited the white truck along with the business from his immigrant father, Max Dugganvitsky. A Russian Jew, Max had Americanized his surname to blend in and assimilate. Dad taught Charlie the baking trade, but died soon after retiring from heart failure and an ensuing stroke. Charlie always craved Dad's approval.

"Doogan Man!" Charlie yelled out the window. He rang bells that drooped from the rear view mirror. Other trucks would whiz through this morning: A milk truck, one selling sodas and seltzer, and a merchant who sharpened knives.

Charlie the 'Doogan Man' sold pastries from the back of his truck. He awoke at three each morning and baked all kinds of pastries in his leased storefront space. Then he placed them on shelves in the vehicle rear compartment. His specialty: Danish, donuts, and marble bread. He mused that when he died and left this Earth he'd distribute free goods to the deceased. They'd love him and know he was the supreme baker of the universe. His savory apricot cheese Danish would transcend time and defy gravity.

Sara bit into a rock hard cinnamon roll while scribbling on yellow legal sized notepad. The pastry she'd purchased from the grocery had turned brittle and overly sweet. Sara scolded herself for neglecting to place it in plastic to keep fresh. She was absent minded when it came to practical matters, too absorbed in other endeavors. Crumbs fell onto the writing pad as she swiped them onto the countertop. Drawn shades blocked out natural light. Sara had turned off the phone ringer, eliminating all distractions, but the odds of someone calling were rare. If a telemarketer or wrong party made contact at a private moment, she'd hang up. Sara sipped her black coffee, and dropped in a sugar cube. She reached for a sharpened number two pencil and placed it between her lips, lost in thought.

Business was good but he had to hustle. On Fridays, Charlie drove his truck into Queens from Brooklyn, delivering to shops and special customers. The old truck's top speed reached forty-

five miles per hour, and Charlie once mistakenly entered the Brooklyn Queens Expressway in fast moving traffic. He thought he'd die of heart failure as drivers honked, jeered and cursed at him for crawling. He now took the Interborough Parkway on Fridays, a meandering highway with narrow lanes and slower speeds. The road wound like a snake in sections. He'd learn that the parkway's name would change, in honor of Jackie Robinson, a favorite Brooklyn Dodger.

That's when all hell broke loose. While negotiating a tight curve, his vehicle swerved, and he landed partway in the adjacent lane. He recalled his recent collision with a seltzer truck and had shuddered at rising insurance premiums. Charlie over-corrected by turning the large steering wheel sharply to the left. He began losing control of the wobbly truck. His baked goods jostled around and fell from their trays. Then he rode over a huge pothole, crater like, which forced the back door ajar. Charlie thought he latched the door, but the bump's impact forced it open. Glancing out the side mirror, Charlie observed pastry hurtling through the air. He saw Danish and jelly donuts splatter onto pavement, as one plopped onto the hood of the trailing vehicle. Charlie slowed down and pulled over. It wasn't easy as the road had few places to pull off. The shoulder was tight and narrow. Cars whizzed by at frightening speed. He exhaled, and stepped gingerly from the truck and walked to the back. Many of his goods were gone, strewn along the highway, like broken glass.

Sara felt empathy for her stranded antihero. Sara didn't drive but rode buses or the subway (off peak hours), and walked everywhere. She imagined being stranded on a busy road, especially the harrowing Interborough Parkway. She'd ridden it with a friend years ago. Her window was rolled down, and she had almost lost her lunch from the monotonous curves.

Her sister Elaine once confided that she'd stalled in the middle of the Holland Tunnel during evening rush hour, submerged under the Hudson River. She'd begun to panic, but a guard in a nearby glass booth phoned for help. The toxic fumes were suffocating, Elaine told Sara. Stalled drivers honked and the blaring noise echoed in the confined space.

Sara bristled, being highly claustrophobic. She'd never ride through a tunnel or sit on a crowded plane, and avoided public gathering places. The exception: an open park or the library reference room. The school where she'd taught in Scarsdale was airy and open and had a pretty campus. There were one or two colleagues she particularly liked, but lost contact after retiring five years ago.

Sara poured herself another cup of hot coffee, her third one, and it wasn't yet noon. She bit into her cinnamon roll, then broke off a piece and dunked to soften it up. It began to sprinkle outside. Sara shut her eyes and heard raindrops tapping the window.

Charlie heard rumbling from above and braced for a summer thunderstorm. He tensed thinking about the impending deluge. He'd drive to the next exit, pull off, and survey the damage. Fortunately, there'd been no accident. How awful if his pastry had splattered someone's windshield causing a collision. He climbed back inside the lumbering truck and revved the motor. He leaned out the window and signaled with his hand, and soon merged onto the busy parkway. The engine hissed and groaned and the tired truck slowed to a crawl. He avoided peering in the rear mirror, knowing others tailed his bumper.

An exit approached. He pulled off the parkway and crept along a service road. Charlie approached an arching iron gate. He drove through the cemetery entrance when the engine died. He'd seen this cemetery before from the parkway and now witnessed a sea of white and gray marble headstones, thousands of them. Steam rose from the hood. Charlie exhaled and slumped to his knees, there being no driver's seat to settle into. He buried his head like a turtle and recited a short prayer. Soon, he emerged from the truck while raindrops pelted his face and torso. He was in trouble and needed help. Lifting the hood, Charlie ducked the hot engine's spewing fumes. His delivery journey to Queens wouldn't happen, disappointing his clientele. Lightning, then raucous thunder claimed the sky as low clouds hovered. He removed his spiral notepad from his shirt pocket and jotted notes with a wet pencil that lay behind an ear. Charlie scribbled into his notebook for another hour.

After a fourth cup of coffee, Sara took a lunch break, snacking on cheese and crackers. Her refrigerator door was plastered with philosophical and practical sayings, garnered from clippings. 'This too shall pass,' was her favorite. Another she adored was 'Don't quit your day job,' and 'Books are my best friends.' She turned on the radio, which sat atop the kitchen counter. It was tuned to jazz. After lunch, Sara decided to continue with her piece, and referred periodically to the notebook she'd discovered.

Charlie ambled over and knocked on the cemetery office door, but no one answered. It was locked. He returned to the truck, his cotton trousers sopped and heavy, and stepped inside the vehicle to wait out the storm. Rain pounded the windshield. It was peaceful and comforting off the nutty highway, and soon exhaustion overcame him. He began to settle in for a long nap, hunched on the metal grating floor. Charlie stretched his torso and legs in the cramped space and then tucked his head between his knees and drifted off. A dead battery precluded his listening to music or the news. The storm raged, rocking his truck. Then he fell asleep, exhausted and resigned.

Charlie dreamed he was at a Brooklyn Dodgers game with Dad. Duke Snider, Gil Hodges, and Wally Moon all smashed towering homers. The raucous Ebbets Field crowd was thrilled. They stood and hollered as a ball almost smacked young Charlie in the head. He used the foul pole for cover. Charlie hugged his Dad, who shouted in his ear: "I told you so, son. I knew the Dodgers would win today. Happy birthday!" Burly hairy hands grabbed his shoulder and neck. Dad's breath reeked from peanuts and beer, but it didn't matter. It was his special day.

Now mid afternoon Sara grew tired and needed to nap. She resisted the urge and pushed herself to finish the chapter, and maintain momentum. She placed a barrette in her hair and poured a glass of orange juice. No more coffee today. Sara lowered her head on the table.

Next, she drifted off for a minute or two, and roused herself, unsure of the day and time. Children shouted from outside her third floor window, which opened to a warm summer breeze. Sara parted the curtains and peered out. Three girls still jumped rope, merrily singing. She felt an urge for fresh air, perhaps a stroll to the park. Instead, she continued with the chapter and seized the moment. She wouldn't abandon her Charlie.

Charlie woke from his nap and stretched. He stepped outside the truck and exhaled. It stopped raining and an impressive rainbow arched over the grounds. He walked to the truck's rear and opened the back, surveying the damage to his pastry. He leaned inside and groped his goods. The Danish were soaked through and through. He was hungry, and began munching on loose pieces of Cheese Cake and marble bread. It was now twilight and Charlie pondered spending the night in the graveyard. He had no choice. He could walk back to the parkway and try flagging a speeding vehicle, but preferred the tranquility of Mt. Judah Cemetery. Charlie grabbed a flashlight from the glove compartment and removed a soggy seeded roll embedded within maps and inventory notepads. Charlie bit into the seeded roll and heard a shrill voice. Charlie looked around for the voice and couldn't pinpoint its source. The squeals, or cries drifted closer. "We're hungry Doogan Man! Feed us now!" A second and third voice cried out. Then a chorus chimed in: **"We're hungry Doogan Man. Feed us please!"**

Charlie recoiled from the shrill, pleading echoes and covered his ears. On cue, he grabbed a tray of soggy and mangled cheese and apricot Danish, and walked to a nearby headstone. His black shoes were caked in mud. An apparition floated over Charlie's head with outstretched hands. It snatched a Danish from Charlie's hand and then swallowed the pastry whole. Charlie heard a burp and gurgle.

"Thank you Doogan Man. Keep feeding us, please!"

Charlie squatted, dazed and confused. Cicadas whined in the near distance. He rubbed cream stained fingers through dark wavy hair, lathering and shampooing root follicles with compote. A crescent moon glowed above, beaming brilliant light onto his hunched torso. Ghosts drifted from monuments and moved toward Charlie, soon encircling him. They clutched hands as if playing Ring-Around-The-Rosie. Transparent bodies soared and descended over headstones. He reached into his pocket and removed scraps of pumpernickel and offered them. They were snatched and devoured. The grateful dead bellowed in unison.

Charlie was pleased his goods were in such great demand and liked the attention. He hoisted gooey hands and addressed the spirits: "Wait here, don't go away. I'll be back with more." Charlie sprinted to the truck, and fell face down in the mud. He got up and gathered remnants from the few remaining trays. Jelly donut filling smeared his white jacket and pants. His hands remained sticky with filling and compote. Charlie grew anxious and concerned over the depleted pastry supply. He didn't want the spirits upset. He'd dash off and out sprint them if chased by the angry throng. Charlie then reconsidered his escape, not wanting to disappoint his new clients, who appreciated his skills. Winning approval and pleasing others took center stage.

Numerous spirits gathered, having summoned their friends, moaning and shouting for more. His baked goods gave life and sustenance to the dead and this was gratifying. Charlie glanced up at the evening sky, lost in reverie.

Now approaching four thirty, Sara lost track of time. A month ago, she'd gotten a picture postcard from a former student. The greeting arrived from Disneyworld. Sara had studied the tacky photo, and placed it on the refrigerator door, a reminder of normal life beyond Brooklyn. People had families and visited places like Orlando or Las Vegas. She hadn't come from an average family, and no longer had one. Her sister Elaine had recently died. Unlike Sara, Elaine loved getting out and volunteering. Sara wished for more postcards, even inane ones, hoping she mattered to former students. Under their breath they'd say, 'Shapiro was loony, but she nurtured me'. She needed confirmation that her life wasn't a complete waste of time, and that she'd contributed or made a small impression. Sara's gray tabby snuggled in her lap. She'd finish the chapter and call it quits. Sara reread and revised and proceeded to scribble. She grabbed a new sharpened pencil while flipping the yellow pad page. Sara liked the feel of a pencil scratching the coarse paper.

Whining voices echoed, forcing Charlie to stuff the hungry phantoms' mouths in rapid- fire motion. He tore chunks of dark rye and pumpernickel but couldn't keep pace with demands. Soon Charlie hoisted his sugary palms to show nothing remained. They'd better not turn on him!

A dozen spirits swarmed above Charlie, locking hands and beaming with delight. Some applauded and whistled. "Thanks dear Doogan Man. Take a bow, a long bow, and now you can go." The spirits waved. "See you back tomorrow night! Don't dare forget about us."

Charlie wanted a return favor. "I need my truck fixed. Is there a mechanic among you? The engine died and the radiator is shot to hell, to purgatory." Charlie covered his mouth. "Pardon the reference. That's no reflection on your current living condition."

A wiry hand grazed Charlie's shoulder and he jumped. Sal, the cemetery's spirit guide made an offer. "We appreciate what you've done. How 'bout a tour of the grounds?"

Charlie shook a transparent hand and was hoisted atop Sal's shoulders. They vaulted over numerous headstones to a sequestered part of the grounds. "This is our weekly potluck site," Sal shared. "This section houses lonely and miserable residents. They lacked social skills when alive. We also invite those with worldly limitations."

Charlie scanned the overgrown weeds and glanced up at the stars. "What kind of limitations?"

Sal chuckled. "We assemble folks who've suffered from neurotic disorders, such as obsessive compulsive complex."

"For example?"

"Just last week we included a friend, who when alive, wouldn't leave his apartment until he'd read every damn word of the Sunday New York Times. Plus the crossword puzzle."

Charlie was aghast. "That takes forever to plow through. He shut himself in needlessly. How sad."

"Yes indeed."

Next, Sal piggybacked Charlie to another section of the grounds, an unkempt mess. Overgrown weeds and broken tree limbs were strewn about. Charlie tripped over a branch but caught himself.

"These deceased inhabitants had accumulated clutter in their homes and apartments," warned Sal. "They lived in chaos and disorder and clutter creates havoc. I don't make the rules Charlie, but Woolworth and JJ Newberry sell binders and bins that make organizing a snap. It takes commitment and discipline."

Charlie stroked his chin and removed his spiral notepad and began scribbling with a wet pencil. "My dwelling and truck are organized. That is, until the recent pothole mishap ruined everything. My business wouldn't survive if I wasn't organized."

"I know. Don't worry. You won't wind up in a disheveled cemetery section like this. You'll be tended to by the maintenance crew."

"You're sure?"

"Yep. I'll see to it. But why didn't you upkeep your truck's engine since it's your livelihood?"

Charlie rubbed smudged stained hands. "That's the result of cutting costs and overhead. It's ridiculous that I drive that lumbering beast."

Sal tapped Charlie's head. "I saw you scribbling in your notepad. Are you spying on us?"

"No, I'm not spying. I need to remember important details and I don't trust my fleeting memory. I've even misplaced my notepad once or twice recently."

"I'd like to transport you to the next section of the grounds. It houses a surprising number of the deceased."

Charlie hopped onto Sal's shoulders and bounded over headstones to a bleaker part of the graveyard. The wind howled and Charlie heard hooting owls.

"These folks are clustered because they were too busy making a living and didn't invest ample time nurturing intimate relationships. All work and no play impacted their lives. Some escaped through silly vices like betting at the track and dallying and daydreaming."

Charlie grew nervous, hoping his work commitments and professional dedication wouldn't doom him. He shuffled his feet and stuttered.

"We can forgive their earnestness and minor mishaps, can't we, Sal? Let's cut some slack. Daydreaming can be productive!"

Suddenly a new spirit hovered above Charlie. Charlie stared and blinked, and recognized his deceased Uncle Benny, a bloated rotund figure with bulging eyes.

"What brings you here, Uncle Benny? This dismal part of the grounds is no place to reside."

"You're my nephew," Benny said, "and to me, always my darling Doogan Man!" Benny smiled, playfully brushing against Charlie. "You'd enter my candy store, rest on a counter stool and pluck pretzel rods from a plastic bin. I'd whip up a splendid chocolate malted on a sweltering summer day and watch you absorbed in Green Lantern comics."

"Great store you had."

"I know. And I've got a fond anecdote for the notepad you're clutching. Pardon my rambling, but we deceased have ample time to reminisce and reflect. It's retirement on steroids."

"Go ahead Benny. I'm ready."

"I loved your father but he was a tightwad. He was known for pinching pennies. Your grandparents infused this habit while trying to survive their impoverished village. Well, when you were born your father wanted to cut corners and hired a rookie Mohel to perform the bris."

"Rookie Mohel?"

"Yes, the rabbi was green and hadn't performed a bris so you'd be his first guinea pig. It was a minimal fee."

"Yuck. I obviously emerged unscathed, except for missing penal foreskin."

"Well, as I watched the rookie Mohel remove his cutting tool, my knees grew wobbly and I got woozy and fainted. I collapsed onto the kitchen linoleum and had to be revived. Your dad wasn't too pleased at the attention I drew."

"You two brothers got along mostly?"

"Not really. He was hard headed and stubborn, but I know he loved you despite being a demanding tyrant."

"Harsh words. But let's change the subject."

Charlie ceased taking notes. "What brings you here, Uncle Benny? I attended your funeral and you were buried somewhere out in the Bronx. Not far from a Kosher deli near Yankee Stadium."

"That's accurate my boy. Good memory."

"So why were you moved? These dismal grounds are reserved for lost souls."

"Says who?"

"Sal, the tour guide. Know him?"

"He's a flake. I don't trust him."

"You're a good man, a decent man, so what happened?"
Charlie observed his beloved uncle blush with embarrassment.

"I worked like a dog and ignored your Aunt Fran. And unfortunately had a fling or two I regret. It got lonely sometimes and my cravings took over. I had fun but ultimately messed up."

Charlie refrained from writing down his uncle's confession and gave full attention.

"She caught me philandering and wouldn't forgive or forget. Carnal impulses wrecked everything."

"I bet you're not alone." Charlie would forgive and show sympathy.

"Right you are. We've got a sizable gathering of fraternal miscreants in this section of the graveyard. But we mostly ignore each other except on birthdays or holidays."

Benny motioned for Charlie to open his notebook. "I suggest you jot this down in bold: 'There's small margin for error and it's damn easy to hurt those you care for'."

Charlie complied and scribbled just as Benny disappeared. He underlined the words 'small margin for error'. Charlie looked around and saw hundreds of headstones but no sighting of Sal or Benny. He rubbed his bloodshot eyes and felt drained. He'd sleep in the truck and devise a plan in the morning. A harrowing day had evolved into something interesting and unusual.

Dad would approve his good deeds and for rising to the occasion. "Now son," Dad would say while watching a ball game from the old musty sofa. "Focus on Gil Hodges at first base. An honorable and modest man, just like you'll be someday. Got that? I know you won't disappoint me!"

Sara placed Mr. Doogan's small spiral notepad in a zip lock bag. She removed her glasses and set them down. Her cat had fallen asleep in her lap and snored. She had produced a working draft of chapter one, based on the journal entries of Charlie Doogan. Sara wasn't sure if she'd continue with the project, and if the writing was of any quality or interest to anyone other than herself.

Sara reread from Charlie's journal and wondered if Charlie lived nearby, and if he still drove his wobbly pastry truck. She needed to be responsible and return his notebook by placing an ad in the local paper, or by phoning her landlord. Or Charlie might retrace his steps and knock on the door with a special inquiry. Sara knew she'd invite him in for conversation. Perhaps he still baked tasty pastries and would let her sample some over strong coffee. It'd be the two of them at her dining room table, snacking and chatting and laughing into the wee morning hours. It would do her a world of good, and she'd adore him and his charming company.

The Sanctuary

The Sanctuary

I missed the boat. The ferry boat that is. I was at fault and messed things up when the ferry left without me on board. Emily and I had been exploring Inishbofin Island on a Tuesday, hiking along the Irish cliffs and rock formations and photographing colorful wildflowers above the shore. We were having fun while leaving our marital routine behind. I loved escaping into this little slice of unspoiled paradise.

We enjoyed a cozy picnic on the craggy rocks, munching on smoked cheese and brown bread. A Dutch family had hiked up, taking a photo of Emily and me holding hands. The bay and mountains surrounded us. Speaking fluent English, we discussed Ireland's beauty and its friendly people. I relayed my bicycling adventures in Holland from years past, before I began instructing full time at the community college. The family lived in a quaint village I'd visited and liked.

The last ferry off the island would depart at five o'clock, which gave us ample time to walk to the pier. Soon it began to drizzle and we quickened the pace. I glanced back at the green hills above and stopped to take a landscape photo, capturing the day's remaining light. We soon arrived at the pier, having an hour before quick boarding and departure. There were two pubs on the island and I sought out the closest one, desiring a fast bowl of soup or fish chowder. Emily decided to wait by the dock and I said that I'd soon return.

After a brisk half mile walk, I entered Leo's Pub and felt instant relief from ensuing chill outside. The wind had picked up, dropping the temperature. Three teens played billiards in a side room while some from the morning ferry ride chatted at tables nearby. They drank beer and snacked on chips, or fries. The Dutch family we'd met earlier waved while I remained at the counter. A nine year old girl ordered bags of crisps for her and a friend. They sat next to me and shared a stool. Patrons huddled together and conversed. Leo, behind the bar, told me he was out of seafood chowder, but had prepared vegetable soup with brown bread.

I ordered my daily Guinness to go with the meal. I sipped the thick foam and liked its rich taste. An old Celtic folk tune played in the background. There would be live music that evening, well after my ferry departed. It'd be pleasant to spend the night on the island, mingle with locals, and drink Guinness. The steamy vegetable soup had a tomato base and was soothing, warming my insides. I dipped the brown bread into the broth and washed it down with thick ale and water. I glanced at my wristwatch. A little time remained before having to walk the half mile to the pier. Emily loved the rain and overcast skies, and I assumed she was fine waiting alone.

I finished the soup and bread and a pint of Guinness, suppressing a yawn. The ale induced drowsiness and I began nodding off. My head soon fell onto my arms, which rested on the counter. During my catnap, I didn't hear anyone move or leave to catch the ferry.

I heard myself snoring and awoke. My watch read five o'clock and I panicked, and almost fell from the stool. My queasy stomach tensed up. I paid the bill and dashed outside into the drizzle, racing along the main road. A slight hangover had slowed me down. Adrenalin was pumping, that's for sure. Rain mist slid from my cheeks as a stray dog chased alongside, barking at my heels. Bells from a church tower rang, echoing in all directions, muddling my thoughts. Why hadn't Emily come for me? She had our cell phone and both tickets. I envisioned her cursing aloud, reprimanding me. Our romantic getaway would turn into a prolonged quarrel. Nasty images of rebuke hampered my strides.

What *had* kept us together all these years? Familiarity, security, established routines, fear of the unknown? She'd be off to the mainland across the choppy bay waters and I'd be a marooned outcast. My new status: Wayward sailor, left behind, AWOL.

The ferry left the harbor, and I deciphered Emily's face from the pier. She didn't look pleased. She gestured and mouthed words from the deck as the boat pulled away. Her look said, 'What in hell have you done?'

I knew she was headstrong, and she wasn't about to alter *her* plans and wait for me. She'd disembark in an hour, check into a hotel and wait for my arrival on the next morning ferry. Or drive off with our rental, explore other parts of Ireland, leaving me stranded. I envisioned hitch-hiking to the nearest large town, and renting a bicycle or moped. I'd never catch her and our vacation would im-plode. I needed faith that all would be okay and that she'd forgive me.

As the ferry boat drifted further away I remained on the dock. I imagined asking Leo, back at the pub, for part time work tending bar or cooking food. I'd organize the even-ing music, sweep the floors, and serve patrons. I was somewhat relieved I missed the ferry, and now felt calm. The guilt abated. I strode back toward Leo's, while light raindrops fell. I soon entered a less crowded tavern and sat back down on the same counter stool.

"You've returned," said Leo.

"I dozed off and couldn't catch the last boat off the is-land."

I felt embarrassed and made light of the mishap. It hadn't been Leo's job to wake me from my earlier slumber.

"Well, sit right down and I'll pour ya another Guinness. It's happened before. And you won't be the last."

Leo was round and jovial. His ruddy cheeks puffed out like marshmallows. He wore glasses and his hair was thinning. I noted thick Popeye forearms as he rolled a beer barrel from behind the counter. Tourists were gone and only locals remained, chatting and drinking. The island had only two hundred full time residents. I had read this in my 'Let's Go' guidebook, along with other tidbits.

The residents were either hearty subsistence farmers, did construction and carpentry, or earned a living from the tourist trade. I hadn't noticed any hotels on the island, but there must've been one or two. Of course locals fished, but this became harder with a dwindling stock over time. I gleaned this from my guidebook and I'd committed facts to memory, in case a conversation materialized. I imagined the island damp, chilly, and isolated during the stormy winter months. These were tough cookies, and relied on one another and themselves.

"Thanks for the ale," I said, recalling the previous one I'd had over lunch before conking out.

"Watch out pal. It's addicting." Leo chuckled while I shook his calloused hand.

"I'm Robert. And I'll be joining you for awhile. Longer than I had originally planned." I liked how that felt.

Leo began rinsing glasses and plates and drying them with a towel. He put muscle into everything he did. "How long is your stay in Ireland? Where're ya from?"

"Connecticut, on the East Coast. We're flying back in a few days, unless, I miss the morning and afternoon ferry tomorrow." I was flirting with dangerous notions as a renegade.

Then Leo bent down and whispered near my ear. "I've a sister and a cousin back in Connecticut. If you ever run across them, don't tell 'em ya saw me drinkin'." Leo's lips parted, exposing a prominent canine tooth.

It occurred to me that I had nowhere to sleep. I had left my guidebook with Emily, and couldn't recall seeing any accommodations on our earlier walk.

"Do you know of a place I can stay tonight?"

"How 'bout here?" Leo replied. "We've a few rooms upstairs. It's not a five star hotel, but there's a bed. May get a wee noisy, but it shouldn't bother ya much."

"Sounds great." I felt relieved. "How much do I owe you?"

Again, Leo leaned in and whispered. "Just don't tell my sister that ya saw me drinkin' if you run into her back home. That's payment enough." Leo paused. "How does thirty Euro sound? I'll include a continental breakfast of biscuits or toast and coffee in the mornin'."

I thanked him for his hospitality and got up and moved to a table by the door. I sat alongside friendly locals. More folks streamed in as evening ensued. This homey place was the living room of the island. The live band arrived in a van and soon set up on a small stage. They began playing lively tunes with amplified guitar and fiddle. An accordion accompanied a female vocalist, who charmed us with traditional ballads. Children squeezed next to grownups and tapped on wooden tabletops while swinging their feet. Portraits of Yeats and Joyce adorned the walls. Many sang along and one patron kept refilling my glass with Guinness.

It was smoky and at times loud, but I tapped my feet to the beat. I thought of Emily and hoped she had calmed down. Our marriage had survived worse distress. I'd buy a lavish dinner the next evening and describe my time here at Leo's. That is, if she hadn't left me. I wasn't sure what she'd do. In some ways she was unpredictable. We've experienced rocky times, and who hasn't, but have always reconciled.

I decided to turn in for the evening as I grew fatigued, and shook hands with those nearby, thanking them for their company. I meandered my way to the back stairwell, and slowly climbed the creaky steps to my room which overlooked the bay. It was a tiny room, but with enough space to fit an old bed and a plain chair that leaned against a hissing radiator. I pressed down on the spongy mattress and wondered how wretched my back would feel in the morning. Then I removed a toothbrush and floss from my daypack.

Next, I walked the narrow hall, while floorboards creaked. Music traveled up from below and reverberated against wooden beams. Being sleepy, I held onto a wall for support. I barely fit into the tiny bathroom with a low ceiling, and hunched over the sink to wash up. Then I had to pee.

A strange noise came from under the toilet seat, a scurrying kind of commotion. I opened the lid and my eyes widened in horror. A speckled rat thrashed and paddled in the bowl water, wanting to climb out. A giant son of a bitch! Jesus, his tail whipped the water, splashing some onto my wool socks. I slammed the lid and flushed the toilet hoping to be rid of him. A minute or two elapsed and I waited, hovering over the bowl, wondering what might happen. Again I heard thrashing noises. I flushed, hoping he'd vanish. My adrenaline surged and I couldn't wait longer to pee. But there was no getting rid of the stubborn creature. I imagined him climbing out from the bowl, making his way to my room and crawling under the covers with me. Yuck!

I dashed back across the hall to my room, slipped into jeans, and sprinted down the wobbly staircase to the restroom below. My stuffed bladder was about to pop. Leo glanced at me from the corner of his eye. My hair was a disheveled mess and puffed up. Then I felt Emily's presence, her spirit enveloping me. She'd be unflappable and unfazed by the commotion upstairs, like her demeanor during our recent power blackout back home.

The jam session ended, and things were winding down. I stopped at the front counter and ordered another Guinness, a nightcap. I couldn't fathom returning upstairs, knowing a live gray mottled rat twice the size of a tennis ball was my immediate neighbor. Who knows where he fled. He'd force his way out somehow. My flustered state caught Leo's attention.

"What's the matter, friend? Seen a ghost?" Leo chuckled. "I forgot to mention spirits renting space above." He pointed at the beams.   "They're harmless apparitions, so don't worry."

"There's a rat in the toilet upstairs, Leo. I flushed twice, maybe three times but he's a survivor." My voice began to rise and quiver.

Leo rubbed his chin. "I'll come on up and have us a look. Gimme a little time to close things down here." Leo placed a hand on my stiff shoulder. He was chuckling.

"Thanks for the rescue," I said, managing a smile. The musicians filed out the door into the chilly night air. A wind picked up off the bay and blew in. I had almost forgotten how fabulous they performed.

Woozy, I remained at the counter sipping my last beer. Leo would know exactly what to do. There were brave souls in this world who took charge, or pretended to, and those who relied on others to clear the way and make everything right.

Leo shut down for the evening. He disappeared into the kitchen and returned, clutching a few items. "Let's go," he said. We climbed the rickety stairs, he in the lead carrying a large plastic bag, a serving spoon, and a plunger. My legs felt wobbly from the Guinness.

Leo squeezed into the puny bathroom. I peered out from behind his wide torso, crouching and straining for a view.

"Are ya married, pal?"

"As of earlier today, yes, but I can't guarantee my marital status tomorrow."

"Oh, she'll forgive ya for missing the ferry. It happens."

"Emily will be quite agitated."

"Maybe she met a handsome lad and had a fine ol' time with him. Ya never know." Leo chortled. "Just jokin'."

I remained crouched behind his torso and my knees ached.

"Are you married, Leo?"

"It's been a forty year sentence so far. But overall, it's been fun. Remember my friend, infuse passion and play into what ya do together. This is what counts in the long run."

I nodded. When *was* the last time Emily and I had a good laugh?

"Maybe," Leo offered, "that rodent provided you a wake-up call. Live for unexpected moments I say."

Leo scooped out the wily critter, who I suppose was dead. I heard no squeals or movement. He plucked the beast out and bagged it. If Leo had needed the plunger for back up, he'd get the job done.

Emily had always reminded me in self assured tone: 'Robert, you need the *right* tool for the job. That's the way things work.' Her unwavering resolve has been the key to Emily's charm. I've admitted to being fussy and too gloomy. Who tolerates a sad sack?

And as color returned to my cheeks a creeping anger

emerged. Emily was sure of everything. I initially liked how she'd always take charge of a situation. Opposites attract. And make each other miserable, they don't say. Emily exuded unflinching nerve by getting on the ferry, and abandoning *me!*

"There ya go, pal. It's taken care of. This one sneaked up from the sewer line, it's no big deal." Leo transported the dead rodent in a plastic bag and strode back down. I soon heard a dumpster lid banging shut outside.

I remained in the bathroom and stared into the bowl. A trickle of water leaked from the faucet. I felt sluggish and dull from the alcohol. I decided I needed to toughen up and vowed to do so.

The urge to sleep was gone. I returned to my room and turned on the light. An incandescent bulb hung from the ceiling. It grew stuffy and I pried open a window. A cool breeze, and then a fly drifted in. I lay down on the mushy mattress and my body kept sinking. I moved to the edge, and away from the biggest lump in the middle. I swiped at the fly buzzing in my ear. I'd forgo sleep.

I stared at the ceiling for awhile. A song performed earlier in the evening, an old ballad about a dirty old town replayed itself. I hummed the plaintive melody over and over, like a nursery rhyme. An hour or two elapsed and I lay awake, relieved that Leo was available to lend a helping hand. And I knew that I'd catch the first morning ferry to Emily.

Irv's Plunge

Irv's Plunge

Irv lived in an old apartment building with peeling yellow paint. The landlord knew of its condition but delayed upkeep. Irv acknowledged other tenants while passing on the front steps and exchanged pleasantries, but no more.

Mrs. Jones once invited him downstairs for tea and Irv had told her that he'd write the landlord and list items needing repair. She encouraged him to do so, but Irv procrastinated figuring he was better off now than where he'd lived previously. Before moving into this building Irv had rented a dark musty basement apartment. It had a central downtown location and was very affordable. Below street level he'd been forced to glance up at people's feet as they strode outside his kitchen window. After retrieving a bill from his mailbox one morning, Irv had hastily scrawled 'The Mole' with marker on the box before descending back to his basement dwelling. A week later, he packed and moved out because he desired a place with more light. Finding a suitable place on a fixed income had been difficult.

Irv stared out his third floor window. A street lamp beamed light onto a garbage can near the curb. Irv recently purchased an inexpensive telescope at the local thrift shop. Since his forced retirement from the post office he became bored and desired a new hobby. Astronomy seemed interesting. He set up the telescope in his living room and held a guide book. Irv looked through the eyepiece and spotted the North Star and Big Dipper constellation. Then he lowered his target to the apartments across the street. He observed tenants engaging in various diversions. A woman watered her patio plants. Next door, a couple sat on a couch watching television. Irv magnified his view and watched the program too. It might have been a game show or a type of dancing competition. Below this window, a man and his cat sat at a table gazing back at him. Irv moved the telescope above two floors and observed a portly man doing sit ups with his feet propped against a wall. He wore a red sweat-suit that may have displayed a monogram in large block letters. After sets of ten sit-ups the tenant reached over and bit into a huge submarine sandwich, and then grabbed a giant thermos and guzzled from it. Irv grew uncomfortable spying on neighbors and stopped. He was no peeping Tom.

An eerie noise from the bathroom startled Irv. He walked through the kitchen toward the bathroom toilet. It sounded like a shrill hissing teapot on high heat. Irv jiggled the handle and flushed and jiggled again. He wondered if an object got stuck in the pipes. A plumber had recently fixed his overflowing toilet or thought he had. The plumber had warned Irv that the toilet was poorly designed and structurally deteriorating. Irv knew that the bathroom floor was caving in and a hole formed under the flimsy rug. The plumber had sealed the hole but emphasized this was only a temporary measure. Corrosion and cracking could render the repair worthless. He advised Irv to phone the landlord immediately. Irv tried phoning and left a voice message but hadn't heard back.

Irv delayed following up with another contact. He didn't want to be perceived as a nuisance by complaining about his bathroom again. Irv feared the frugal and grouchy owner would raise everyone's rent or sell the decaying building forcing him and everyone out. Irv played with the handle and vowed to call again or write. The clanking and hissing continued, like an old noisy living room radiator. Irv removed the top encasement and stuck his hand into cold water. He rattled the chain twice while swishing his wrist around looking for a clue to the problem.

Frustrated, Irv gave up and plopped onto the toilet seat. His mood darkened while reflecting on his serious work injury at the post office which had forced him to retire. He'd been loading a mail truck and fell injuring his back. Irv took a leave of absence, but his back pain continued and he applied for disability which is a long process. He lost contact with former colleagues and now needed new structure and daily routine. He considered applying for part time work after his back healed, which would supplement his government pension.

Irv continued sitting on the toilet. He scratched his scalp feeling sorry for himself. Then he felt a sudden jerk as if an earthquake was occurring.

A rocking motion dislodged him from the toilet seat and he fell onto the moldy rug. He got up and sat back down. The toilet was sinking and the floor underneath cracked and began splitting in sections. Irv heard a rumble and felt vibrations underneath. Petrified, he reached out to grasp the tub. Irv sank violently while on the seat and screamed. Next he plunged through the floor and temporarily blacked out.

Irv's plunge was stopped by Mrs. Jones' bed one floor below. Fortunately, she wasn't in bed but in the kitchen baking brownies. She jumped and dashed toward the bedroom. Irv lay flat on his stomach with his face pressed onto the padded mattress. He squirmed and wiggled and then raised his bruised head. Irv scanned the room and squinted wondering where in hell he landed.

He heard approaching footsteps. Irv sat up and saw Mrs. Jones, his neighbor, running toward him. Her heavy shoes stomped the wood floor while hustling down the long narrow hallway. Irv saw her enter the room and straightened. He was a disheveled mess.

"Mrs. Jones?"

"Irv?"

"Mrs. Jones?" Irv felt groggy and disoriented.

"My goodness! What happened? You poor man."

"I'm really sorry, don't know what hit me."

Mrs. Jones approached the bed and reached out to Irv.

"Do you need medical attention? I can call an ambulance."

"Oh no, that's not needed." Irv felt embarrassed and didn't want to create additional drama or fuss. He sensed the room spin and hoped he wouldn't black out or succumb to a concussion.

"Call me Ann. Take my hand and let me help you straighten up."

Irv refused assistance. "Again, I'm sorry. I'm in my bathroom one minute and the next thing I'm here. Incredible."

He nervously tugged on his torn trousers which had fallen below the waist. His boxer shorts ripped at the crotch seam. Irv rolled onto his side and gingerly sat up. He wondered if his speech was slurred. He felt punch drunk from the trauma.

Ann sat down on a chair next to the bed and stared. She wore a cotton apron tied around her broad hips. Irv pointed to the ceiling and they both gazed up at the hole and damage.

"I came from there. It's implausible!"

"I better call an ambulance. You appear ashen."

Irv stood, and tugged on his baggy trousers. "No need. I've got it under control. I'll reimburse you for the damage once I contact the landlord. I'm so sorry."

"It's okay. Sit back down and rest a bit. There's no need to go anywhere."

Irv raised his voice. "These shoddy apartments are no

good. I'll sue that son of a bitch!"

Ann winced. She'd never seen him so upset.

"Please calm down and don't worry. The ceiling will get fixed. What's important is that you're not injured."

Irv mumbled to himself.

"Besides, what will you do about your apartment? You can't live up there with that horrible hole in the bathroom."

"What screwy construction. Why didn't I land in your bathroom? It violates every safety code in the book. Is this building from the nineteenth century?"

Irv stroked his whiskers and realized he hadn't shaved in three days. He liked to stay clean and tidy and organized. Irv glanced in the mirror above the dresser and shuddered. He looked like a monster with wild tousled hair and rubbery skin. Irv transformed into Frankenstein's twin brother.

Ann got up and reached over and patted his shoulder. Irv shook. He hadn't been touched by anyone in ages.

"Don't worry so much. You can stay here for a day or two until that thing gets fixed. The couch in the living room opens up. My last roommate was my late husband and he'd sleep out there."

"He did? Why?"

"Cause he claimed I snored, which might be true. He did as well, and he gnashed his teeth into a pulp. Chomp chomp grind."

"You miss him?"

"No, I don't. He wasn't shall we say a very pleasant person."

Irv slid along the bedspread inching further away.

"You're not imposing at all. I'll put bedding on the sofa for you, while I sleep in the spare bedroom. So clean up, shower if you'd like and we'll eat a late dinner."

Irv wasn't used to being attended to or nurtured. He sometimes felt like the stray neighborhood cat without a home base.

"Stay tonight and maybe things will appear more normal tomorrow."

Irv twirled his hair and tried parting it on the left side. His limbs ached and were sore. "I should probably ice my knee and back. Thank you for the dinner invitation and I'll reimburse you for food. You're very kind and generous."

"Good. All settled. Wash up and we'll have an appetizer."

Ann left Irv to himself. Pieces of his cracked toilet lay strewn about the room.

Irv cleaned up and soon joined Ann by the kitchen table. Ann's hair was usually braided but tonight it unraveled into long strands.

"Let's open a bottle of wine I've been saving for special occasions."

"Does this qualify as a special occasion?" asked Irv. "A little lift would be nice."

"Better than a tumble."

Irv forced a clumsy smile.

Ann opened the utensil drawer and removed a corkscrew. Irv admired how she took everything in stride. Another tenant would act horrified and panicked at his unplanned descent into their life, and cast him out immediately. He'd help Ann clean the bedroom debris after dinner if not sooner.

"What in heavens are you plotting, Irv? I understand why you're preoccupied. Don't obsess."

"Before we eat, I'll clean up the bedroom. I insist."

"Forget it. I know it's odd to put off clearing the debris

right away, but we'll do it later before dessert to work off dinner. Look, I'm upset too, believe me, but I hide it better than you. We won't ignore the disastrous mess much longer."

Ann poured two glasses of merlot and set out cheese and crackers.

"Shall we toast?" said Ann. "To an unexpected visit."

"Here's to life after death," declared Irv. "And to kind neighbors."

"Cheers."

Irv scanned the tidy living room and noted a tall antique radio with push buttons. On top stood framed portraits, perhaps grandchildren. Black licorice cubes lay in a porcelain bowl on the coffee table. The apartment looked as he remembered it from his previous visit.

"I've been here before."

"Of course you have. I invited you down for tea when you first moved into the building as a neighborly gesture."

"I remember now. It's been a couple of years. You were the first person I met in the building."

"I think you stayed for ten minutes and made some excuse to run off. It was a nice short visit."

Irv enjoyed the wine and finished his glass, gulping instead of sipping. Ann poured a refill.

"Any kids, grandkids or current sweeties in your life," asked Ann.

Irv scrunched his nose. "Nah. Not much luck on the romantic front I'm afraid. Call me clumsy and lazy in that department."

"Been married?"

"Was engaged in my early twenties, a long time ago."

"What happened if you don't mind my asking. I'm curious."

Irv put down his glass after drinking his refill and suppressed a burp. His face turned crimson.

"Well, my best buddy, the Best Man at my upcoming wedding stole her heart and they ran off together. A bad movie. You know that song, 'Tennessee Waltz'? I was stranded on the dance floor without a partner. Brought down a few notches. Humbled. I never forgave the interloping bastard. Or myself."

"That's bad luck, Irv. And it was obviously tough rebounding from that heartbreak."

"Calamity. Greek tragedy. Never quite got my footing again."

Irv fidgeted and tried to change the subject. "Umm, those brownies smell good. I'll often do take out dinner but it's expensive. I sometimes microwave something frozen that's fairly high in sodium. It adds flavor but it's not healthy in the long run."

"Do you exercise? Go for walks?"

"My back went out on me at work not long ago and I'm a bit stiff. And somewhat lazy."

"Well, I can inspire you to get moving. Wait right there."

Irv picked up the wine bottle and scrutinized the label.

"You know this wine, Irv?"

"Nope. But it's from Central California so it must be good," he improvised.

Ann walked into the living room and Irv tracked her movement while she gathered a CD player and a CD. She placed the music box on the kitchen counter and plugged the cord in. Then she inserted the disc and turned up the volume. Irv was on his third glass of wine and felt drowsy but much calmer.

Ann untied her apron and kicked off her shoes. She twirled her hands above her head like a ballerina. "Come on Irv! Let's go."

"You mean dance? I had a work related back injury that prevents me from moving too much."

"Just try," Ann exhorted. "Give it a go."

She took his arm and gently guided him across the linoleum toward the center of the room. They huddled together under bright lights.

"It's been years since I've done anything like this," Irv said.

"Who says you can't teach an old geezer new tricks," Ann teased.

Big Band swing music inspired Ann to hip swivel. She showed Irv what to do and how to lead. He moved like a clumsy robot but the wine made him less self conscious. Irv twirled Ann under his arm as they rammed into the refrigerator. He fixated on her lingerie which hung on the outside line in the alley. The glowing moon beamed light onto her brassieres, which swayed with the summer breeze. Ann pulled him closer and they rocked on their heels while bumping into a chair. Irv forgot about his sore back and limbs and let go. He panted and wheezed but didn't care. Beads of sweat covered his brow as he led the length of the kitchen in closed position, twirling her round and round. He glimpsed assorted crockery suspended from above. A ceiling fan cooled the air. Irv looked out the open window and watched her flapping lingerie again. The song stopped and they sat to recover.

They remained on the floor exchanging flirtatious glances. Spices and cooking utensils hung on a wall rack above the stove. Brownies had been cooling off on the counter. The chocolatey aroma sedated Irv.

"Will you assist me with something Ann? I have unfinished business to tend to."

Ann refilled their glasses. "Can it wait?"

"I don't think so. Come upstairs to my apartment."

"Now?"

"Now. Please."

Blood raced through his veins and he tingled all over.

They walked arm in arm out of Ann's apartment and mounted the stairs to Irv's place. He opened the apartment door and let Ann in. She noticed the telescope by the window.

"A hobby? Have you observed anything interesting?"

Irv fidgeted and then straightened his torso. "Nothing worth noting, just the North Star."

Ann was the first person other than the plumber or landlord to set foot in his apartment. He led her through the kitchen and down the hallway.

A picture postcard fell from under a refrigerator door magnet.

"So this is the abbreviated grand tour," said Ann. "No marble staircase and antique wall hangings?"

"Guess so. Wait just a second, please."

Irv ducked into a hallway closet and reached inside for an implement and eye goggles. When Ann spotted the hammer she froze.

"Don't worry. I know what I'm doing. It's under control."

Ann couldn't fathom what he might do but trusted him.

"I'm leading you to the crime scene."

Irv entered the damaged bathroom and asked Ann to stand back. He lifted the hammer over his head and whacked down hard on remaining toilet debris. He smacked porcelain pieces sending vibrations up through his hands with each blow. A few pieces scattered and some lay under the sink. Irv inhaled through the nostrils and tightened his stomach muscles before letting out a piercing scream. This woke the neighbors. A dog barked and wailed in the back alley.

Ann watched, not knowing when he'd call it quits. She was fearful that he'd injure himself or her. She stood back and didn't stop him.

"Be careful Irv that you don't fall through that nasty hole again. We don't want another long plunge." Ann had to shout to be heard.

Irv ignored her warnings and continued ramming and battering debris while straddling the enlarged hole.

"Awwwwwright. Awwwwwwright!" Irv yelled. "Yes! Screw the son of a bitch!"

He put down the hammer and crouched near where the toilet had been. Irv wiped his brow with his shirt sleeve.

"I'm done, Ann. Sorry if I scared you."

"See Irv, all the pieces are fitting together. You're releasing your rage at that negligent landlord."

"Must be." He reached over and clasped her hand.

"May I still take you up on your dinner offer? And anything else that develops in our relationship."

A Tryst in Room Seventeen

A Tryst in Room Seventeen

Daniel had never been so nervous. He'd do anything for Caroline, including spying on her husband Richie, tailing him like a private detective. He had no professional training doing this. Again, Daniel waited in his VW Beetle, peering out from behind the steering wheel. His eyes scanned the parking lot for signs of Richie. Daniel wore cheap sunglasses and a rumpled baseball cap. It was an overcast winter day. Caroline sat beside him, slumped in the passenger seat, her magenta wool hat pulled down over her forehead. She wore tinted glasses.

"You know this is dangerous. What're we doing, Caroline?"

She placed a chilly delicate hand on his knee, then let go. Her pretty green eyes numbed Daniel's semblance of clarity. To his amazement and utter frustration, Daniel had never kissed, caressed, or fondled Caroline. The urge haunted him, and he held back, knowing he'd be rebuffed, sweetly though. And then she'd disappear for good, vanish permanently, knowing he'd upset the balance of their friendship and her marriage.

"I appreciate this so much. I think Richie's cheating on me and I've got to find out who she is. I wonder if she's even a friend of ours." Caroline muttered under her breath, her voice trailing off. "Maybe it's someone I know."

Daniel imagined himself as Caroline's husband, doting on her constantly, massaging her tired muscles at the end of the workday, scrubbing her soft skin while she soaked in a warm tub.

"Why would he fool around? Richie adores you, he'd do *anything* for you." Daniel wanted to say, 'I would too!'

Caroline stared out the window, turning away from

Daniel, shoulders stiffening. "Maybe I'm jumping to con-clusions. I hate feeling this insecure. Richie's *so* sweet, too nice."

Daniel wanted to lay a comforting hand on her shoul-der, but didn't. He felt envious of Richie, of his power to spark Caroline's vulnerability. She turned back toward Daniel. Her dark eyebrows enhanced her lure.

"Why don't you plain out ask Richie if something is go-ing on.....if he's unhappy about anything in your relation-ship." Daniel wanted to slap himself for sounding like a therapist. It was painful playing this detached role, know-ing his heart was bursting at the seams.

Caroline sighed and began muttering, and then stopped. Her eyes fixated on an imposing figure exiting the natural food store, a handsome and rugged dude in a green flannel shirt. Daniel tracked Caroline's eyes and al-so stared at the man, who might've stepped out of an LL Bean Outdoor catalogue. With long strides, he straddled a puddle as raindrops bounced off his torso. Daniel recog-nized Richie as he completed his Thursday shopping rou-tine. He'd soon pamper Caroline with another nourishing dinner. Groceries rested against his broad shoulder. Dan-iel and Caroline waited nearby, parked in front of Bagel land, a few stores away. In one fluid motion, Richie got into his car and drove off.

Daniel could hear Caroline's labored breathing. It grew damp and chilly in the car. Daniel broke the silence.

"Our work is done for the day. See, he'd never fool around. Richie loves you, cooks for you, and he's loyal, true blue. I wish someone at home had a hot meal waiting for me."

"Maybe you need a kind husband too," Caroline teased.

Daniel wondered if this was all a ruse, a strange game she was playing with him. "A month of this spying is enough, don't you think?" He turned the ignition key. A hand reached out, stopping him.

"Please wait. Let's see if someone attractive emerges from the store and follows him. Maybe they're meeting up somewhere."

"Somewhere clandestine?" Daniel emitted a faint smile. "Motel 6?" He caught himself sounding sarcastic, and frustrated. Above all, he still wanted Caroline's approval.

"I'm serious. I'm not joking," she said, looking right at him.

"You have no evidence of anything, just your suspicions."

"It's intuition. Mine is never wrong." Daniel noted her tight jaw, and saw she was determined.

Daniel had known Caroline three years, meeting around the time she had married Richie, a former heartthrob from graduate school days. Daniel and Caroline worked for a software design company, next door neighbors in tiny windowless cubicles. Daniel had enjoyed their weekly lunchtime banter. On Fridays, he packed a tuna sandwich and chips, and they ate in a nearby park. Sometimes, Caroline made him laugh, and he had to keep from gagging. They discussed new films, dream travel escapades, and silly tales about her pet macaw, Henry. Occasionally, Caroline gushed on about Richie, and about their cute Tudor home nestled in the hills. Daniel grew jealous of these simple pleasures and longed for someone special. He berated, no, flogged himself for imagining that this person could be Caroline, a futile attraction to an unavailable woman.

Daniel designed educational software for schools. Caroline had recently left to pursue an evolving interest in jewelry design and painting. Richie worked as an independent contractor, dutifully supporting both on one paycheck.

Daniel knew Richie adored her, observing them embracing at an office holiday party not long ago. Daniel had staggered home that night, tipsy and depressed. He had entered a deep funk that snowy evening, his soul mired in doubt and self pity. He was a mess.

"Your intuition isn't perfect, you know," countered Daniel. He watched it piss down, raindrops striking the windshield, while mist obscured shoppers in the lot.

"Yesterday was a close call," he warned. They'd been following Richie on a narrow stretch of road in Caroline's neighborhood and almost rear ended him when a cyclist darted in front without warning. "Yesterday was a sign, a bad omen, and we need to stop spying."

"You're imagining things," said Caroline. "It wasn't even close. We were way behind, but just skidded a bit, that's all." Caroline moved her hands apart and smirked. "We missed him by at least three feet."

It rained harder and grew dark. Daniel wanted to wait for the storm to pass. He again wondered why she would fabricate notions of infidelity, but didn't want to completely discount her fears. He knew that the attention and time spent with Caroline was addicting. Daniel removed the sunglasses and cap. "Do you still love him?"

Caroline rubbed her eyes, peering straight ahead, somewhat in a daze. "Of course I do. He's my little world."

"Your protected, safe world." He didn't want to sound harsh.

"Speaking of 'safe', Richie's going away this weekend and I hate being alone in that big house at night. It spooks me."

Daniel wondered if this was a veiled invitation. He became aroused, wanting to make a valiant offer to help comfort her fears. Ah, he mused, they could rent a video, drink wine, and laugh the night away. Or do more.

"Where's Richie going?"

"Hiking with his brother somewhere on the coast. I'd go, but it's an annual brother bonding thing they do."

"Well, I have nothing going on this weekend." Daniel's voice climbed an octave before trailing off. "I'd be happy, um, to keep you company. I could, um, crash on the couch......"

"Oh, that's a sweet offer. But I guess I'll be all right."

She patted his shoulder. Daniel knew she was letting him down, and needed to change the subject to conceal his embarrassment.

"Henry's a good pet watchdog, even though he's a bird." Daniel forced a smile. "He'll alert you to intruders, a built in house alarm."

Caroline began fidgeting and twirling her hair.

"How goes the work-crew? Enticing gossip to report? Fill me in on pregnancies, deaths, divorces."

Daniel felt despondent, like the bottom had fallen out. He wanted to get the hell out of there. Instead, he stroked his chin. The rough five day stubble would become a full beard in a month. He stopped shaving each February during his week- long vacation, out of habit. Daniel reached into the glove compartment for a chocolate energy bar, offering one to Caroline, who politely refused.

"No marriages or funerals in the past month," said Daniel. "We're a bunch of content drones chained to our computer terminals all day. I'm not complaining though. It keeps me from roaming the mean streets."

"Your job keeps you from roaming your apartment," Caroline countered. "Why not quit like I did and follow your passion."

"And what might that be? And who will support me?" said Daniel. He wished life was that simple.

Caroline arched her eyebrows. He knew she would tease him. "What's stopping you? Let go. Take that enticing Carnival cruise adventure you've been postponing. Play poker on deck with the Captain and invite the first gorgeous babe you spot to dinner." Caroline elbowed him. "You'll schmooze with the house band on the high seas. It's Madagascar or bust, friend!"

"You've got it all wrong." Daniel's eyes narrowed. "My true passion: stay home for a month, lounge on the sofa with pasta and wine, nap a bit, and then devour the list of books I need to read. That's paradise." Daniel lowered his raised index finger.

Caroline checked her watch. Daniel knew that someone was waiting back at her house, someone who adored her.

Daniel wished he had inherited her straight teeth and unblemished skin, and good looks. Once, on a bright day, he could decipher tiny hairs on her arms. Daniel had studied her face and her contours and now could only imagine what lay under the wool sweater and jeans.

"I think I'd better go," Caroline said. "Why don't you drop me off at my car and we'll talk soon. Thanks."

Her dark green Honda was parked a few blocks away. With its new clutch, it could easily go for fifty thousand more miles. Daniel had named it 'Green Hornet,' after the sleek action hero, because of the lumbering way it climbed hills and navigated turns. Caroline kept the inside immaculate and the body in perfect shape.

"Don't leave yet," Daniel said. He wanted the conversation, the moment, to last. "Are you painting anything fun? Feeling inspired? You've got all the time in the world now." Daniel wanted to sound upbeat and encouraging, and not like a sad sack. "I'd love to see what you're doing."

Caroline sighed. "I'm afraid nothing much is happening. I can't seem to get untracked. My wheels are spinning, but not the right ones. Thanks for asking." Her torso slumped a bit.

Daniel hated saying good-by, reluctant to return to a sparse apartment. He'd return home, whip up macaroni and cheese and settle into routine. Then he'd unleash a pep talk monologue. Why not volunteer on weekends, he'd say aloud. Plant trees, paint houses for the needy, do nature hikes, a Big Brother. The talk would continue: get married, have children (and a cat), purchase a home in the burbs, swing the kiddos in the backyard, go furniture shopping, do home repairs, and do more shopping. His adoring sweetie would bestow a Home Depot gift certificate and plant a kiss for being so damn handy. Soon Daniel would run out of ideas, and steam, and then drift off on the living room sofa. This was what he imagined doing after saying good-by to Caroline.

Three days later, Sunday morning light streamed through Daniel's bedroom window. This pleased him. The dark Oregon winter days grew depressing and natural light was a gift. He remembered that Jay, an old college buddy, would fly in at noon and needed a ride from the airport. Former roommates, they maintained contact over the years. Daniel looked forward to company. They'd play chess, take in a movie and go out for pizza and beer. He enjoyed their conversations and easy banter. Jay was recently divorced and would need a temporary diversion surmised Daniel.

Daniel showered, all refreshed and energized. He studied the plaintive image in the mirror while drying off.

It was time for change, time to overcome innate shyness and its burden. He was through feeling awkward around others, especially women he liked. Caroline accepted his quirks and despondent moods, and listened sympathetically as he described a few strained on line dates a year ago. Daniel hated to date women he didn't know.

He wondered what Caroline was doing right now. Then he remembered that Richie was at the coast with his brother. There was no reason for Caroline to suspect her husband of infidelity. Anyone lucky enough to win her heart would never consider straying. Thinking about Caroline had become a habit, offering solace and escape. She had recently coached him on romance, covering its delights and pitfalls. Daniel felt a compelling urge to put her advice into action and start dating again. Unfortunately, he felt an opposite equally stubborn urge to do nothing.

Daniel shuffled into the living room wearing a slightly tattered robe, and put on a blues CD. Daniel prepared breakfast at the kitchen counter, mixing berries and almonds into plain yogurt. He popped two waffles into the toaster and waited. He'd smother the waffles with fruit and yogurt and take two multi vitamins with black coffee.

He peered out the window and saw an attractive neighbor below walking her Chocolate Lab and stooping to scoop up remains. Daniel picked up a library book about meditation and Zen Buddhism. He had books about religion and philosophy by Alan Watts and Krishnamurti, and read excerpts daily. The past no longer exists he ruminated, and the future hasn't yet happened. There is only Now. Daniel kept repeating this while closing his eyes. Waffles popped from the toaster forcing his eyes open.

A brief notecard from his mom lay on the counter wishing him a Happy Birthday. The generic card featured an everyman casting a line from a small fishing boat on a lake. Daniel reread the card's trite inscription about having dreams come true. Mom lived on the East Coast, in Maryland, and they conversed monthly. He flew out to see her once a year. She had visited him a few years back, and they had an okay time, but soon exhausted things to do and say. Daniel glanced up at the clock and placed the card with a stack of bills.

He decided to take a brief walk into the nearby park. His friend's airport pickup was a few hours away. Daniel put on jeans and a flannel shirt and stepped into fresh morning air. He felt light on his feet and buoyant. He'd enroll in a beginning dance class, ballroom or Latin, and shed a few insecurities. Crocuses were sprouting, and the sky opened up, which was rare for late February. Daniel entered the park and strolled up the path while glancing at the reservoir below. He'd soon see his apartment building from the ridge on top. Daniel vowed to make a fresh start and venture out more often.

Soon Daniel reached the top and sat on a bench. He thought about recurring insomnia and how watching My Little Margie reruns at three in the morning reinforced his stupor and lulled him to sleep on the sofa. It was time to return home and prepare to get Jay at the airport. A squirrel approached and begged for a handout. It perched on top of the bench, but Daniel had nothing to feed him. Then Daniel rose and slowly ambled down the marked trail, keeping his hands in his pockets for warmth.

Back home, Daniel read a bit and washed up. He got into his car and decided on a different route to the airport, wanting to shake routine. Sunday traffic was light. On the way he drove past a ball field opposite a closed Mexican restaurant, and then approached a stretch of tacky motels. In the corner of his eye while stopped at a light, he spotted a familiar vehicle parked by a beige stucco building. A neon sign flashed: 'Vacancies $39.00 Special'. Impulse forced him to swerve right and enter the motel lot.

The dark green Honda's front end faced a window with drawn curtains. A garish palm tree sculpture, metal like, hovered over a balcony railing. The flimsy structure would topple over if met by a strong breeze. Daniel envisioned pink flamingos encircling the palm tree and nesting in its fronds. He imagined blue colored lights and a fountain, like he'd seen on a trip to Miami Beach, with its hotel row along Collins Avenue. Daniel guessed this might be *Caroline's* dark green Honda.

He pulled completely into the motel lot, inching closer to the Honda's rear bumper. The license plate numbers and peeling university decal seemed a plausible match. It was Caroline's Green Hornet.

Daniel had ten minutes to investigate and then he'd leave for the airport. His stomach got queasy and knotted up. Daniel reached into the glove apartment and put on gaudy sunglasses and a ragged baseball cap, a silly disguise. He felt like a complete idiot sitting there.

Blinds were drawn in the occupied rooms while air conditioners hummed. Windows were sealed shut. Daniel feared that the manager had seen him and was phoning the police, thinking a drug dealer or gang member was on the premises. He'd enter the motel office and claim to be friends of the party in room seventeen, the one under suspicion. He'd ask to phone the room, to confirm a prearranged breakfast date at the International House of Pancakes, just down the busy main road. Daniel rehearsed the silly lines he'd give the manager, lame excuses to contact the occupants and uncover what Caroline was doing and with whom. His pulse was racing, but he'd wait another minute and then drive off.

He was about to turn the ignition, when Caroline, sleepy eyed and groggy, opened the door leading onto the walkway. She and the stranger locked hands and embraced. Daniel observed that she appeared oblivious to everything around her. They remained outside their door and kissed. She leaned back with eyes closed and her tousled hair moved with the late morning breeze. Daniel wanted to reach out and stroke each strand. She tilted her neck back as Dracula licked and bit into her exposed flesh.

They were no more than thirty feet away. Daniel was reduced to voyeur and mesmerized by the spectacle. He released a muffled grunt and was about to go mad. A shrill and annoying ringing inundated his eardrums. He distracted himself from the carnal display by recalculating his recent 1040 tax form. Daniel alternated between peeking out at Caroline's lustful pleasure and ducking back down, fiddling with a pocket calculator, punching in random numbers. He recited aloud his annual adjusted gross income, minus deductions and personal exemptions, plus charitable contributions and medical expenses. The numbers became a muddled mish-mash as the ringing and buzzing in his ear got louder. He was getting nowhere!

Daniel popped above the surface and witnessed Caroline passionately engaged, her angelic face flush with excitement and surrender. Daniel hunkered down while peeking above the steering wheel. Finally, they stopped smooching. Caroline turned around and closed the room door. She bent down to grab her small suitcase and walked toward her car, which was parked in front of Daniel. As the couple approached, Daniel noted a serene and satiated grin covering Lothario's face. The stranger wore a floral aloha shirt and pleated tan trousers. He was at least fifty pounds lighter than Richie and wasn't nearly as handsome. A dark moustache added a bit of dazzle to his pale face. To Daniel, he swaggered, brimming with confidence. Daniel wished he could be that cocky. Daniel flung his calculator to the mat. He'd bolt from behind the wheel, dash out, and smack the swashbuckler on the nose. A wave of shame then overtook him.

Daniel's small VW blocked Caroline's vehicle and he needed to back out without being seen. They were just feet away. He ducked completely under the steering wheel, blind to his surroundings. Daniel turned the ignition, shifted into reverse and prayed that no one blocked the way. Then he backed out the driveway into oncoming traffic and braked with a piercing squeal, averting a nasty collision. The car stalled and he mistakenly turned the ignition in reverse gear, and stalled again, rocking forward. His torso jerked like a marionette.

He sped off, leaving exhaust fumes behind, and glimpsed outlines of Caroline and her Casanova in the rear mirror. Daniel craved a triple espresso, something hot and nurturing, but was running late. Perspiration formed in clumps under his armpits, soaking his shirt. He began hyperventilating and rolled down the window.

He'd have an unusual story to tell his buddy Jay, but decided to keep mum. If Caroline contacted him and asked questions, he'd deny and play dumb. No, he didn't witness anything. What motel, or liaison?

Confronting her would lead nowhere, and trigger shame and embarrassment over his inane obsession. He no longer found Caroline alluring or special, and conceded he'd been a willing dupe. He'd become a sidekick to her concocted fantasy world. Yet he wished that it had been *him,* and not that weasel, making passionate love to her.

Daniel drove in prolonged stupor, unaware of his surroundings, including the passenger jet flying above. The waters of the Columbia flowed nearby, and Daniel hoped to eject from his vehicle and glide down the river, to the Pacific and beyond.

A flashing neon sign broke his trance. It was off to the side, up ahead: Waddles---Eat Now!

He needed a nurturing cup of coffee. He craved a warm counter, a hideout where strangers sit in peace, alone and anonymous. He'd perch on a stool, drink coffee, and eat pie too. Humble pie. Why had he chosen to drive himself crazy with his silly obsession? Or did the obsession choose him? He'd ask the wise sage behind the counter, the wizard of Waddles. Daniel would demand a simple answer and leave a generous tip in appreciation.

Daniel glanced up at the jet hovering above, now half a mile ahead. The plane cast a long shadow on the asphalt, and Daniel watched its rapid descent, his limp hands clutching the steering wheel. The aircraft steadied itself for a landing.

The Waiting Room

The Waiting Room

Carlos woke from a fitful dream and wiped flush skin with a tissue. He was a patient in the county hospital recovering from an abdominal stab wound. Soon, his girlfriend Mimi would arrive and comfort him. She'd run her smooth palm along his pale cheek and breathe life into sore limbs. The pain had been intense at first, and then the sedatives took hold and made him drowsy and able to cope. The nurses were responsive, though harried, and watched over him when feasible. He liked to joke with one particular nurse about silly things and though groggy, he tried hard not to laugh or his insides would rattle around and jab him.

Carlos was attacked by a couple of thugs at the city bus depot just ten days ago, on his birthday. It happened so fast he didn't see it coming. Before that, he'd been conversing with two senior ladies seated nearby on a wooden bench in the depot waiting area. That's the last thing he remembered.

Carlos had experience in waiting rooms: Escorting mama for chest x-rays and medication prescriptions, updating forms at the local employment office, and sitting in jury duty rooms waiting to be called for trial. Waiting was an art, a technique, and Carlos often brought a book or sketchpad along. He'd compile portraits of strangers, those waiting their turn. Carlos drew in pencil or charcoal and was discreet, but occasionally showed his finished work to an inquisitive subject. He turned down compensation and donated the rough portrait to a grateful stranger, who usually liked the attention. One day, if he ever focused, Carlos would re-enroll in school and work toward a Fine Arts degree. This was a fantasy. For now, he labored at temp jobs, boring stints that paid the rent and allowed him to treat Mimi to dinner and a film once a week.

A pretty woman approached Carlos and he sat up. Her bright red lipstick accented lovely brown eyes. She looks dazzling, Carlos thought. He sniffed the purple irises Mimi placed under his nose, while a pedal dropped onto his belly. He inhaled Mimi's scent and got aroused. She bent over, kissing him gently on the lips and then ran her tongue down his neck. Next, she rested her cheek on Carlos' chest. His heart pounded.

"I've been waiting for you, love. Thanks for not deserting me even though I'm lookin' haggard and puffy and like crap."

"Stitches and surgery will do that," said Mimi. Carlos ran a hand through Mimi's thick hair and kept it there.

"I came right from work, sweetie. And you're looking better every day. Promise me I'm the only one to touch that nasty scar on your belly. It's a badge of honor, remember that."

Mimi reached into her backpack and retrieved a few magazines, placing them on the bed.

"Is there a catalogue I can use to order a new face?"

"Before you delve into some intense reading, try some of this." Mimi reached into a white freezer bag and pulled out sweet and sour soup, his favorite. "It's not homemade, but take-out will have to suffice." She removed the lid and let him ingest the aroma while handing over a plastic spoon.

"Now get cracking on your research project," said Mimi. "Scan 'People' magazine, take notes, and find out what's really important in the world."

"Like what relationships are teetering and who's having plastic surgery?" said Carlos.

She winked at him. "When you walk outta here, I want you *informed* so you'll keep a civil conversation at the next highfalutin cocktail party we're invited to."

Carlos smiled, patting her on the bottom. Then he whispered in Mimi's ear. "I'm going mad, stir crazy in here. The guy next to me has the goddamn T.V. on all day and night. Slim down commercials, cholesterol busting drugs, Viagra, Humvees. The blabbering nonsense is decimating brain cells and I'm turning into a zombie."

Carlos examined the earplugs Mimi had brought. "I thought of a new way to make money. I'll sign on as spokesman for reconstructive surgery." Carlos broke into a deep tone. "I too have joined this unique club, but it wasn't my choice. Avoid getting mugged!"

Mimi ran delicate fingers along his cheekbone and stroked his forehead with a knuckle, resting at the place where a chunk of skin had been torn, the spot where his head banged hard, causing him to lose consciousness.

"You're looking better each day, I swear, Carlos." Mimi sighed.

"You're repeating yourself. It must be true."

"Oh baby, you'll be discharged in no time, for sure."

Mimi ran a hand through his wavy dark hair, sweeping it away from his face in a fluid motion. He imbibed her warm sweet breath.

"Discharged soon?" Carlos said. "Hope so."

He kissed Mimi again on the lips. She wore tight jeans and a black turtleneck. She lay to the side as they caressed. Carlos kept a palm on his belly, the stab wound entry point. He was still bandaged up and his ribs ached.

"Are they taking good care of you? I know the food sucks," Mimi said. "Greasy fish sticks and lime Jell-o again?"

"Jesus, it's not that bad. The macaroni and cheese is edible, and loaded with tons of salt or preservatives. I wonder if it's easy to die in one of these places."

"Food poisoning," Mimi said. "There's tons of lethal germs round here. I'm not kidding."

"Now you're sounding like my worried mama," Carlos said. "But please keep fussing over me. Don't stop."

Mimi handed Carlos a Consumer Reports magazine she'd brought, one featuring an expose on choosing the best hospital and the best specialty surgeon. Carlos held it up to the light and wrinkled his nose.

"Lots good it does me now. For not having insurance, this place will do. It could be worse you know."

"Sleeping all right?" Mimi said. "Do you need anything to help you sleep?"

Carlos grinned. "Yeah, I need *you* here next to me. Let's sneak you in for the night after visitor hours."

He chuckled, then felt a sharp pain in his gut, and moaned. Carlos had recurring nightmares, bad ones, but didn't want to share these with Mimi, or anyone, just yet. He figured his subconscious was working overtime, gathering pieces of his nasty experience in the bus depot, forming a collage of events.

"Next year we'll celebrate your birthday somewhere exotic," said Mimi. "Not in a hospital. Let's fly to Spain or Italy and nestle in a villa on the beach. You can paint to your heart's content, and we'll have candlelight dinners."

Carlos saw her eyes glow with passion. He wanted to ask Mimi to tango, right then and there.

She whispered into his ear. "You can paint nudes of me. Shoot for the stars! Be my Dali, darling."

Carlos glanced down. "My work is far from perfect. Is there room for creative failure? I expect to produce something memorable but can't."

"Lower your standards. Produce occasional crap. Slay your inner critic and let loose."

Carlos nodded. He knew Mimi was right but if he

wanted to succeed in an arts program or make a living doing what he loved, he'd have to deal with internal pressures and lack of confidence.

"Don't compare your style and results with others. It'll drive you insane and lead you to give up. It's easier said than done and I'm behind you all the way. Your portrait renditions of strangers are fun and zany."

"It doesn't pay the bills."

"I don't care. I'm not a gold digger. Again, produce crap, I don't care. We'll make it somehow."

He felt her warm hand stroke the contours of his face. She rested her head on his chest and he wondered if his heart was thumping in her eardrums. And, he was told, this very heart had about permanently stopped ten days ago. He had lain unconscious, in a coma, and adrift somewhere else. Not in Italy or Spain. Nor was there candlelight on a villa terrace. It was a void, a black hole, a moment where the brain hallucinates and drifts in and out of strange, exotic dreams. Neurons, synapses, and errant chemical secretions created havoc across pathways. Whatever the hell it'd been, Carlos could only retrieve tiny fragments from the bus depot attack and its aftermath.

Meanwhile, Carlos got aroused and held still, somewhat embarrassed. A full moon shone light through the window while it got dark. Carlos sipped from a cup of day old mineral water. A band on his limp wrist dangled. With a marker, he'd crossed out Carlos and written 'Zorro', his boyhood action hero. He folded his arm around the nape of Mimi's neck and held tight. She smelled sweet, like a wild spring rose.

Carlos had tried describing the assailants to detectives but couldn't juggle fragments in a logical fashion. His memory was cockeyed, and this was frustrating as hell. He, the detail artist who absorbed new faces and sketched couldn't visualize his attackers.

Carlos did recall some of his public portraits. They were the faces of flawed, yearning, and passive strangers in transition. He kept sketchpads of strangers riding elevators, standing on train station platforms, and those lingering in amusement parks and midnight diners. Carlos filled these transition spaces and eavesdropped. He respected privacy and would stop sketching if glared at, but this rarely occurred. There's magic in the ordinary he'd tell Mimi.

An hour flew by and visiting time ended. Carlos hoped Mimi would return the next day with Swiss dark chocolate. He knew that Mimi's job as a paralegal was draining. Once discharged from the hospital, they'd marry and honeymoon somewhere low key, away from loud tourists and sleaze. Maybe their savings would be enough to pursue this. Or he'd borrow money from his older sister and go.

The television droned on, putting Carlos in a semi hypnotic state. A stupid laugh track hopped off the bright screen. He wanted to tell the dolt nearby to shut the goddamn thing. Soon Carlos felt groggy and dozed off, and wondered if his recurring nightmare of being chased would continue. He had dreamed of blood and spilled guts, of missing pieces and parts. But tonight, he'd compile mental snapshots and glimpse what had happened that ugly day in the bus depot. His brain began putting memory fragments together: splicing, editing, cranking out truth, being objective.

He remembered two senior women approach him. One had large eyes and wore gobs of mascara.

"Excuse me, young man. Would you be kind enough to take our picture?"

He placed his suitcase down and smiled, taking the

camera. A garbled intercom voice announced the next arriving bus. Carlos snapped the photo of the two women, both dressed in long beige coats. He captured the gray marble walls in the background. It framed a border around a wooden bench the women sat on.

"Thank you kindly," said the one with layers of makeup. Words rolled from her mouth in a twang. Carlos surmised a Texan drawl, but wasn't sure.

"Where ya off to, sir? We're on our way to Las Vegas."

She tapped her companion on the shoulder. "Mary, my darlin' sister, just turned *eighty* and we're goin' to raise hell!"

Mary nodded on cue while gazing at Carlos.

"I'm Claire." Carlos took her moist hand and bowed.

"This is our first vacation together in a while," Claire announced, "and we're goin' to party hearty!"

"Am I invited too?" said Carlos. He was in good spirits, this being a twenty-fifth birthday. He was off to a family celebration a few hours away. He'd blow out candles and roughhouse with nephews and nieces. Carlos could've driven, but despised freeway traffic and wasn't patient behind the wheel. The bus would be relaxing, and he could look out the window and think about Mimi. She had to work that day and couldn't join him. Her boss was insecure and controlling and Carlos suggested she search for something else, but the job market was horrendous.

The strangers giggled at Carlos' request to join them. They flirted back. "Of course you may join us." Claire, the outgoing one, had straight teeth and a small mole on her chin. Then her eyes narrowed.

"We hope you like playin' the slots because that's where we'll be the whole darn weekend. We're takin' no prisoners."

Then Mary whispered aloud while covering her mouth.

"Guess what else we're doing?"

Carlos paused. He'd never been to Vegas but Mimi's sister had visited and mentioned the Eiffel tower replica built near a five star hotel. Carlos preferred the real McCoy though.

"Guess what else we're doing?" repeated Mary, waking Carlos from his reverie.

"Going to a show," he said. "You'll catch Wayne Newton if he's still performing." Carlos had heard of crooners like Newton and Tom Jones, but would these ladies still find either appealing?

Claire poked her sister. "We're on a mission. Goin' to drink a bit and pick up some unsuspecting honey and......" Then she whispered into Mary's ear, shielding her commentary from Carlos.

Carlos leaned forward, blocking out the muddled intercom announcing the next departure. He almost didn't care about his bus and entertained the notion of joining his newfound companions. His large extended family included boisterous uncles, aunts, and cousins all lying in wait, miles up the freeway. And he wouldn't disappoint by running off.

"It's never too late for sultry romance, is it young man?" said Claire.

Carlos liked how she pushed the limits or pretended to. He acted nonchalant and thought they were joking and goofing around. He hoped Mary found a willing partner in the casino bar, at the craps table, or wherever they might get lucky.

"Of course it's never too late for *anything*. And I want the medication you're both on. Can you spare any?" Carlos winked.

He'd tell Mimi about these fun sisters. Ceiling fans whizzed overhead as it grew humid and stuffy in the depot. He stripped to a light shirt and scanned the posted schedule on the departure board. His bus would leave in twenty minutes, the one heading north to Fresno on the interstate. Next, Carlos picked up his travel bag and was about to wish the adventurers bon voyage. Their bus would depart in an hour.

"Do y'all have a girlfriend, a fiance?" Claire asked.

Carlos was about to reveal how he'd met Mimi, as freshmen in the same dorm. He'd share how they reunited, and how occasional tension and conflict fueled passion and desire. Then Carlos spotted two gritty and bedraggled teens and as they shuffled over, he sensed trouble. They looked like street kids. One wore a bandanna around his forehead and tinted shades, and baggy pants that exposed striped boxer shorts. Splotchy tattoos covered his right arm. His taller and lanky partner chewed pink gum, blowing and popping bubbles. They appeared as hip hop caricatures, cursing under their breath, dissing and strutting, acting like jerks.

They glared at the sisters and leaned forward with menacing postures. Their eyes were cold, zombie like. One grabbed Mary's leather purse and yanked, but she held tight, dragging the punk partway down. He sneered, and whisked out a long switchblade from his jeans pocket, placing it near her throat. The blade tip glittered under the incandescent lights.

"Give me the fuckin' purse or I'll hurt you." His eyes were bleary as if he'd been drinking, or doped up on meth. His breath reeked with a foul odor.

Carlos scanned for security, police, anyone. Even God. The ticket counter windows were glazed over, its metal bars obscuring the clerks' view. Passengers had boarded other buses and the lobby was deserted. Petrified, Carlos didn't know what to do. He opened his mouth and gasped for air.

"Com' on, leave the lady alone. Take my wallet but please leave her be." Carlos couldn't believe his resolve considering his heart was thrashing about. The scene flowed like a silent movie reprint: blurry, slowed down and out of focus.

"I'll take your fuckin' wallet and the ladies' too. Then I'll cut you, you whining prick."

The teens towered over Carlos, who clutched his luggage straps. He perspired and shivered and his body disengaged. Desperate, Carlos tried reasoning.

"Please, man. It's the lady's eightieth and they're off to Vegas to celebrate." Carlos hoped that by stalling, help would arrive. His cell phone was buried in his luggage.

"Don't give two shits 'bout fuckin' birthdays. Shut the fuck up."

Then the tall lanky tough grabbed Carlos's neck, forcing him forward and onto his toes. Carlos stared, transfixed, into the punk's eyes. He glimpsed a faint image of himself in the pupil. The neck grip tightened cutting off blood flow. Mundane images flooded his brain and emerged: A ballpark vendor hawking doughy salted pretzels while weaving through the grandstand; also, a theatre matinee usher in gaudy red uniform, vest chains protruding while clutching a flashlight, leading patrons to their seats. Were these vintage images from Life magazine?

Carlos felt his body further disengage, like it wasn't there. He motioned to the sisters, urging them to run. Carlos heard a piercing wail, or an echo of one and collapsed. He slumped when the sharp blade penetrated his gut, slicing a hole that forced his legs to buckle. He couldn't breathe and was drowning on fluids. Blood leaked onto the depot floor and he remained still, his wallet gone. He had no idea when the paramedics arrived.

Carlos bolted upright from his horrid flashback in the middle of the night, his gown dripping wet. Raindrops struck the nearby windowpane. It was stormy and gusty outside. He lay in the hospital bed surrounded by birthday and get well cards, dangling silver balloons with designs, and assorted knick knacks. A box of crackerjack hung over the nightstand. Carlos grabbed the box and reached inside, hoping for a prize. He rattled the box and tried again without luck. Carlos stared at the ceiling and was about to summon the nurse for additional valium. He needed to calm down.

Instead, Carlos reached for his sketchpad and pencil, and drew the bus depot station, the crime scene. Soon he'd sketch the sisters on the bench. He wondered if they pursued their ambitious plans despite the trauma. He hoped they reached their destination and celebrated. Claire and Mary would be reliable witnesses when located. He hoped they escaped unharmed and filed a report, but Carlos couldn't recall the results of the criminal investigation. Perhaps Mimi had taken notes and would share these soon. Carlos worried for the sisters whom he'd bonded with. Fragments of the investigation were surfacing in his mind.

Carlos needed to contact the head detective and urge him to pursue new leads, even though no witnesses had emerged. Someone called an ambulance and perhaps glimpsed the fleeing thugs. Were surveillance cameras working? His memory was reviving and he wanted this resolved.

He sketched into early dawn, vowing to recover full memory and help officials identify the vermin who'd extracted chunks of his soul.

Carlos began outlining scenes that would evolve into an

action comic book, a 1930's gangster tale. It cast him as benevolent hit man, mowing down the depot scum with machine gun fire, their torsos flailing like marionettes. He'd leap over their prostrate bodies into waiting white limo and wave to adoring crowds. He'd blow kisses into the wind, sending a fat juicy one to the Vegas sisters. They'd lean against the station wall with purses intact and wave back, rescued from harm and peril.

He'd add a sketch panel depicting him wooing Mimi for the first time. Feigning indigestion, he had knocked on her college dorm door, seeking a soothing remedy for an unsettled intestinal track. He needed an excuse to talk to her and by the time he summoned the nerve, a real bout of indigestion ensued. *This* part was true.

In Carlos's evolving tale the hero crushes evil, winning the day. He knew his fantasy yarn was silly concoction, "fools gold", yet seductive for a battered body and ego.

Meanwhile, Mimi would visit later and offer comfort. She'd clutch his wet clammy hand and soothe him. She'd make everything right again and help shoo the ugly rage away.

Carlos dropped the sketchpad and pencil onto the floor. He refused to forgive the jerks, now or ever. He'd be chasing an elusive shadow if seeking a rationale for their cruelty. Carlos was grateful and lucky to be alive, but still wanted revenge or at least justice.

Then a cajoling voice emerged. He vowed to retrieve his old self and dormant spirit and coax it from hiding. With effort and persistence he'd let laughter and light through, and transcend the pain. And when Mimi arrived he'd let her nurture him and he'd follow her steady lead.

The Bare Bones

The Bare Bones

Naomi struggled to make ends meet and needed to do something about it. She grew deflated and bored waitressing, making lousy wages, a dead end. Naomi sipped on imported coffee and ignored this week's tight budget. Then she got an idea. She'd strip to enhance her income.

And why not, she thought. She loved theatre, everything from Shakespeare to campy musicals, even opera. Naomi lounged on the sofa and pulled a blanket over her torso. She recently graduated with a Psych degree and had interned her senior year at a mental health clinic. Naomi had developed engaging rapport with clients, combined with a healthy detachment when not working. Now she'd apply these traits to her new temporary vocation. Naomi would commit to a year of stripping, and accumulate savings toward beginning a graduate degree in clinical psychology or counseling.

She'd hire herself out as a party entertainer or erotic telegram, but wasn't yet ready to be independent and start her own business. Instead, she glanced through the back section of Seattle's alternative weekly and found a possible lead. She didn't think the work would be dangerous but was prepared to take all necessary precautions. Naomi sat up, then cracked her knuckles and rotated her neck, making a popping sound. Yoga postures and classes had created a supple torso. She envisioned using subtle charm to entice partygoers and ensure that everyone had a fun time. Naomi saw herself as flirty erotic entertainer, exuding grace and sleazy humor in her role. She'd done nothing like this before, but once loved performing in high school plays and amateur theatre.

The next day, Naomi contacted the agency she'd found in the alternative weekly. She was accepted for the party entertainer position after submitting an on line photo and describing her personal background and interests. Her enthusiasm won over the agency owner, who'd started the business three years ago. She'd earn a set wage per performance, making more in half an hour than she would waiting tables over the course of a week. Naomi was told that Mr. Lopes would accompany her on each assignment to ensure security in case anyone overstepped boundaries. Lopes would carry a boom box of music CD's and remain on the periphery. He'd be the man who wasn't there, unless an emergency required that he whisk Naomi away. She liked the terms of the informal agreement and was comfortable going ahead and giving it a try.

Naomi decided to adopt the persona of a bedraggled homeless bag lady, and at the opportune time, strip down to reveal her enticing alter ego. The next day, she went shopping at Goodwill with her friend Roberta, and procured a frumpy overcoat and baggy skirt plus numerous tacky polyester sweaters.

The agency called two days later on a Friday and arranged Naomi's first gig, a birthday celebration at a local private residence. They urged her to contact the best friend of the birthday 'boy', who was turning forty. She'd glean valuable tidbits and background trivia about him and string Mr. Forty along while in bag lady disguise.

Naomi soon reached the best friend by phone and informed him that she'd be arriving the following afternoon at the assigned address. Naomi conversed with Alan, the informant, about his buddy Steven Gold. She jotted notes during their fifteen minute conversation. Naomi explained that Steven would be pleasantly surprised, and that she'd deliver an entertaining show. Steven's wife Susan would be privy to the prank. Naomi put aside her laptop and removed a scratch pad and pen for note taking.

"So, how did Steven meet Susan?

"They met on a blind date back in college. We saw the film 'Rocky Horror Picture Show' at a local theatre and then ended up at a deli for a late evening meal."

"What did your friend Steven order?"

"Chicken salad on dark rye."

"How can you be sure? It was years ago, wasn't it?" Naomi jotted key words on scrap paper while sipping mineral water. Then she put down her drink and twirled strands of auburn dyed hair. The dark red highlights accented her almond eyes.

"I know what he ordered because Steven's a creature of habit. He orders the same goddamn thing every time we go to that deli."

Naomi decided to amuse him and probed further. "Why always the chicken salad but not chopped liver? Isn't it any good there?"

Alan continued rambling, ignoring her comment. "And write this down: The leach practically begged Susan for her fat dill pickle. He loves sour stuff. Almost swiped it off her plate like a thief."

Naomi heard Alan chuckling.

"His favorite dessert?" said Naomi.

"A toss-up between chocolate Danish and a black and white cookie. Tough call."

They continued discussing personal things Naomi would spring on Steven. She'd pretend that the two of them were long lost lovers, old romantic flames; and she'd force him to remember her, or be embarrassed. Naomi assumed Steven would play along and be a good sport.

"One last thing before you go."

"What's that?" said Naomi.

"You must say that you know Minnie Minoso. You have to."

"Who's that, a relative?"

"No," said Alan. "That's Steven's all time favorite ball player. Minoso was born in Havana and entered the majors in 1949, ten years before the Marxist Revolution took control."

"You mean when Castro seized power?" This was before Naomi's time. She wasn't enthused about baseball or politics.

"Yes. Minoso played infield for the Indians and the White Sox and moved like lightning around the base paths. Hit .300 a few times. He played until his mid forties, retired, then returned for a brief spell in his mid fifties. An icon, part cult figure."

"You're telling me more than I want to know," said Naomi. "But okay, I'll mention Minnie's name at the right moment."

Naomi enjoyed eavesdropping, uncovering Steven Gold's nuances and quirks. She wondered if Alan was stretching facts, and what other little secrets would unravel. If the work panned out, she could write about her experiences and accept a lucrative book offer. Was it wrong to write a kiss and tell piece about vulnerable men turning forty, anxious men, some fearing they missed the boat. Naomi finished her drink, gathered notes and locked key phrases and names in her memory. Naomi neglected to get a physical description of Steven but assumed Alan would point him out. She looked forward to the party.

Mr. Lopes picked Naomi up at her place around noon the following day. She wore a polyester baggy skirt and flannel shirt, covered with multiple layers of clothes. There were baggy sweaters piled on top of other knick knacks. Fake gaudy jewelry hung from her neck and wrists. Naomi's disguise added bulk to her slender frame. She puffed out like an inflated balloon and strained bending over. She donned an oversized felt hat with a protruding feather. Cheap Coke bottle glasses from the '40's added to her downtrodden street charm.

They drove to the address on Harrison Lane. It was brisk and chilly out. Naomi's clothes swayed with the breeze as they stepped onto the front porch. Lopes carted his music box to the door and rang the bell. He had a stout shape, barrel-chested and appeared quite ordinary. His pencil thin moustache highlighted puffy jowls along with a pot belly. He could've been anyone's middle aged uncle visiting relatives for weekend brunch.

The revelers consumed appetizers and salads in both the living room and kitchen. Naomi exhaled and made her grand entrance. Lopes followed, lugging a giant boom box. He remained by the door, an unimposing stick figure. Naomi scanned the room for Alan, the man of honor's confidant, but couldn't locate him. Was he in the bathroom? She had memorized their phone conversation in its entirety and was ready to deliver her lines.

"Okay," Naomi blurted out, "where's the birthday boy?" She became the center of attention.

A helpful woman in a plaid skirt guided Naomi toward a tall slender man raising a glass of champagne.

"That's him," she told Naomi. "But who are you, and who do you know here?"

Naomi noted her puzzled expression and understood that others would question what galaxy or underground world she emerged from. She looked forward to shedding her frumpy clothes and revealing her wild side.

"You'll soon find out who I know but can't reveal anything yet. Is that him slurping champagne, the man of honor."

"Yes."

He also bit into brie cheese and French bread. Guests in the kitchen came over to see the odd looking bag lady. Naomi sauntered over to the birthday guy and wrapped her arm around his stiff shoulder. She delivered her opening lines.

"So how 'bout treating me to a *chicken salad* sandwich at Dave's Deli sometime. I'll even give ya my *pickle* if you're good. You won't have to beg for one if you do as I say."

He blinked a few times and tilted his head to the left while clutching his champagne glass. Naomi expected this confused reaction. Others stared.

Naomi placed a warm hand on the back of his neck and rubbed her hips alongside his. "Don't you remember me, Steven? We were inseparable back then. We were a hot couple before ditching me for another sweetie. Boy, it was sultry!" Naomi tried slurring her speech to sound like she'd been drinking, fresh from the gutter. She roasted under multiple layers and couldn't wait to strip down.

"Com' on Steven honey, we double dated with *Minnie Minoso, your college homeboy, and wasn't he a hoot!*" Naomi hoped to win him over by dropping Minnie's name. This would loosen him up. "Can't you see that I've fallen on hard times, but still have a hot thing for you."

The Birthday Man's face turned crimson. Naomi would work him over and wipe away his perplexed expression through sweet talk and humor.

"I'm not......," he stuttered. His mouth opened as if to yawn, exposing numerous gold crowns and porcelain fillings. Naomi waited for him to play along, to say *something,* but he wouldn't.

After another attempt to get him talking, Naomi gave up

and stripped layer by layer, shedding the Bag Lady identity. Off came the bright orange sweater, then the lime green one, and then the brown one, and finally the striped pullover, all tossed aside, revealing a black lace bra. The rumpled skirt slid off her svelte frame and landed on her shiny high heeled boots.

She leaned into the befuddled man and swiveled her buttocks near his chest, exposing a skimpy bikini.

She glanced toward Mr. Lopes, who appeared confused and unsteady. Naomi noticed her pale assistant fumbling through his appointment book while arching an eyebrow. His moustache drooped and he turned ashen. Naomi was down to fishnet stockings, thong bikini, and sexy bra. Her black leather boots tapped the hardwood floor. A plate or glass crashed onto the kitchen linoleum.

Naomi noticed Mr. Lopes waving, urging her toward him. She circled the room, prancing and twirling like a prima ballerina. Why no boom box music she wondered. Had Lopes forgotten the sultry hypnotic tape she'd given him? He'd better get with the planned program, and soon. She imagined a roomful of judges penalizing her score.

"Naomi," Lopes whispered from across the room. "This is a terrible mistake. We've got the wrong address!"

Naomi stopped strutting and twirling. A seated guest behind her blushed, his eyes fixated on Naomi's bottom. The wildflower tattoo on her left buttock lay inches from his nostril.

"Wrong address?" Naomi shouted in Lopes direction. "What are you saying? And where's the music, goddammit!" The room stopped swirling, and her dizziness and giddiness dissipated.

"It's across and down the street. We blew it," whispered Lopes. "It's 936 Harrison, not 963. Oops." Lopes crumpled scrap papers into a fist and moaned.

She turned toward the reveler she thought was Steven Gold, her prime target and client. His torso began to twitch and shake from all the flirtatious attention. He now resembled a flaccid Gumby toy doll she had adored as a child. A Van Gogh print displaying a vast sunflower field hung above his shoulder on the wall. Naomi would dive into that luminous field and vanish.

Naomi faced him. "Steven? Steven Gold?" Then Naomi knew she'd made a rookie mistake by not confirming his identity from the onset. It was a birthday party but unfortunately the wrong one. And why hadn't the befuddled birthday fake spoken up earlier? Jesus!

"Okay, I'll be Steven Gold if you want. You've convinced me." He straightened and thrust out his chest, having recovered from shyness and stupor.

"You found your voice," said Naomi. "It's too late, too bad." Naomi reached for a sweater and slipped it on. She perspired all over, and wanted to clobber someone. Who dumped new batteries into this dude's brain cavity?

The Birthday Impostor turned toward a few buddies. "Okay, who hired her? I admit I was fooled. She's gorgeous." No one spoke. "Com' on guys, fess up. What a fabulous treat!"

"I know Steven Gold," said the woman who'd earlier guided Naomi to the birthday fraud, now full of bravado. "Steven had invited me to *his* party down the street, but told him I'd be here first. I'll take you there if you want." She placed a hand on Naomi's shoulder. A pendulum clock on a corner wall produced a bird call. Naomi waited for the cuckoo bird but it didn't show.

Naomi muttered under her breath. "Count your lucky stars folks, you witnessed a free peep show."

Then party guests passed a jar and placed numerous bills inside, and handed the money to Naomi. She lightened up and laughed. Naomi walked over to Lopes and patted his shoulder, telling him it was an honest mistake.

"Shouldn't we contact Steven's wife Susan with an update and clarify why we're running late," said Naomi. "I assume they've put a deposit down and I hate to disappoint by not appearing."

Lopes nodded. "She'll understand our predicament but we can make our way there and check in. If you're up to it."

Naomi was offered food and drink and invited to stay, but she politely declined. Then she and Lopes stepped onto the front porch and into a drenching downpour. Her clothes were soaked through and through and adhered to clammy skin. Her tangled and knotted hair was a soggy mess.

Naomi insisted they walk down the block to the intended birthday party and see what she was missing. They braved the wild downpour while still on Harrison, and then crossed over. She stopped in front of a bungalow dwelling and noted a festive gathering through the window. Naomi stood by the front gate and watched. Her heart raced while getting drenched. Naomi told Lopes to please return to the car and wait as she'd only be a minute. She felt too drained to perform again so soon.

Naomi opened the gate and stepped across a damp muddy lawn until reaching the front living room window. She pressed her nose against the outside glass and witnessed wild dancing. A striking man wearing a garish party hat circled the room and began hugging and kissing everyone. Naomi noted how light and bouncy he was on his feet, and how he radiated charm. When he stopped whirling he glanced outside at Naomi. They locked eyes. She tried to smile, but a lump or obstruction tightened her throat, and she felt chilled to the bone.

Oblivious

Oblivious

You could say Jerry Hoffman was distraught when his secure manufacturing job disappeared. He was replaced by an industrial robot, which performed the job of ten. Complaints about injury, fatigue, or stress also vanished with layoffs. The company's profit rose along with output. Jerry was livid at the damn robot, and derisively named him Battling Kelso. Kelso made Jerry obsolete. He imagined luring the robot to an isolated tavern by the river, getting it drunk and woozy, and then tossing it into the icy waterway. He'd watch Kelso float away, its circuitry and chips a soggy mess. Jerry would beat the murder or manslaughter rap by hiring a sharp attorney, then plead temporary insanity to a sympathetic jury. He knew his job was permanently gone.

Jerry and his cohorts had imbibed a bitter pill, and convened daily in Troy's oldest tavern over pitchers of ale. Robots didn't need health or pension plans, days off, or vacations. Automation and outsourcing was the death knell. Jerry was luckier than others as he had no dependents or outstanding debts. Jerry believed in 'pay as you go' and lived modestly. He lived alone in a two-story brick house inherited from his parents, who'd died a few years back.

Jerry grew bored and restless one November evening. He'd soon pick up a corned beef sandwich at the Italian deli and an evening edition of the Sunday Times. Troy was gritty, industrial, and somewhat bleak and desolate in winter. There wasn't much to do though Albany wasn't far off.

Jerry had worked with former school buddies in a tool making plant, and found comfort in the freight trains that rumbled by below his third floor shop window. He imagined hopping one and riding away to an unknown destination. Jerry sometimes daydreamed at work, and on lunch break read books on Eastern philosophy and religion. Perched on a hard metal stool, coffee thermos nearby, he'd read and listen for the trains. Occasionally he brought a whistling yo-yo and practiced new tricks, keeping fine motor coordination sharp. He showed these tricks to his buddies' children at family gatherings and potlucks.

Folks liked Jerry and who wouldn't? Pals fixed him up with a sister or cousin, wanting him to taste romance. Few dates developed further as he could be shy and fussy about a potential partner. Even before the layoff Jerry had considered leaving Troy. Monotonous routine was dulling his spirit and a fresh start was needed.

Over corned beef and ginger ale at the kitchen table, Jerry scanned the Sunday Times. He sorted through sections, being careful not to stain the newsprint with mustard or greasy French fries. He removed the magazine section and skimmed fashion ads and feature articles. A blurb toward the back described a retreat that sounded intriguing. The ad was positioned near others offering discount Caribbean cruises and Cape Cod bungalows.

He stared at the photo of trees and rustic cabins. Jerry had been to the Adirondacks and Catskills for hiking and fishing and enjoyed the autumn mountain colors. He knew he'd have to get away again. Jerry adjusted his reading glasses and sipped ginger ale. The ad described a unique retreat. It outlined a variation of Zen Buddhism, and offered a discount on food and lodging. The package included meditation and body movement classes. He had tried meditation a few times, and even self-hypnosis to mitigate floating anxiety when meeting new people, especially women.

Jerry clipped the discount offer and placed it on the counter top. He put his plate and glass in the sink for soaking. Then he went to pack for an extended weekend, intending to phone the next morning and reserve a place at the center. What the hell, he muttered. Unlike automated plant robots, people still craved getaways, fresh air, nature, and damn well deserved it.

Jerry drove off the next morning, leaving his house and Troy behind. A neighbor agreed to keep an eye on things and had a key. A harsh cold snap, though unlikely, could freeze the pipes. Troubles behind, he'd explore the offerings of this Zen Buddhist retreat center.   If it didn't pan out, he'd stay at a motel and fish along a pristine stream or lake. The Catskills offered lovely charm, and autumn's peak had passed, keeping tourists and big city folk away. He'd make out well either way. His reservation confirmed, the promo ad with directions lay on the passenger seat.

Route 44/55 became 209 as Jerry negotiated curves, passing small towns, farms and rolling hills. Jerry stopped for gas in one town, somewhere between Monticello and Kerhonkson, and asked for directions to the retreat center. No one had heard about it, but he sensed he was close. In the gas station lot, Jerry pulled to the side and parked. He rolled down the window and removed a peanut butter and jelly sandwich from a rumpled bag on the seat. A few crumbs fell out the window and onto the pavement while a couple of pigeons pecked at the crust. The cool breeze brushed against his pale skin. Jerry dozed off and his head rocked forward. He soon awoke and forgot for a moment where he was. Then Jerry started the ignition and drove back onto the country road. He glanced out at bare branched oak and maple and ingested a lingering apple cider scent.

Jerry spotted a colorful sign to the right and hit the brakes. He pulled off the main road and turned onto a dirt lane marked with potholes. Dust and pebbles landed on his windshield, reducing visibility. He drove on a half mile until reaching an iron gate. He finally arrived at his intended destination.

Jerry had read Zen Buddhist essays, piecing together its philosophy and principles. In his suitcase he had packed a worn copy of Siddhartha, a tale about a wandering disciple searching for truth. He had gotten a used edition at a Saturday flea market sale. Jerry parked in the dirt lot, the ground hardened from a recent cold snap. He needed a bathroom and a hot shower and was relieved the long drive ended. Jerry decided to leave his suitcase in the trunk and walk to the main lodge for check in. A map encased in glass attached to a wooden post guided him. He walked a winding dirt path, which led to an open grass meadow and then continued to the lodge entrance.

Jerry stepped inside and looked around. A tall lean man smiled from behind the counter. On mounted shelves lay an assortment of reading material, sundries, soaps, and art supplies, including watercolor paints.

"Welcome to Catskills Paradise. I'm Joseph."

"Hi. Jerry Hoffman." He shook Joseph's outstretched hand. "I've got a reservation for two nights."

Joseph checked his ledger. "Good to see you." Joseph was cheerful, his voice upbeat. Balding, he had just enough hair on the back for a short ponytail. He wore horned rimmed glasses that concealed dark hazel eyes. His teeth were bright and straight, except for one canine protruding from the bottom row. A rush of chilly air swept through a crack in the window, though the lodge was heated.

Jerry removed his wallet and a credit card. "I know it's unlikely, but I thought I'd ask."

"Sure. What is it?" Joseph leaned forward.

"Do you offer AAA or AARP discounts? Many hotels offer them."

"Sorry. But we offer a three-day package to new guests. This includes hearty meals, access to classes and free use of our tubs, sauna, and hiking trails. Is that acceptable?"

"Yes. I'll book an extra night."

"After you're settled," said Joseph, "come back for a personal tour of the grounds. Perhaps you'd like a soak first."

Joseph pointed in the direction of hot tubs and a herb scented sauna. He also handed Jerry a map of the sleeping quarters and highlighted his cabin in yellow marker. Jerry had never been in a hot tub, and looked forward to soaking in one.

Jerry already liked it here, and pondered staying longer. He'd join the maintenance crew, or cook meals for guests. This was only a fleeting fantasy, an enticing one. Jerry found his cabin in a cluster of elm and maples. A few guests ambled down the path from the main lodge. He heard a rushing stream by a footbridge that led to hiking trails.

Inside the cabin, Jerry lay down for a refreshing catnap and slept well. The bunk bed mattress was firm, not spongy. There was ample heat, and a small window that looked out toward the surrounding woods.

A half hour later, Jerry awoke and decided to accept Joseph's tour offer. He got dressed and grabbed a book and jacket before stepping outside into brisk cool air. He retraced his steps to the main office. After knocking and entering, he saw Joseph scribble in a notebook behind the counter.

"Find your cabin OK?"

"Yeah, no problem," said Jerry. "Are you free to show me around?"

"I'd like to, but I'm tied up for another hour. Do walk around and enjoy the grounds. Stop back at four o'clock and we'll see the sights together." The phone rang and Joseph picked up, booking a new reservation.

"Sounds good," said Jerry. He waved and stepped onto the porch. A fresh cool breeze tossed his thick unkempt hair into a disheveled pile. He wore a wool flannel shirt and jeans. Clutching the iron railing, he peered into the distance while descending narrow steps. His black Converse lost traction and slid on muddy spots. He moved cautiously onto a dirt path covered with small rocks. Jerry strolled past hot tubs and a sauna before taking a new meandering path toward a footbridge. The rushing water below soothed him. Jerry sat on a stone bench in the middle of the bridge. The rolling Catskills stretched across the horizon. Being laid off wasn't so bad after all.

He crossed the narrow bridge and spotted a small brick structure off to the side, not far from the stream bank. It stood apart from other buildings, with clumps of ivy clinging to the brick. Jerry walked over and noted a painted sign hanging on the door. Neat black lettering featured a name: Mel Eisenberg, Tax Accountant---CPA.

Jerry knocked on the door and a muffled voice responded. Jerry stuck his head inside and glanced around. The ten by twelve foot room had tiny windows. A balding man in his sixties sat behind a wide oak desk, an adding machine to his left. He chewed on a hamburger while scribbling with pencil into a bulky notebook. A sliver of meat juice dripped onto his chin, which he wiped with a napkin. Thick bifocals covered an angular face. He motioned for Jerry to sit on a hard wooden chair. A diploma or certificate hung above the man's head. A seal was stamped on the bottom of the framed certificate.

"What can I do for you today, sir? Need assistance preparing your tax return? It's early in the season but never too soon to get a head start."

The stranger tapped a pencil against his cheek and leaned forward.

Jerry said what popped into his head. "Does it get busy in spring?" Mel Eisenberg had to be playing a joke on visitors. Jerry was open to harmless diversion.

"Uh-hum. It gets busy, but November is slow so you're in luck." Mel bit into a thick pickle as a droplet of brine juice slid onto his sleeve. Jerry's mouth watered, and hoped dinner would soon be served.

"Would you like one of these? I've got an extra." Mel reached for tongs and pulled a pickle out from the jar.

"No thanks." Jerry craved juicy dill pickles, and had second thoughts but didn't want to impose.

Mel wiped his moist hand on a napkin, and then tapped Jerry's arm. "My rates are reasonable, but it'll cost more if you itemize your return. Weekend guests receive a ten per cent discount. Shall we begin?"

"I've brought nothing with me, Mr. Eisenberg."

"It's Mel."

"My documents and statements are at home."

"No problem," Mel said, waving off Jerry's admission. "We can work with what we have. Let's get started." Mel rubbed his hands together.

Jerry exhaled. The river flowed in the near distance. Mel was harmless and Jerry played along having nothing better to do.

"Okay. Let's get started," said Jerry.

"First, let's calculate interest and dividends for this year so far. Have you performed any helpful deeds or assisted someone?"

Jerry thought hard. "Can we come back to this? I need to mull it over."

Mel tapped his pencil on the desktop. Another one lay across the top of his earlobe. "I apologize, your name again?"

"Jerry Hoffman."

"Sorry Jerry, but I'm not set up to computerize your return. I've got to do it by hand. But I'm pretty quick."

"Sure. What do you need to know next?"

"Describe the failed relationships and blown opportunities you've had with the opposite sex over the past year. Assuming you're heterosexual. Now be truthful. If you claim zero, then I know you're not taking risks." Mel's eyes bulged.

"You're kidding. How'd you know I was filing as single, and not a joint return?"

"It's written on your face. Accountants can read between the lines." Mel leaned forward, his neck veins protruding. The light beam from above shone onto his bald pate, forming a splotch or halo.

"I admit I've blown a few personal encounters. I'm in my early fifties and still single. I've been hurt, sometimes depressed, even anxious."

"Good."

"Why?" Jerry didn't mind the probing questions and liked the attention.

"Because you'll take the standard deduction for things you could have done but didn't. You're given leeway for benign neglect, or what's deferred to as 'opportunity costs'. After all, it's hard to be perfect. That's why a higher standard deduction and personal exemption is given each year." Mel smiled. "We just write it off. Now, feel better?"

Jerry snapped from his trance. He was disclosing personal information and shortcomings to a stranger and he needed to exit.

"Thanks for your time Mel, but this is too awkward. I think I'd better go."

"But we're just getting started. We can devise all kinds of exemptions, credits, etc. Upper income filers do it, and so can you. Remember, nobody's perfect!"

Jerry shook Mel's hand, turned and shut the door behind him. He stepped into crisp mountain air, shaking his head. Who else knows about this nutcase accountant, this charlatan? He began crossing over the river, taking unsteady strides. Then Joseph approached, walking across the footbridge toward him. Joseph's gait had a bounce.

"Finding your way around I see. Isn't it delightful here?"

Jerry stopped in the middle of the bridge and clutched the railing. The river below picked up speed. "Are you aware of a strange man pretending he's a tax accountant?" Jerry pointed to the small brick building fifty feet away. "He's like a fortune teller, but uses an adding machine."

"Yes, Mel. He was here before the retreat opened, over a year ago. Mel had claim to that piece of property first. Now he contracts with us and provides specialty services. He's an honest guy and knowledgeable too." Joseph tapped Jerry's shoulder. "I'll show you around. Let's go."

They crossed back over the footbridge and climbed along a path. To the right was the kitchen and dining hall. Behind this, a small greenhouse stood on an incline, containing various plants and herbs. They soon stopped at a circular structure with a domed roof. A taped door sign announced a meditation session in progress. Joseph opened the door, and invited Jerry inside. A dozen guests sat cross-legged in a circle on thick carpet, eyes closed, palms turned up. Chanting ensued.

Jerry observed portraits hanging along the wall toward the front. Candles and coconut incense burned on an altar below the black and white prints. "Are these revered men?" asked Jerry, pointing to the photographs. One appeared to wink.

Joseph whispered. "They're former nightclub comics who once performed on these very grounds."

"You're not serious."

"Before this retreat officially opened, the property was a resort. I discovered discarded relics, these portraits, in a closet. They were in bad shape and smudged, so I restored the prints the best I could. What a shame."

"Anyone I recognize?"

"Probably," said Joseph. "There's Buddy Hackett, and on the far wall Shecky Greene." Joseph swung his torso and pointed. "Over in the corner, Joey Bishop." Joseph shrugged. "These stand ups may have performed in this very room."

"No kidding."

"Sh. Hear that?"

"Hear what?"

"Listen. Buddy Hackett is mumbling."

Jerry cocked his ear and pretended to also hear. "Yes, he's speaking to us." Buddy's portrait struck the wall it was mounted on.

"His voice is fading. What's he saying, Jerry?"

Jerry decided to contrive a pep talk that might inspire. "He's telling us to never quit no matter how challenging life is."

"What else? His voice flows in and out each day depending on his mood. He mutters a lot when he's grumpy."

"He's saying that when times get tough or rocky, keep punching. And remember to duck!"

"Thanks for interpreting."

"And if you don't mind, I need to get something off my chest."

"Sure, go ahead."

"It's a bit humiliating, but I was laid off from my job and replaced by an arrogant robot I named Battling Kelso."

"That's too bad. But how can a robot be arrogant? They have no feelings."

"True. But the bastard is efficient, and I give him credit."

"Being laid off and displaced is a bummer. But you have the ability to imagine, unlike the robot."

"True. I'll chase away the blues and revive here."

"We'll give it a go," said Joseph. "Here's to a good time."

The room grew louder with chanting and deep breathing. Guests meditated in unison exhaling on cue.

"Care to partake?"

"No thanks. Perhaps tomorrow," said Jerry, shaking his head.

"Good.   A body movement class starts before breakfast, sometime around six."

The mention of food roused Jerry's gurgling stomach. A shrill ringing ensued. Some ceased meditating, and began text messaging and conversing on tablets and on Smart phones. The babbling reminded Jerry of day traders buying and selling livestock futures on the Mercantile Exchange.

"Don't you marvel at their ability to multi-task?" said Joseph.

"Suppose so," Jerry replied. "But they're ruining the calm and peace."

Joseph grinned. "We encourage constant communication with the outside. It enhances the experience."

"Why?"

"Our philosophy is not to deprive guests of worldly comforts. Most Zen Buddhist practices require abstention from excess food, banter, and frivolous distractions. Here we promote comfort and convenience. Why swim against the tide? We integrate our practices with the twenty first century."

"I see," said Jerry.

"Instead of blocking distractions, we incorporate the clatter as focus training. It's an evolving process of systematic desensitization."

A guest on a laptop chewed saltine crackers and bit into a Snickers bar while logging onto a NASCAR website. A younger woman viewed an action movie on her screen. Jerry flinched at the battle scene depicting swords and decapitated limbs.

Joseph grabbed Jerry's arm. "Let's move on. I suggest a relaxation class tomorrow morning."

They ambled down the dirt path, and stopped at a building constructed from natural cob. It appeared energy efficient and welcoming from the outside. Joseph explained the design and origin of the structure. Eco-friendly materials were used on the retreat grounds.

As he pressed an ear against the doorframe Jerry heard a ball tapping against a paddle. It sounded like a loud ticking clock.

"It's our workout room. Let's go in."

Two intent competitors played Ping-Pong in the middle of the room. Drawn shades blocked any natural light. A hairy man resembling a mountain gorilla sucked from a camelback water bottle. He whacked the tiny white ball. It zinged and hummed as it flew over the net. Joseph pointed at the player with wild bushy red hair and drooping beard. Jerry marveled at the long scraggly beard and thought of the wild-eyed Smith Brothers on an old box of cherry cough drops, straight out of a gun-slinging western.

"That's Robbie Belzer, the local table tennis champ. Determined fellow, and never lost a match." Joseph corrected himself. "Actually, he did lose once which was disastrous."

"Did he throw a tantrum?" Jerry wondered what shenanigans lay ahead. This wasn't a normal retreat, or at least how Jerry envisioned one.

"Yep. He began harassing his opponent, threatening to run him off the grounds. We don't tolerate bullying and intimidation."

"So if I challenge him and beat the pants off him he'll come after me?"

Joseph shook his head. "Cry baby, sore loser. We don't sympathize with whiners like Robbie."

"I love Ping-Pong. I'll challenge the grouch. It'll restore my confidence after that deflating job layoff."

"Anyway, he vowed not to lose and agreed to vacate the premises if he threatens anyone again. And he won't lose. Robbie's won hundreds of consecutive games. He gets better and more determined."

Jerry shook his head. "What's he trying to prove? Why all the machismo posturing?"

"You've got to understand Robbie's past. He comes from an abusive home. Robbie arrived with a thick file from a foster agency seeking an appropriate setting. I'm paid a stipend to be a guardian or Big Brother. He's only seventeen."

"Seventeen? He looks twice that."

"Yes," Joseph continued, "and I feel sorry for him. As long as Robbie's playing ping pong, his anger is displaced."

The game continued, the volleys going on and on.

"What about counseling?"

"Doesn't work with Robbie. He can't sit still. He's got attention disorder, and drugs or medication won't sedate him.   We've tried everything and repetitive activity works."

"So he competes here all day?"

"And night," added Joseph. "He never sleeps, or so it seems. At least he's content."

"Until he loses," said Jerry.

"Yeah, then watch out."

Jerry observed for a moment.   Robbie's backhand was powerful and his reach expansive. He consumed an energy drink and kept focus. To Jerry, Robbie could eat or sleep and compete, and he yearned for this intensity and concentration. He'd accomplish great things and demand his old job back and prove his worth.

Then Jerry approached the table.

"Where ya goin'? Don't get too close," cautioned Joseph. He grabbed Jerry's shoulder.

Jerry whispered in Robbie's direction. "Great strokes champ. Good rhythm you got going."

Robbie's face reddened and he flinched. He turned toward Jerry, and this diversion cost him. His forehand slam hit the top of the net and bounced back onto the table.

"Get lost asshole or I'll chop you up!" Robbie faked throwing the foam paddle at Jerry, who ducked and backpedaled.

"Sorry.   I'll leave you be." Jerry offered advice from a safer distance. "You shouldn't get attached to the result. A Zen Buddhist principle."

Robbie scowled and lost another point. Then he shook his fist and spit.

Joseph interceded and tapped Jerry's elbow. "We've seen enough from that hothead. Dinner will soon be served." He led Jerry out the door.

Jerry anticipated a wholesome meal, perhaps a hearty vegetarian one.   Jerry was used to meat and potatoes but craved a dietary change, and a chance to shed pounds and acquire more energy.

"What's on tonight? Veggie lasagna and Caesar salad I hope."

"You'll see," Joseph said. "It'll be nutritious."

They walked the main path while Jerry tucked his hands into his pockets. He gazed up at an emerging crescent moon. A cloud formed a halo around it.

"What were you doing before the retreat?"

Joseph stared ahead. "I attended chef school where I met my ex, and then we opened a restaurant. It was fun but we couldn't make a go of it. Then I managed a bookstore after the divorce and eventually found my way here. I procured loans to purchase the property, plus I inherited money from a relative."

"Thanks for showing me around." Jerry didn't want to intrude by asking more personal questions.

"No problem. It's not busy today and I've got time. My assistant is helping out with reservations and booking and I need a break."

The early evening air became chilled.

"I'll take you to the dining hall in the main lodge. There's an adjoining room where we conduct seminars and workshops. Adventurous souls gravitate to these classes. Last week, we hosted a dream therapy group."

"I remember some dreams," Jerry offered, "but usually the frightening ones."   They stepped onto the front porch and entered the main building. Jerry poked his head into the adjacent space Joseph had referred to. He glanced around. Two back doors led to a porch and a grass area, perfect for a picnic on a mild day. The room had beige walls and an old sofa by a bookcase. A flower vase lay atop a nearby piano.

"We have concerts here," said Joseph. "I'd play for you now, but these ladies want no distractions."

At a square table, four senior women sat on metal folding chairs. Hands swished around colorful ivory tiles. A rattling sound echoed from the ceiling, while an animated discussion brewed over strategy.

"What's happening?"

"Our annual Senior mah-jongg gathering. The game originated in China and made its way to American cities and suburbia," explained Joseph. "These ladies are bonding and sharing the game's nuances."

Money was wagered as the game concluded. Jerry thought about poker and how he once played on Friday evenings with friends. Maybe he'd start up again. A new round began and Jerry sauntered over. Not wanting to intrude, he stood apart from the action. Then an errant tile flew off the table and landed on his sneaker. Jerry bent to retrieve it and examined the intricate designs. A red dragon was etched onto smooth fake ivory. The tile appeared to glow in his palm.

A moist hand reached over and snatched the tile, and slapped down hard on his wrist. The player glared at Jerry.

"Mind your own business, creep," she mumbled under her breath.

"Excuse me?" said Jerry. "I wasn't taking it. What's your problem?"

"Scram, Junior! We're territorial and you weren't invited to our gathering."

"Com' on. It's dinner time," said Joseph, placing a hand on Jerry's stiff shoulder.

"What a nasty piece of work," mumbled Jerry.

"Sorry 'bout that. My apologies again. Muriel was out of line and lost her composure. When her adrenaline gets going, she gets locked in and forgets it's a game."

"You suggest I ignore her?"

"Recent divorce and health issues make her grouchy and crabby. She gives me a hard time so don't take it personally."

Jerry turned and glared. "Hard not to."

Dinner gongs rang. Guests entered the lodge and lined up behind a glass door. Jerry smelled corn chowder which he craved. The door opened as separate lines formed by a long table. Jerry popped open a metal food bin exposing giant size waffles. A separate bin contained whipped cream, and another walnuts or almond pieces.

"Waffles?"

"Yes," said Joseph. "They're delicious cornmeal waffles made from natural cornmeal flour and free range eggs. Only the best ingredients."

"Interesting dinner choice."

"We shake things up now and then," said Joseph.

Jerry felt a body graze his hip. He dished up and moved, not wanting to delay others. With tongs he dropped a waffle onto his plate. He took a spoon and sprinkled nuts over mounds of whipped cream. Jerry sat alongside an affectionate couple who smooched between bites, and devoured his dinner while glancing around. He was open to meeting someone new and interesting. Jerry peered out the window and noticed an attractive woman. She sat under the front porch lights, absorbed in a novel. Then she glanced at the night sky, and next his way. They locked eyes. He wanted to wave but nervously turned away. Jerry needed to meet her, but by the time he stood to go outside she was gone.

Jerry indulged in calm and refreshing sleep. He enjoyed being removed from ordinary routine and loved the pretty surroundings. It was a treat to enjoy food cooked by someone else. The cabin had a bunk bed, a desk and chair, and sufficient heat. Jerry hoped he'd bump into the attractive woman he'd seen from last night. He craved female company.

At seven the next morning he was roused by gongs, the breakfast signal. He rose slowly and stepped outside, and then washed in a bathroom along the footpath before continuing on toward the dining hall. The air was crisp, a brilliant morning in the mountains.

On the breakfast buffet table were fresh cold cuts: salami, ham, corned beef, pastrami, and sausage. Cream cheese and lox caught his eye. While poking slabs of pastrami with a fork, Jerry noticed the alluring babe from the previous evening. A salami piece dropped from his plate and he couldn't catch it. Then she approached him.

"Isn't this a wonderful breakfast?" she said.

"It's unusual, like the dinner choice." He wanted to make a good first impression and join her.

"Care to join me?" she asked. They sat by a window and absorbed morning light. Jerry maneuvered his knife and fork and cut small pieces. He wanted to avoid a mess. They made small talk while he noted her high cheekbones and full lips. She told him about her graphic design business. Jerry yearned to spend the morning together. Then Hillary invited him on a hike and he quickly accepted.

It was a bright gorgeous morning. Jerry returned to his cabin to retrieve a small backpack and water bottle while his heart raced. He packed a whistle in case they got lost. The trails were well marked and he wanted everything to go right. A half hour later, he met Hillary at the lodge. They walked to the trailhead and began their hike. Jerry spotted Mel's brick building in the distance. He wanted to tell Hillary about the interesting tax accountant, but decided not to. She'd think he was goofing around, or imagining things.

They hiked on the path passing pretty foliage. Jerry wondered about black bear and had asked Joseph about wildlife. He was told to watch for hummingbirds and the eastern meadowlark. Hillary carried binoculars and a bird watching guide borrowed from a friend. Soon they stopped and rested by the river. They ceased chitchatting and listened to birdcalls.

Then Jerry noticed a furry dark form sweeping through the bushes. A black bear was foraging. He nudged Hillary's arm and pointed toward the rustling sound. They observed a small black bear scampering through brush.

"Wow. First time you've seen bear in the wild?"

"Yes," whispered Hillary. "Let's turn around."

They turned back and continued hiking. Lunch would be served at one o'clock and there was no hurry. Jerry enjoyed Hillary's company and liked her keen eye for color. He wanted to know more about her.

"How'd you hear about this place?" Jerry asked.

"A friend recently visited. Do you like the retreat?

"I do." Jerry paused. "But stay clear of odd ones who are rough and hostile."

"What do you mean?"

Jerry savored the moment with his newfound companion. Stay positive, he thought. "Nothing to dwell on. Just riffraff here and there."

Morning light filtered through open branches, creating faint shadows on the ground. Jerry again spotted Mel's small brick building by the footbridge. He sipped water while resting on a fallen log. The sun's rays warmed his face. He desired continual contact with Hillary though Boston was far from Troy. He wondered if she had a boyfriend.

"I'm curious about the hostile people you encountered," said Hillary.

"Let's say disagreeable," said Jerry. "But I'm having a great time with you." Jerry sneezed and grabbed a tissue. "It's not allergy season, is it?"

"I love a good yarn," said Hillary. She moved closer, her legs almost touching his, and leaned toward him on the log.

Jerry hesitated but figured he'd amuse her and share a laugh. He wasn't adept at telling stories but would give it his best shot. He exhaled through the nostrils.

"Where to begin. Well, people are meditating in this large open space, chanting and humming. Next thing I know, i Phones and texting dominate. There's discombobulating buzzing, like swirling gnats." Jerry waited for a response.

"Continue. Let's hear more."

"There's a young gal absorbed on a laptop when she's supposed to be chanting. Portraits of nightclub comedians are mounted. I recognized Phil Silvers. He later played Sergeant Bilko on the television comedy. Great show."

"Before my time. But I suppose," Hillary offered, "there are reruns in syndication."

"This place used to be a popular resort, a hotel. We could be sitting on sacred ground this very minute."

"You're kidding."

"Nope. Joseph the owner and tour guide relayed this. You'll have to meet him."

"Go on. But slow down. I'm trying to absorb it all." Hillary arched an eyebrow and blinked. Jerry thought it was a slight twitch.

"Then Joseph escorts me to the workout room and a hothead named Robbie Belzer is smashing Ping Pong balls and feigns hurling his paddle at me." Jerry's voice climbed an octave while conversing in a flurry. "He's downright livid because I want a close up of his playing technique. And the guy never sleeps!"

Hillary discreetly backed away. She blinked again, scrunching her nose. Jerry told himself to slow down. He didn't want her believing he was fabricating everything or was a paranoid nutcase. 'Slow down', he told himself.

"And there's more. Shall I continue?"

Hillary stared. Jerry decided to talk on to fill the awkward gap. He needed reassurance from a caring attentive woman.

"Finally, there's a Senior mah-jongg retreat in the main lodge. They're tough cookies."

"Mah-jongg?"

"Ladies are tossing tiles, part of the game. Then one lands square on my foot. I retrieve it and I'm called a creep. She thought I was stealing."

"That's awful," Hillary said, sliding further away on the log. She was about to get up and leave. Jerry reached out as she broke away and began walking. A Pandora's Box had opened and he perspired all over. His shirt now soaked, Jerry needed a shower to wash away cumulative stains. He'd douse his body with cold water.

"Please wait up, Hillary. This all happened." He walked behind her and stared at dirt stained heels, needing to shut up or change the subject. He avoided stepping in deer dung. As she quickened the pace he tried keeping up.

"I'll prove it."

Hillary stopped and turned. "I don't know if I want to hear more."

"Have I mentioned the interesting accountant who works in the building up ahead? His name's Mel Eisenberg and stays here year round." Jerry scratched an annoying itch. "I met him yesterday."

"Yeah?" said Hillary, averting eye contact.

"Let's stop for a short visit and he'll confirm our recent meeting. He's not an ordinary tax accountant."

"Was he mean to you too?"

"Not at all. He's insightful, and we're almost there."

Hillary patiently agreed to a brief stop and meet Mel. They soon arrived, and Hillary examined the business sign that hung on the door. Jerry knocked and waited, and then poked his head inside. Mel looked out from behind the wide desk.

Joseph sat on a wooden chair across from Mel, his back toward Jerry.   A lamp stood on Mel's oak desk. Hillary stepped inside and leaned against the door.

"Hey Jerry."   Joseph turned and smiled and raised a porcelain cup. "Join us for tea."

Mel gathered fluffy cushions and placed them on an area rug. Jerry inhaled soothing peppermint aroma from a kettle on a hot plate.

"Have a seat folks," Mel said, bowing. "Good to see you again Jerry. Here on business or pleasure?" Mel nodded at Hillary, and then winked at Jerry. "Wishing to file a joint return?"

They drank herbal mint tea while relaxing on cushions. A crow on the roof cackled. Jerry was overcome by a brash alien voice that rose up from within. Jerry knew he was losing control. He glanced up at the ceiling beams and unexpectedly blurted out: "Do you believe in love at first sight? Love at first sight!"

Hillary glared at Jerry and he gleaned shock and horror, not unlike viewing an impending collision of two trains. He liked Hillary, and wanted to undo the babbling mess from earlier on the trail.

"Any thoughts, Mel," Joseph said. "Attraction is an intriguing mystery."

Mel shrugged, pointing to numerous tax manuals behind his desk. "I wouldn't know about love at first sight, but I know the marriage penalty is gone."

"You gave helpful advice yesterday. Recount the highlights from our discussion."

Jerry knew Hillary was departing that afternoon. He wanted this moment to last. He'd miss her, and suspected his brain was playing deceitful tricks, projecting more than existed. He'd forgotten how to display charm and discretion.

"More tea?" offered Mel, breaking Jerry's ruminations, and ignoring his request for a recap of yesterday's conversation.

Jerry passed his cup.

"Yesterday, let's see," said Mel, stroking his chin. "I need to open my appointment book for a refresher."

"Tell Hillary about our encounter, and how we deduct for risks and opportunities not taken. You equated accounting practices to life and making choices."

"Yes,"confirmed Mel. "I do recall our session. Shall we recalculate your return?"

Jerry turned toward Joseph. "Please describe what we saw yesterday in the meditation room. You witnessed the shenanigans, the silly distractions too."

"What's to tell?" said Joseph. "The guests were meditating."

"And what else?"

"Nothing else. Normal routine."

"Huh? And the workout room?" said Jerry.

"Table tennis. Great action though a bit dicey."

"But that firebrand Robbie Belzer almost mugged me with his paddle!"

Hillary stood and backpedaled toward the door. "Thanks for tea gentlemen but it's time to go."

Jerry started after her but then hesitated. Hillary bolted out the door and scampered across the footbridge. Jerry soon followed but lost her. He wanted another chance and knew it likely wouldn't happen. He'd apologize and begin anew, and omit anything out of the ordinary. He had blabbed like a damn fool.

Jerry winced as Joseph approached with hands outstretched. "Come join me for a hearty lunch. There's room at the table."

"Thanks," Jerry whispered. "My body aches and I'm experiencing vertigo. Maybe it's stress."

"And," Joseph continued, "I suggest you remain for Bingo game night. You might get lucky and meet the next woman of your dreams. Or win a prize."

"Why didn't you corroborate my previous encounters? Hillary thinks I'm delusional or paranoid. But I'm not oblivious to what's happening."

"Making good impressions is an art. Then you have to close the deal. When pushed into vulnerable or awkward situations it wakes you up a bit I'm told."

Jerry scratched under his chin.

"Guess I've been caught off guard despite good intentions. I'm out of my comfort zone here."

"No worries. We overlook perceptual blind spots that come with aging." Joseph winked. "Even your robot nemesis Kelso has limitations."

"Guess so, though not obvious."

"We're considering utilizing robotic technology to lead our personal growth seminars. We may not need people to facilitate group discussion." Joseph placed a wad of chewing gum in his mouth.

"I hope our guests get used to the potential change and won't mind disclosing personal issues with a robot. They can be programmed to be very objective."

Jerry nodded and paused. "Is lunch on?"

"Not so fast," said Joseph. "I'll take you inside one last attraction before lunch. It's a valued addition to our facility. But first I'll show you something under construction but won't be ready for another year."

They walked to a vacant site and Jerry observed a dump truck on the lot. He wondered if a miniature amusement park was planned, complete with carousel and roller coaster.

"I'm building a twenty-four hour Pancake restaurant that's insomniac friendly," said Joseph. "It's modeled on a Portland diner called 'The Original Hotcake House'. Mine will be named 'The Original Original Hotcake House'." Joseph's eyes widened. "We'll have a long counter and small cozy booths. It'll open within a year."

"You're joking of course. And into playing pranks, aren't you Joseph. Is anything normal around here?"

"Well, insomniacs get lonely and the nights stretch on. An informal eating spot offers company and camaraderie. Guests can cut loose if desiring to. There's divorce, impotence, unrequited love, job layoffs, and other painful topics to explore at three in the morning."

"I'd share a silly joke or two over flapjacks and strong black coffee," said Jerry, playing along with Joseph's bizarre vision.

"You get it."

"Clarify this please: Would hypochondriacs like me find acceptance in this diner? Complaining about health issues might bore or alienate patrons." Jerry grew less skeptical and interested in Joseph's project, knowing it was a bit loony.

"Take that risk. It's feasible that insomniacs exhibit hypochondriac tendencies as well. You'll fit right in, Jerry. I'm in your corner."

"Thanks for your time and company, again. I can tell you've got an interesting sense of humor."

"It just worked out plus you've been a good sport. My sweetie is off visiting with her mom. I enjoy meeting new guests and playing host."

Jerry nodded and loosened his shoulders.

"Besides, we pick on lonely and vulnerable souls like you to toughen them up."

"Huh?"

"Just giving you a hard time. No worries. Follow me to a recent addition on the grounds. It'll impress you."

Joseph led them to a hidden grove off a side trail. Then they entered a stucco building with a tiled roof. Jerry noticed the large copy machine in a corner of the only room. Above the copier, framed documents lined the wall. A computer and printer stood opposite the entrance.

"Welcome to the sacred room on the grounds."

"How so?" asked Jerry.

"We produce and distribute certificates and awards to special guests before their departure. Note the enticing samples posted on the far wall."

What departures? Jerry concocted a dark fantasy about hapless victims butchered in this remote room, the body chopped and disposed of in the overgrown weeds behind the building. He released his unsettling vision and relaxed.

"I'll explain what happens here."

"What kinds of awards are you giving? Perhaps I deserve an Oscar for forgettable performance."

Joseph cleared his throat. "As you're aware, important milestones are recognized. Diplomas and awards honor accomplishments in the workplace, at school, and for athletics."

Jerry flashed back to receiving his perfect Attendance award in Third grade. He remembered bowing on the auditorium stage, wearing a red clip-on tie attached to a starched collar.

"Let's create an award for you Jerry, and pardon my brief spiel without note cards." Joseph chuckled.

Joseph led Jerry to the computer and turned the power on. His new certificate would be framed.

"Ready?"

"I need to think. I've accomplished little recently I'm afraid."

"Have you enjoyed your weekend?"

"At times," replied Jerry, "despite my having to navigate a human obstacle course."

"Then let's produce an award for living in the moment and enjoying the company of others."

"But I don't always enjoy company, especially those I don't know well."

"Pretend you do. It's a start. We can always revise your award."

"Living in the moment? This sounds vague. What moment?"

"You've been open to new experiences, though not all have been pleasant."

"By not pleasant, are you referencing rejection." Jerry drew a breath. "No more mishaps thank you."

"Let's focus on the upside of your visit. You maintained composure when facing adversity. You take risks and don't get easily rattled."

"Other than to relax, why do folks come here?"

"Many come for a personal transformation, or makeover. Sometimes folks repackage themselves to be well liked."

"Well liked? It's not obvious that's happening here. Why is that important?"

"Now Jerry, accumulating friends and contacts is important during these challenging times. It's an asset to be well liked."

"Then perhaps I'll grow old, decrepit, and lonely. Romantic connection would be comforting though."

"You're onto something there."

"Perseverance counts. Or ability to absorb blows and recover."

"Yes, I agree. Would you like a certificate honoring that quality? We have a similar prototype hanging on the far wall. Let's print one out, frame it and it's good to go."

Jerry rubbed his scalp. "Let's go with your award recommendation for being a good sport. I like that one. I'm a good sport, I roll with the punches, so why not."

Jerry surveyed various frames from a crate and selected one. He'd stay for Bingo night and mingle, and if very lucky meet someone special or interesting. He believed in luck and in humility. Jerry clutched his printed certificate and placed his prize in a simple but appealing frame.

Gremlin

Gremlin

Dusty hit the jackpot when he beat out a hundred applicants for a teaching position. He was just out of college, in debt, and still living in Eugene when he applied for the third grade opening. His buddy Jon had driven him to the interview in a wobbly Volkswagen bug, a black Beetle with a shaky clutch. On back roads to Veneta, a rural town fifteen miles from Eugene, Dusty hoped the rickety bug would deliver him on time for the meeting. He was nervous all right, and half hoped he'd bomb, to avoid the pressure of taking over for a teacher in the middle of the year.

Long story short, Dusty got the job. He attributed his success partly to the new Irish tweed sport coat purchased in Donegal the previous summer. He told Jon the hand woven tweed bestowed Irish luck, and his buddy treated him to Guinness stout that evening. They celebrated way past midnight and closed the place down after many beers.

The celebration ended the next morning, a damp Saturday in late December. Dusty awoke groggy and stuffy, staving off a cold. He lay chilled, knowing his new position would soon begin. He had no vehicle, and little money to purchase a used one. He'd never applied for credit, eking by on college loans and work study jobs in the campus library. He had met Angela while working there two years ago.

Dusty got around on a Univega ten speed bike, and when it rained wore a flimsy vinyl poncho that flapped in the breeze. He'd roast inside while climbing steep hills, grinding toward his girlfriend's ceramics art studio. He'd regretted not having money to take Angela to nice restaurants or to the theatre and hated being poor. Layers of clothes had adhered to moist skin while biking in the rain without fenders. At night, Dusty strapped a cheap plastic light around his ankle. It bounced around and dangled, shaking the worn batteries. Now he needed a reliable car, one that would get him to his new job.

Dusty dressed and left his apartment, moving in slow motion. He stopped at the 7-11 market down the street for orange juice. Outside the store, he examined a Nickels Ad paper. He stood under the awning, and shivered in the damp downpour while scanning the auto section for a cheap car, hopefully one under four hundred, providing its engine functioned. He thought he got lucky, again, when the Gremlin ad appeared. Dusty hadn't the foggiest what a Gremlin AMC was, but knew that AMC had made the Rambler in the '50's. He folded the paper under his armpit and jogged home in the rain.

Dusty contacted Fred Johnson, the Gremlin's owner, and they agreed to meet at his mechanic for a vehicle inspection. Tony, Fred's trusted mechanic, would do a cursory inspection and list needed repairs, if any. Tony's shop stood next to Dunkin' Donuts, along the main thoroughfare. Dusty walked the mile to Franklin Boulevard and met Fred outside the donut shop. It was pouring buckets, a gray chilly day. Fred parked the Gremlin in the lot for Dunkin' Donuts customers. The lot was also used by the cannery plant crew who plucked defective corn and beets from roving conveyer belts. The cannery was behind the repair shop.

Dusty and Fred stood outside, pelted by raindrops. Dusty eyed the Gremlin and saw a spacecraft, its rear windows and body arched like a bubble. He'd seen a similar module on a futuristic cartoon series called the Jetsons. White paint chips peeled in spots, but overall, its shell looked fresh and well maintained. The Gremlin stood atop a deep puddle, and to Dusty, treaded water to stay afloat. He imagined snapping his fingers and the vehicle would rise like a blimp.

Dusty knew nothing about cars and instinctively kicked all four tires, hoping the car wouldn't collapse. Fred invited Dusty to take her for a test spin, but Dusty feared skidding on wet pavement and crashing. He needed to relax before driving a strange vehicle on slick roads.

Dusty got inside Gremlin and sniffed. It had a homey lived in scent. The interior, vinyl red, appeared sharp and clean. Dusty sat behind the large steering wheel, and fiddled with the lights and wipers. Fred showed him the defroster and heater and how best to start the engine when cold. Dusty pulled a knob, the choke, and then turned on the radio. The station was set to a Ducks football game. Absorbed by the game, Dusty and Fred cheered a Ducks touchdown. It was late December, and a Bowl berth was at stake. They forgot about the car and why they were there.

Gremlin was a five speed manual powered by a six cylinder engine, nothing fancy. A worn owner's manual lay in the glove compartment. A new clutch had been installed, and now reenergized, neared one hundred and fifty thousand miles. Fred, the original owner, had it twelve years. He'd given it to his son Willy, but Willy no longer needed Gremlin. Dusty would soon find out more about Willy. The name rang familiar when Fred mentioned who'd driven it last.

Tony needed an hour to inspect Gremlin so buyer and seller moved to the donut shop next door, to wait out the storm. They sat at the counter making small talk before ordering donuts and coffee. Dusty was warm and cozy, and protected from winter chill. He'd been here before, at midnight, studying for midterms. The noisy lights blurred night into day.

The donuts looked the same, and after a while, tasted the same. A long mirror reflected a line of torsos bent over coffee. Dusty imagined leading an Eastern philosophy seminar right here at the counter: Time is transcended and no one hurries to be somewhere.

Dusty recalled the cannery crew on midnight break. They'd huddle and chitchat over black coffee, while a full moon hovered above the shop. Dusty liked the chocolate honey glaze and butternut donuts. He'd order three or four, and devour them with hot coffee. The donut grease would plug his intestines and induce constipation. Sometimes, the cannery stench of pulverized green beans or corn seeped through the donut shop window.

Dusty observed the efficient baker through a glass partition, noting his white apron stained with jelly, custard, and flour. He hoisted metal trays with mitts, and slid donuts into the oven in one motion. Next, he dumped and mixed fresh batter in a giant vat, a pastry chef on an assembly line.

Fred ordered a jelly donut and strong coffee, and offered to treat Dusty. A wiry woman behind the counter took their order. She possessed a beak like nose and Dusty had nicknamed her 'Bird'. A pleasant smile revealed a set of crooked teeth. Her pink striped apron matched the store decor.

"So, how long you've been in Eugene?" Fred asked.

Dusty bit into his crusty donut. Crumbs fell onto his lap and napkin. Then he swiveled on the stool toward Fred.

"I arrived in Eugene to attend college, maybe five years ago. And I graduated on time, unlike others I know."

"What'd ya study?"

"Psychology and Elementary Education. I did my student teaching at a local school nearby."

"I grew up here," Fred said. "This has always been home. Was in the merchant marines in my twenties, saw the world a bit. But I love it right here." Fred scratched his chin.

"Yes, I agree, and I'm starting a new teaching position. I'm replacing someone on maternity leave, but it's a temporary assignment."

"Fantastic! What grade?" Fred's eyes widened.

"Third grade. But I'm a bit anxious about taking over in the middle of the year. It'll be challenging replacing a popular and well liked teacher."

Dusty stiffened when thinking about his previous teaching internship. He'd felt thrown in without much guidance, and had gotten eaten alive by rambunctious fifth graders. Practically run out of town. He'd still have occasional flashbacks of his charges gone hog wild, feeling impotent to stop the mayhem. HIs mentor supervisor was hardly there. Dusty discovered he'd been conducting real estate business on the side and worked two jobs at once. Other interns or cohorts had it rough too, but nothing like this. Dusty referred to his recurring flashbacks as 'post traumatic battle disorder'.

"You'll do just fine," offered Fred. "It's rough landing any work around here. Bad recession. Very bad times." Fred rapped his large knuckles on the counter. "*Everyone* likes Eugene and no one wants to leave. You've got folks with advanced degrees making minimum wage."

"I know. It's downright depressing."

Fred scratched his head and tugged on long earlobes. "I bet the opening was cutthroat competitive. It's always been an employers' market here."

Dusty nodded. Then Bird returned with refills and he noticed dark hair strands on her forearm.   A prominent mole sat above her wrist and Dusty wondered if it might be malignant. He enjoyed Fred's company, which diverted him from nervous thoughts and worry. The caffeine and overhead lights pumped his adrenaline.

"I think I got lucky," said Dusty.

"Why say that? You obviously made a great impression during the interview. Don't sell yourself short."

"I relaxed when the principal said he was considering two other candidates. He shared this from the get-go, and I figured I have nothing to lose. So I went for broke, really puffed myself up. And he had me teach an impromptu math lesson afterward, and I hit all my marks."

The outside rain dropped in buckets. Dusty hoped Gremlin checked out because he liked Fred and wanted to inherit *his* car.

"See, so it wasn't *only* luck that got you the offer. It's also talent and focus and good preparation."

"Do you believe in plain Lady Luck, outside of our control?" Dusty asked.

Fred sneezed into a napkin. Wild bushy eyebrows added bulk to his frame. To Dusty, he could've once been a mill worker or lumberjack. Fred's calloused hands lay on top of the counter. He wore an extra large plaid flannel shirt and jeans with suspenders.

"Absolutely, yeah. I believe in random luck plain and simple. We don't choose our parents or where on Earth we're born, or when."

Fred moved closer and continued, while Dusty finished his assortment of donuts with coffee.

"Let's examine a worst case situation and luck, or lack of. Suppose you're Jewish in Berlin, 1938 or '39, and you own a shop or business. You wake up the next morning to shattered store glass and menacing scorn followed by malicious beatings."

"You're right," Dusty whispered. "Humans inflict needless suffering onto others. Being at the wrong place at the wrong time is tragic."

"Exactly. Luck, plain and simple, that determines our fate. But we *do* make choices: Some big, some not so big. Many make the best of a bad hand they've been dealt."

Fred rested a palm under his chin and sighed. "Don't want to bend your ear back, but here's an example of unusual luck. Want to hear it?"

"Sure." Dusty glanced at the wall clock and knew that Gremlin was in Tony's capable hands. Anxious thoughts about teaching abated.

"I've got a younger brother, Paul. He wasn't very kind to his wife Rita. Downright mean at times. Controlling son of a..... So she considers leaving him, waiting, waiting for the perfect opportunity. This is what Rita tells *my* wife, who then informs me. They're pretty close. Then one day, Rita finds out about the young man across the street. He needs a house sitter while he visits his parents out of town. It's just for a week. Well, without telling my brother, Rita takes the guy up on the offer. She packs a suitcase and leaves while Paul's at work. The homeowner pays her to care for the plants and house cats."

Fred paused to blow his nose. "A refill? On me."

"Sure. Thanks."

"Shall I continue?"

"Sure, go ahead." Dusty was enjoying the moment and liked the diversion. He blocked out snippets of nearby chatter. Soaked patrons entered the shop and being Oregon, no one carried an umbrella.

"So Rita moves out. She's just across the street. When

Paul gets home he shouts for dinner and there's no response. He looks for a note, some sign, but she's gone. He calls my house and we know nothing about her plan. Then he phones the police at midnight and Rita's listed as missing the following evening."

"Did this really happen?" said Dusty.

"Meanwhile," Fred continued, "she's having a blast hiding out: watching videos, eating popcorn and chocolate, cats curled on her lap. Free to do as she pleases for once. She views the evening news and sees an outdated photo of herself as a missing person and watches the newscaster going on about possible foul play. The police question Paul and he contacts an attorney."

"It's getting out of hand," said Dusty, who squirmed on the stool and had to pee. But he didn't want to break Fred's momentum.

"Yep, it's getting out of hand all right. Rita thinks about coming clean and ending her charade, but can't. She's right *across* the street, maybe thirty feet away. She opens the living room blinds and peeks through, and observes her distraught hubby pacing the living room floor. She mocks him, whispering, 'poor baby doesn't have his dinner.' It's obvious who I sympathize with."

"What happened?" Dusty noticed hairs protruding from Fred's nostrils.

"Well," Fred continued, "Rita's celebration suffers a temporary setback the next morning."

"Why?"

"She discovers the toilet overflows after flushing, and the shower won't work properly. There's a massive leak, maybe a break in the water pipe. It's winter and frigid outside that day. So she calls a plumber and neglects to contact the owner. She's panicky."

"A referral?" asked Dusty.

"Probably," said Fred. "So a plumber comes over to fix the pipes. Young, handsome guy. He's got his tools spread all over the bathroom floor and tub. It's a complete mess. Wrenches, hammers, drill bits, even a small blowtorch. Then Rita and the plumber start chatting about family relationships and divorce while she watches him work. Sometimes it's easier unloading with a stranger who you think you'll never see again."

"That's true, Fred."

"Well, this is Rita's version as told to my wife, after the fact. She wants the water problem fixed but relates to the plumber's recent marital woes, offering snippets of advice."

"Advice? Not a good idea," said Dusty. "Bad timing."

"She sees that the plumber's agitated, and shaking his wrench. Rita wants him to do his job and stops her compulsive yapping. She nods her head while he blows off steam and resumes work. He soon fixes the leak and Rita's mighty relieved. She alerts the homeowner later that morning and explains what happened and apologizes for not contacting him first."

"Close call," said Dusty, who'd already devoured his fourth donut and felt his stomach knotting.

"Rita was afraid at one point," said Fred, "that the plumber would drop his tools and not complete the work. Those who fix broken pipes hold all the cards. Hell you don't want to distract or agitate them for any reason. Let 'em do their job."

"So Rita returns to her husband after the week?" asked Dusty.

"Yes. But not before she observes him through the blinds each evening, noting a beaten and weary figure hunched over the sofa, while the T.V. runs nonstop. Meanwhile, a detective stops by now and then to interview

Paul. After the week, Rita tidies up, packs her bags and returns to her home across the street. She feels remorse for dragging her husband through this ordeal. She apologizes to my brother for running away, and cooks him a sumptuous lasagna dinner that first evening."

"Isn't Paul upset, even livid?"

"He's relieved she's back," said Fred. "Very relieved. They kiss and make up. But Rita should've left for good. Just postponing the inevitable in my opinion. Can't say I'm optimistic about their future together."

"How does luck figure into this?" Dusty asked.

Fred scratched his chin, rubbing a stubble growth. "Well, I'm not quite sure to be honest, but it's a bizarre tale. Absence makes the heart grow fonder they say."

"I suppose," Dusty offered, "that now he'll appreciate her. Unless the feeling wears off and he acts the jerk again."

"Who knows," Fred said, while checking his watch. "Tony should be through in a short while. A refill?"

"No thanks." Dusty left for the bathroom and the rain tapered off. Low lying clouds hovered above the donut shop. Dusty returned to the counter and gazed out the window at the menacing clouds drifting across an ashen sky.

"What about you? Got a girlfriend or fiance, young man?"

"I did. But she recently left me for a law student, a serious fellow with career goals. Someone with potential earning power."

"Is that what she told you?" Fred leaned over and squinted.

"More or less. But I wasn't ready to step up and buy a home and settle down. She was moving so fast and I couldn't keep up with expectations. I'm an immature ado-lescent delaying adulthood, I guess."

"Not true!" Dusty received a nurturing pat on the back. "You're a late bloomer. Go see the world, explore a bit. Then there's time to settle down."

Dusty wanted to change the subject and distract himself from becoming despondent. He was still upset about the rejection and felt hollow inside. He missed Angela's company after two months of no contact, and would do anything to win her back short of applying to medical school. Dusty wouldn't inform Fred of his expertise at sabotaging close relationships, and avoiding the hurt and conflict that accompanies intimacy. Angela had wanted commitment, a future together, and he'd sidestep this by acting distant and by withholding affection. He'd keep this unappealing secret to himself and focus on Fred.

"I think I knew your son Willy."

Fred's pupils widened. "You did?"

"I'm sure he was in one of my education classes. We probably played a pickup game of hoops now and then."

"Willy studied music education and wanted to teach. My boy loved music: Blues, jazz, rock, classical. He played bass in a blues band and wrote songs. Did you know that?"

"Is he teaching somewhere? Did he stay in town?"

Fred's eyes grew bleary. He hunched over, staring straight into his coffee. He looked like he aged instantly.

"Willy's no longer with us. He died last year. Brain cancer got him."

Dusty felt nauseous and didn't know what to say. "That's awful. I'm sorry."

"Rips your goddamn heart out. My only son." Fred's voice quivered while he pounded his chest. "It's true what they say: The pain never goes away. I'll take it to the grave."

Fred pressed on his gut and wheezed, taking shallow breaths. Dusty noticed drooping bags under his eyes and surmised this grieving dad needed potent sedatives to help him sleep. Fred was dealt a horrific blow thought Dusty, who was adept at keeping frightening emotions like loss at arm's length. He envisioned Fred being jolted awake at three in the morning with grief. He saw Fred up and about all night pacing the floor, perspiring and cursing aloud. Perhaps he'd remain on the living room sofa frozen and catatonic. Insomnia was a curse that drained the soul and depleted the body. Dusty wished he had comfort or release at three in the morning when hopelessly awake. He rejected lame excuses that tragic blows were all meant to happen. Who said so?

Dusty heard the Burlington Northern freight train whiz by. The tracks lay behind the donut shop, by the Mill Race waterway, which fed into the Willamette. The men remained silent for a while. A long train passed, its freight cars rattling and swaying. A plaintive whistle sounded, and a foghorn echo, its vibrations dispersing into the atmosphere. They sat still, absorbing fragments of nearby conversation. Then Fred suggested they go over to Tony's shop and retrieve Gremlin. Dusty offered to leave the tip but Fred refused. He placed a couple of bills on the counter.

Gremlin had passed with flying colors and Tony jokingly predicted it would outlive them. He had run a compression test as well, and the cylinders and pistons were humming in sync. Fred and Willy had taken good care of her: diligent oil changes, a new alternator and recent tune up, sturdy belts and hoses, and fresh brake pads.

Dusty offered to pay Fred's original asking price, four hundred and fifty, but Fred insisted on three hundred and a congenial handshake. "You get a good deal being you knew Willy. And I like you," added Fred.

The title signed over, Dusty took command of his first used car. Or Gremlin took command of him. He got in and buckled up, then slowly backed out, taking his time. Dusty rolled down the window and waved at Fred, who stood somewhat shorter than before. His shoulders drooped and he scratched his chin, lost in reverie.

"Can I give ya a lift home?" Dusty shouted. "It's no problem."

"No thanks. My wife's coming to get me. Good luck." He gave Dusty a soldier's salute.

As Dusty maneuvered down the wide street he thought he heard a high pitch rattle from the engine, but it was just the wind seeping through a window air pocket. Gremlin was smooth, homey, and purring along. Dusty reached over and felt something thin and worn clinging to the console by the shift lever. Stopped at a light, Dusty stuck a hand down further, as if panning for gold. Slender fingers gripped a concert ticket that had been tightly wedged between the seat and the shift lever. He held onto it while driving back to his apartment. The ticket stub fell onto his lap.

Dusty soon arrived home and examined the artifact. He discovered that Willy, Fred's boy, had initialed and dated the back of it with a Sharpie. Here lay a treasured memento from a local Blues show, and possibly his very last one.

Dusty hoped that Willy hadn't lingered and suffered. He envisioned Willy near the end with headphones and listening to soothing tunes. A warm blanket covered frail bones, while Fred stroked his flush face. He saw Fred tucking his son in, keeping him safe and protected. Dusty shivered and almost sobbed but held back.

He craved company and glanced around his stark, chilly apartment. Dusty longed to contact his former girl-friend and reconcile, and to make everything right again. He wouldn't be aloof and disengaged and would give it his best shot. And he was about to earn a real paycheck and do a bang up job, despite the unknowns. But he knew it was too late to win her back. He'd have to do better next time.

Dusty thought again about Willy and decided to leave the concert ticket stub on the dashboard, a good luck charm for himself and for Gremlin. He thanked Willy for the gift and hoped it brought good fortune and protection from events beyond his control. Better yet he'd phone Fred and offer to treat him to dinner, or at least a beer, and escort them in his new Gremlin. He looked forward to this.

The Matchmaker

The Matchmaker

Back in 1960, an October breeze carried Bill Mazeroski's ball over the left field wall at Forbes Field and Pittsburgh won the World Series. Alice sipped coffee at the breakfast nook, adjusting her glasses. She studied the album's grainy news clipping of Yogi Berra in left field, buttocks wedged against a Double mint gum advertisement, neck cocked and helpless as the ball sailed into a jubilant mob of Pirates' fans. Alice wondered if this Mazeroski fellow possessed a guiding angel that bestowed good luck.

Her late husband Frank had cursed the Pirates' hero infielder. Alice heard Frank's ghostlike voice grumbling from afar: *An errant bounce, an unlucky hop, could've smashed his Adams Apple, and he never would've made it to the plate in the ninth inning!* A bad bounce had injured the Yankees shortstop earlier on. Alice bit into a peach Danish and glanced outside, relieved at being alone, finally. Frank loved baseball and while alive shared sports trivia gems with her. She had pretended to listen but really thought how she'd like to kill him and not go to prison.

If the surgeon had successfully repaired Frank's diseased heart or if he'd stop smoking and overeating, who knows, he'd be alive today. If Alice could bring him back for an hour, would she? Not a chance in hell. Frank had badgered, berated, and ignored her. She called him an insecure bully, a sourpuss. Alice wanted to leave him but lacked the resolve, being short on savings or a place to live. They'd met in high school and married after graduating. Alice wanted to escape an abrasive controlling father and Frank seemed like a calm, reasonable person back then. He'd soon train as an apprentice longshoreman and provide stable income. Over time, Frank grew sullen and depressed, exacerbated by excessive beer drinking and belly-aching.

Alice thumbed through Frank's baseball scrapbook and would donate it to Goodwill. She wanted to rid herself of these obnoxious and meaningless mementos and start fresh. Her eyes glazed over other sports photos and clippings. Alice cringed upon hearing Frank's blaring hoarse voice: *Yeah, that team SHOULD be cursed for trading that moron for a more hapless lemon.*

Alice knocked the scrapbook off the table with her elbow, and gritted her teeth. She saw Frank's faint image on the beige kitchen wall. Alice saw him gagging and coughing up corn flakes. He ground his molars and sneezed while milk dribbled down puffy cheeks. Alice loathed this bloated ghost, all 250 pounds of him. She picked up the scrapbook and hurled it at the vacant wall, while muttering a half apology to Mazeroski, whose home run photo landed near her feet.

Alice had contacted a divorce attorney twice, but Frank, classic abuser, reverted to false charm. He'd plead, beg, and sweet talk her into submission and wear her down. Finally he died and she was free from the rascal. He'd left behind a healthy pension and savings.

Still, Alice was lonely and somewhat melancholy. She missed male companionship and genuine physical intimacy. She'd been single for three years and enjoyed her independence. She traveled a bit and liked her freedom, but desired a sweetie to share new adventures with. Alice wanted to meet someone special, someone kind.

This wouldn't be easy. Segments of the male population were lost to war, post trauma stress disorder, and chronic illness. Men of all ages were conscripted into the armed forces to fight abroad. Toxic chemical agents had ravaged a large chunk of the male population. The coward label branded those refusing to fight, those coveting their intestines and limbs. These men were imprisoned for treason or went into hiding. If Alice protested government policy, which she despised, she'd be arrested. She was not optimistic that prevailing fear would abate and wanted her remaining years to be tolerable and decent. Alice had just turned sixty and was ready to risk meeting someone new and add hope to her days.

She was in luck. Within the past few years, an enterprising team of female engineers had designed a male facsimile, a prototype model. It was programmed to talk, move like, and impersonate a real man. As the model evolved it became affordable. Alice grew interested and anticipated choosing a model, but one unlike Frank. She'd use part of Frank's pension and savings to purchase a tender, responsive mate.

Scouring a mail order catalogue, Alice scanned ads describing available male prototypes. The ads appealed to many women, some who'd taken on their late husbands' passions, such as bowling, fly fishing, deer hunting, golf, and poker. Some male models claimed to enjoy fly fishing, deer hunting, Scrabble, and even baseball. Alice shuddered at anything sports related. She loved to paint and work with her hands, having nothing to do with moving balls, bulky equipment, or hurtling objects.

An hour later, Alice phoned her friend Pia and invited her to go shopping for a man model. She knew it was time to share life with a new companion. Pia lived down the street and offered to drive. They agreed to lunch in the super mall and perhaps take in a movie. Alice knew the demand was intense and hoped for remaining models in stock. Rain-checks had been discontinued at most major outlets. Alice gathered a catalogue insert from the local paper. She noted that intricate chips, wiring, and programming designs offered choices in personality, temperament, and appearance. Even minor quirks, charming ones, could be pre programmed, though this risked a refund or exchange, which could get messy.

Alice and Mia fought traffic but arrived at the super mall in good spirits. They discussed some popular models from the glossy catalogue pages. She wondered why and how she put up with that louse of a husband for so long. Alpha human males like Frank were dwindling, and seemed cranky and boring. They soon approached an espresso vending machine and parked alongside. Alice reached out the window, inserting a digital card through a tiny slot and selected an iced vanilla mocha. She raised the plastic cup to her lips and licked foam from the rim.

"I hope the kindest, sweetest, most considerate man of the twenty first century is available," said Alice. "I'll even lower my expectations if I've got to."

"Are you sure that's what you want?" said Pia. "Wouldn't you get bored with Mr. Perfect?"

Alice brushed her auburn hair and glanced in the compact mirror behind the visor. She applied eye shadow, desiring a neat and attractive appearance before meeting her potential date.

"No, I wouldn't be bored. We'll discuss films, exotic getaways, even play scrabble. I wouldn't object to romantic sweet talk in Italian or Portuguese, if he's programmed that way."

"I'll help you throw a housewarming party for your new man," said Pia, with an edge of playful sarcasm. "Let's invite the whole neighborhood. We can orchestrate a backyard barbecue. Can they program robots to flip hamburgers and hot dogs?"

Alice finished her drink and rode across the expansive lot to the super store. They found a parking spot nearby. Heat baked the asphalt. Alice's adrenalin flowed, a combination of caffeine and anticipation. They locked the car and then walked toward the store entrance. A greeter, or associate, opened the door. He wore a white shirt with red pinstripes and a flimsy straw hat. His outfit could've been grafted from a barbershop quartet. A plastic smile coated his rubbery skin.

"Welcome to our 24 hour sale," chimed this male facsimile greeter in tan polyester pants. "Make yourself at home." His outstretched arm pointed to numerous aisles. To Alice, he looked like a real human male, the genuine article, if not for the patch of dull rust primer protruding from his nostril. It appeared a mix of snot and open sore blister. His right thumb was swollen, and twice as big as the left one, a nasty inflammation. Alice wondered if he or it had been pulling dandelions in the store nursery, and gathered soil infested bacteria under his nail causing infection or abnormality. Or was this a defective model removed from the shelf, and not for sale. Alice couldn't help staring at him.

As Alice and Pia walked the aisles, they encountered numerous male models, finely honed shiny robots posed in various positions in front of mammoth boxes. These were demo models and looked eerily authentic. Alice reached into her purse for glasses and craned her neck toward the high ceiling, noting layers of cardboard boxes stacked under florescent lights. Nostalgic rock tunes played through the intercom. Women shoppers strolled aisles with large metal carts, plucking sale accessories from shelves.

Shoppers grabbed male pajamas in various waist sizes and patterns, including terrycloth robes and slippers. A nearby sign read: "Outfit your man in the style *you* desire. Work clothes, leisure wear, gardening overalls. Even charming Irish tweed coats with matching merino wool sweaters."

"I'll get creative," whispered Alice. "I like the English professor look."

"Hey, don't steal my look, girlfriend," said Pia.

They burst out laughing like two silly schoolgirls.

"May I help you?" A handsome man with dark features winked at Alice. He reminded her of Cary Grant emitting a mischievous twinkle. Alice envisioned herself as Princess Grace Kelly, strolling along the Parisian riverbank beside a suave dandy clutching a picnic basket. The agent removed a business card from a sport coat pocket. He wore strong cologne, a woodsy scent.

"Help me? I hope so," said Alice. Was he authentic and not a facsimile? Alice stared at him, attempting to discern the difference. The face, the torso, and the lower trunk all seemed proportional, a designing marvel. Pia nudged her, breaking Alice's trance.

"What kind of man are you looking for?" asked the agent. "We stock shy types, and more outgoing ones, or even a hybrid blend. And for a nominal fee we administer a reliable survey and match *your* interest level and type with our men. It's based on the outdated Myers-Briggs, but we've updated the questions to cross reference personality type and preferences. Interested?"

"Are you available?" whispered Pia under her breath. Alice couldn't believe her friend's chutzpah and elbowed her.

"I'm afraid not. I haven't left the store since it opened a year ago. My hefty work schedule prevents me from doing so. I want to be the *best* matchmaker around here and land a promotion."

Alice felt her foot cramp and shook it. "All work and no play," she started to say. She loved his dreamy brown eyes and clear skin.

"What kind of man would you like, um...."

"Alice." She extended a hand. "Someone the complete opposite of the lout I was married to."

The sales agent perked up. "Someone earlier said the same thing. We have models programmed to be athletic, if you like the jock type. They golf, water ski, play tennis. And some are more erudite, the cerebral type."

Impressive vocabulary, thought Alice: Erudite, cerebral.

"A popular prototype is the lighthearted humorous man. We have dry, absurd, off beat, and all kinds to tickle the funny bone. These coveted models go quickly. Never underestimate a sense of humor in these challenging times."

Alice pointed to a floor model behind the agent, one with a transparent honest appearance. He'd be open and flexible, and willing to try new adventures she assumed.

"I'm afraid we're out of stock, being he's last year's design. We can order another one from our warehouse but it'll take two weeks. Mind waiting?"

"Can I take the floor model? I want to walk away with one today."

The agent stroked his cleft chin. A tiny birthmark lay on the lower half of his right cheek. Alice gazed at him under the bright lights. She still couldn't tell if he was real or designed from scratch.

The agent cleared his throat. "It's no problem taking the floor demo. Please be advised that a minor kink or two may surface, being last year's model. Overall though, he should perform well, especially under stress. We programmed this particular model to withstand anxiety-producing situations, be it crowds, loud noise, or dealing with aggressive types. And best of all, no medications or antidepressants need be administered. He's a package of pure bliss."

"Then I assume," said Alice, "that he's mellow and compliant and sweet natured."

"No problem, no worries. I guarantee the polar *opposite* of your deceased. May I surmise the cad was a loser. We sell only winners around here."

The agent then asked Alice to accompany him to a glass partitioned office to sign sales documents. She climbed a stairway to reach the office, which afforded a better view of the shopping area. Alice observed women shopping, some jotting notes onto a pad or Blackberry while inspecting the wares. The agent offered a half- year warranty on parts and labor, but Alice wasn't concentrating. He also tried to sell her an extended warranty by offering an employee discount. Pia advised against the extended warranty, which would jack the price considerably.

When Alice asked Pia if she too would purchase a model, Pia said that she'd first see how Alice's new companion functioned. She had warned Alice earlier that she didn't think advanced technology could deliver unblemished goods. Alice assumed Pia would help her rectify any problems should something go awry.

The agent lifted and wheeled Alice's new companion into the paneled office for closer inspection. He removed a comb from his coat pocket and stroked the model's dark hair, picked lint from his shirt, and patted him head to toe. The rollers under the robot's spiffy shoes were removed. He came with the name Hank. He was clean and handsome, and dapper with open blue collar and charcoal sport coat.

Hank's program was lodged in his skull, where the human brain resides. Brain research had evolved, and important cognitive areas were mapped and diagrammed. Alice wondered if she was deluding herself into believing that a robot companion could allay loneliness and provide companionship. But she convinced herself to go along with the plan, and pretend Hank was the genuine article and not a programmed facsimile. Alice seized this second chance with gusto. She thanked the charming sales agent.

"I'm very grateful, Mr.?"

"Smith. That's the name we've been given. But call me Larry."

Alice handed back the pen, and placed folded documents and receipts into her purse. "I can't wait to take Hank to a loving home."

Pia whispered into Alice's ear. "He's not an adopted pet from the Humane Society. Make sure you have all his papers and ask for instructions or a maintenance manual."

Alice ignored her. She was wrapped up in the moment.

"The pleasure's mine," said Mr. Smith, shaking hands. "Please don't hesitate to call if minor glitches or problems ensue. We'll take care of it. We have an excellent service department." Next, the agent escorted the women and Hank toward the front entrance. Alice noted that a few customers cast a jealous glance while sizing up Hank. One shopper smiled and wished Alice luck and success as they exited. Mr. Smith opened the glass door and waved, thanking them again for their business.

Alice and Pia walked alongside Hank in the parking lot, and located their battery powered vehicle. Alice gently guided Hank inside by the elbow, and observed Hank easily strapping on his lap belt, as if he'd done this a hundred times. Hank had changed clothes in a back room while the papers were being signed. The agent had suggested more informal attire once purchased. Now, Hank wore stone-washed jeans and a rayon floral Aloha shirt. The top two buttons opened, exposing chest hair strands to sunlight. What a handsome devil, thought Alice.

Hank, six feet tall and designed to please, displayed a prominent nose and chin. He was given salt and pepper hair, especially around the temples, and a neatly cropped beard. He appeared bright eyed and alert, and in decent shape for sixty, as the manual had stated. Sleek and slender boned, Hank hadn't an ounce of fat. He was the Real McCoy. Any minor defect in Hank, last year's model, wasn't apparent. Alice would celebrate that evening by baking homemade lasagna. She'd uncork a bottle of red wine she'd been saving, light candles, and begin life anew.

Hank arrived at Alice's house with two pieces of luggage containing clothes and sundries. Mr. Smith, the sales agent, had slipped three one hundred dollar bills into Hank's jacket pocket to help defray restaurant and entertainment expenses. The contract that Alice signed stipulated that she provide food and lodging for up to ten days, and if not satisfied with the living arrangement, could exchange Hank for another model, or return him for a full refund. There were no refunds or exchanges after thirty days. Parts and labor were guaranteed should Hank need a tweaking or rewiring or replacement of chips parts. This also included a six month tune up that regulated mood and behavior if necessary.

Hank retrieved a canvas duffel bag from Pia's trunk. It wasn't completely zipped and a plastic bottle of Dr. Bronner's Peppermint soap fell onto his trousers, the lid having popped open. Some of the liquid soap spilled down his leg, then socks and shoe. A yellow puddle formed a ring around his heel. Alice took a tissue and began wiping the soap from his trousers while suppressing a chuckle.

"Clumsy me," Hank said. "Maybe my lack of coordination is culture shock. I'm not used to suburbia."

Alice touched his shoulder. "No problem. You'll adjust in no time. Check out the pretty ranch and bungalow homes on my street. There are flower gardens, not many kids, and quiet."

Hank nodded and picked up the soap bottle, closed the lid and placed it into his duffel. He used Alice's tissue to wipe his gooey hands. Hank walked past the lavender and sage in Alice's garden and stepped onto the porch. He shielded his eyes from the afternoon sunlight and blinked. "My sunglasses are buried somewhere in my bag. I'll get it all sorted out later."

Pia waited in her car and observed. Alice motioned that she could leave, and that everything was fine and dandy. Pia waved and drove off after wishing them luck.

Alice led Hank inside the house. She planned on separate bedrooms at first, allowing time to get acquainted. It'd be odd sharing home with a stranger after living alone. Frank would be jealous and livid, knowing that she handpicked Hank and liked his style. Alice imagined Frank's reaction to being replaced by someone the complete opposite of his twisted tormented personality. Despite Alice's residual anger at him, she knew it was time to release pain and move on.

At this first stage, she envisioned Hank as a companion and sleepover guest. Hopefully, it would evolve into something long term. Alice wanted to go slow, or it'd be awkward and their relationship wouldn't work. Hank was programmed and designed to act cool and calm. Alice had known ugly drama and abuse, and now needed to adjust to someone caring and attentive. They stood in the hallway.

"You get the house tour in a minute. Put down your bag, sit, and please make yourself at home. Something to drink?"

Hank glanced up above and then back at Alice. "Lemonade or club soda sounds good. Thanks." Hank sat on the sofa, his back to the front window. He exhaled as if he'd been on a long rail journey. He placed a hand on the soft cushion, stretched his long legs forward and yawned, covering his mouth. Alice yawned too.

She noticed his long svelte fingers with rounded tips. She observed his non calloused hands and knew that he'd done no farming, heavy hauling or manual labor. She recalled eyeing a model at the store earlier that morning outfitted in overalls and straw hat. He'd held a pitchfork of hay at his side, posing stiffly. The robot farmer had reminded Alice of a famous depression era portrait.

Next, Alice walked to the kitchen to get Hank's drink, and then shouted while peering into the fridge. "How bout lemon 'n lime seltzer?" She poured him a glass and took his drink into the living room.

Meanwhile, Hank fidgeted with his shirt, placing a hand inside as if adjusting a wire on his chest. Alice thought he was swatting a fly or bug. Alice walked back over to the sofa and handed Hank his drink. He stood like a gentleman, and sat back down.

"Thanks. I need to rehydrate. It's warm out there today."

"I know," said Alice. "You've been cooped up in that musty store all morning. Invasive bright lights and noise."

"Don't remind me. I've been cooped up longer than that. I'm grateful for your invitation and hospitality. You'll be pleased you chose me."

Alice didn't want the conversation to be stiff and unnatural. She sat opposite from him on an oak rocker. Light filtered through the curtains. She desired to initiate natural conversation. She'd ask him to introduce himself, similar to a first date. He could say that he'd been programmed in an engineering lab and was now available, the hot new stud around town. She'd pretend, and pretend hard that Hank was real. Alice hadn't been on a date or met any new man in ages.

"So Hank, tell me about yourself. What do you do for fun?" Pia had reminded her that he wasn't an adopted pet from the Humane Society. She advised Alice to be observant, and assume that he was a real man, but to also expect the unexpected.

Hank straightened up and his posture grew relaxed. "Funny you should ask. I was going to ask you the same thing."

"Well? Your turn first," said Alice.

Hank stroked his neat whiskers. "As you've likely surmised, I don't have an extensive history. But here goes anyway." Hank again fidgeted with something inside his shirt and appeared to be tugging at chest hairs. "Let's see, college.... I graduated cum laude from Brown University and changed my academic focus from Accounting to Fine Arts my junior year."

"Wow. That's quite a ninety degree turn," said Alice.

"It wasn't too hard of an adjustment. After graduating, I apprenticed in graphic design applying visual and spatial skills. I like to problem solve using my eye, hands, and brain. I didn't pursue accounting, though numbers and statistics intrigue me when applied to something meaningful and useful." Hank paused. "What about you? Fill me in on the past fifty or so years."

Alice couldn't hide her astonishment. This facsimile of

a man conversed in an intelligent manner. Someone sharp had scripted and programmed his background story. She sipped from her glass of lemonade. She exhaled and began recalling her past.

"I started out with great hopes, great ambitions. I wanted to paint or design clothes, something creative. Then I married young, a colossal mistake. Now I see what could've been and it's depressing. My past has gaping holes and I'm trying to forget."

Hank leaned forward and smiled. "I know what you mean about not taking the other road or path. Forget about what you didn't do. Let's take it from the top, from today, looking ahead. Sound good?"

"I agree. Tell me more about your interesting background. What are your passions?"

Hank stroked his chin and then tugged on his earlobes. He squirmed and began to stutter while straining to retrieve the right words and tone.

"Being the floor model robot, you'll need to cut me slack as my history is rather limited. I'm somewhat self conscious and need time to think."

"Of course, no problem. Share what you're at ease disclosing," said Alice.

Hank pressed on his chest as if pushing a replay button.

"Well, let's see. I worked on a cruise ship briefly. The Carnival or Princess line. It was interesting work."

"Tell me about it."

"I was initially brought on as entertainment director. For example, I organized shuffleboard tournaments and table tennis matches. I even learned to be a blackjack dealer when I wasn't taking everyone's money in late night poker competition." Hank grinned. "I played occasional harmless pranks on folks to stir things up."

"Sounds like fun. You were the life of the party."

"Indeed. Then my role shifted when the cruise director discovered a vast shortage of older mature men to dance with an abundance of unattached women. I learned tango, salsa, fox trot, waltz and became damned good at it."

"I bet you flirted quite a bit." Alice thought she saw Hank blush.

"Yes, that was part of the job. I never got emotionally or romantically attached to anyone. My job was to please and entertain and provide diversion."

"Like now, with me?"

"Exactly. Does this align with your expectations?"

"Sure." Alice needed to remind herself that Hank wasn't 'real', and that his emotional range and capacity for involvement was limited to his wiring and programming.

"Perhaps you can demonstrate a few slick dance moves sometime. I'll play an engaging tango beat and you can strut your stuff with me."

"Absolutely. I aim to please."

Alice was beginning to like Hank and looked forward to their first homemade lasagna dinner together.

Exhausted from the busy day and the heat, Alice napped. Hank stretched out on the couch and also napped. Alice thought she heard him snoring but wasn't sure. After napping, they decided to prep dinner together. First, Hank was shown his room and given another house tour. In the kitchen he prepared a green salad, cutting and slicing tomatoes, lettuce and cucumbers from the backyard vegetable garden. Alice boiled the lasagna noodles.

"Do you know what today is?" asked Hank.

Alice looked up from the stove, a pot of water rolling to a boil. She adjusted the burner. "It's Friday."

"Guess again. It's a surprise." Hank grinned as if he

was about to propose marriage by whipping out a fancy ring.

"Okay. I give up. What day is today?"

Hank perked up, having stumped her. "On this date back in 1960, Bill Mazeroski of the Pirates won the World Series at Forbes Field with an explosive ninth inning homer. They beat the Yankees by one run. Can you believe it?"

There was silence and then Alice flinched. Her head rocked back as if avoiding a punch. "You don't say?"

"Are you a baseball fan?" Hank asked.

Alice felt her adrenalin racing. She recalled the scrapbook of photos and news clippings she'd found in the bedroom closet that morning while sorting and gathering items for Goodwill donation. She wouldn't tell Hank that she'd stared at the Mazeroski scrapbook photo earlier. Her stomach churned and rumbled.

"Everything okay?" said Hank. "You look pale as a ghost. Do you need to sit down?"

Alice backed up, and gathered herself. "I'm fine. Sorry, but I'm not a baseball fan. My late husband was but I'm definitely not." Alice felt light headed and prayed that Hank was not another rendition of Frank in some cruel and perverse way.

Hank handed her a glass of water and to Alice, looked concerned and remorseful. She was relieved when Hank abruptly changed the subject.

"Did you raise children?"

"Yes. I raised three daughters, all grown and out on their own. They went to private Catholic schools and I attended soccer and volleyball tournaments. And oh, swim meets. Good kids, good students."

"What kind of work did your husband do?"

"He worked in manufacturing and shipping, a steady

job with a decent salary and pension. But he worked graveyard and wasn't around a lot, which was fine by me." Sarcasm oozed from her voice.

"Did he choose that shift, or was it forced on him?"

"He liked those hours. A good way to avoid a relationship." Alice's jaw tightened, suppressing her resentment. She wanted a fresh start with Hank, if possible.

"That's too bad. A stranger living under your roof for so long." Hank stopped tossing the salad and leaned against the kitchen counter. His elbow almost landed in the oil and vinegar dressing. "Why didn't you leave him?"

"Look around, Hank. What do you see?"

"A nice and comfortable home."

"Exactly. Comfort and security. He made a decent living. I lived a conventional life with a conventional husband. I placed my dreams on hold while being supermom." Alice took a shallow breath. "And we reach a certain point in our lives, look around, and realize that all the things we said we'd do and become will never pass...and that we're *ordinary*."

Hank nodded while she spoke.

"If I may be honest with you Hank, I wonder something."

"What's that?"

"Don't take this the wrong way, but you're assembled from scratch. Without human genes or DNA, that is. How can, pardon the term, a 'robot' ask such insightful questions and display this depth of understanding?"

Hank moved closer to Alice, just inches away. She hoped he didn't take offense at the truth.

"I was programmed to ask questions like: 'Why didn't you leave him sooner,' and 'Are you really being true to yourself.' My hardware is wired for sensitivity and empathy. My training also included viewing hours of videotape of late afternoon talk shows broadcast on television many years ago."

"What kind of shows? Soaps?"

"No, shows that targeted a female viewership and audience. I learned from watching the host what types of questions show concern and caring. I learned a lot about broken hearts and loneliness."

"Wow," said Alice. "You're well trained indeed. But can you feel anything original?"

"I can only be," said Hank, "what I was designed for, nothing more, nothing less. This is the whole package, as they say."

Alice peered into his eyes. Hank was already a colossal improvement over Frank, and provided more comfort than living alone. The lasagna would soon be ready and they'd continue their conversation over a sumptuous meal. She'd move on to lighter topics, listen to soft jazz, and share a pleasant evening together with her newfound companion.

A week passed, and then two more. Hank was delightful company. He did chores around the house, like the vacuuming and cleaning and laundry, and prepared tasty curry dishes he improvised from Alice's Asian cookbook. Hank fixed little things too and was handy. He'd surprise her with a meal out, dipping into the stipend provided by Mr. Smith, the sales agent. Hank was agreeable, and compliant. Alice became light on her feet, and giddy. The couple expressed mutual affection. Hank was hardwired to please a woman in many ways and didn't disappoint. He was adept at massage and back rubs. His delicate and smooth hands were expertly designed and attached, oozing magic.

The only oddity was Hank's habit of napping for long stretches with their bedroom door shut, which they now shared. Alice once sauntered in and unexpectedly found him on all fours in her closet, nose to the carpet and sniffing for a scent like a bloodhound. She ignored this quirk, attributing it to a slight program malfunction. Hank was too perfect to consider taking back, even for a minor tune up. She had asked him if he was panning for gold and instead of a chuckle, he appeared mildly annoyed at her teasing.

Alice wasn't used to this bliss, and waited for the shoe to drop, for something to go awry. One morning, while Hank was out getting the Sunday Times, Alice phoned her friend Pia. She'd given Pia updates over the past month, but these became less frequent.

"I hate to say this, but this man,"

"Man," affirmed Pia. "Good job pretending he's human, like I told you to do."

"At first I was charmed, and still am."

"But?"

"Am I bored? Complacent? He's too good, too perfect. I'm afraid I'll sabotage our relationship by being nasty or mean. I wouldn't mind an argument, a little tension. He could use a few rough edges."

"Be careful, Alice. You've experienced that twisted drama and now have hit the jackpot. Enjoy the ride!"

"It's time for you to meet him again."

"Why don't we," suggested Pia, "have our monthly book gathering at your place?"

"Okay. A Coming-out party. He blends well with women."

"Blends with *you*. Now, you don't want him flirting with your friends."

"Not to worry," said Alice. "Remember, he's not a *human* male.

"All right, let's keep our usual meeting day. I'll contact

everyone. See you this Monday evening, seven o'clock. And by the way," Pia continued, "does Hank have an unattached friend?"

"You'll have to cruise the superstore stockroom. Chao."

She had parting advice for Alice. "Until then, keep appreciating Hank's good nature. Enjoy the gift. But step back occasionally and observe."

"Why?"

"It's best practice. It keeps you on your toes and humble."

An hour later, Hank returned from the store with the newspaper and shared the lead story. The government would continue inducting all remaining men into the armed services, and enlist younger women for frontline combat and logistical support. Troops were bogged down in hostile places, and Alice had stopped reading the paper. Hank listened intently to Alice's opinions and nodded, but wouldn't offer any of his own and apologized. Alice surmised that Hank knew his capability and limits, or didn't want to upset her by engaging in discussion that could lead to conflict. Hank held no opinions on political issues. Robots weren't forced to serve but Alice assumed younger male robots would soon be given combat training to shore up depleted ranks.

Hank was charming, and Alice suggested they create fun art to cement their bond with shared purpose. She suggested designing earrings and necklaces, and selling at the local Saturday market. Hank had expressed interest in using his eyes, hands, and brain. He agreed to the art projects and on Alice's credit card, they shopped and purchased materials. Hank's delicate fingers and fine motor skills were helpful and they'd make a great team.

Alice anticipated the monthly evening book club gathering. Thirty days had passed since Hank entered her life. She stashed the robot warranty and paperwork in a utility file, and from now on there'd be no refunds or exchanges. He was hers for keeps. They shopped for deli food in preparation for the gathering. She looked forward to introducing Hank to her friends, and hoped he looked forward to meeting them. Alice liked how he wasn't possessive of her time or friendships. They napped that afternoon and Alice awoke first. Hank slept a while longer, and when Alice walked into the bedroom sometime later, she found him again on all fours in her closet, nose to the carpet, his backside arched high. A yoga or meditation posture Alice thought. She ignored him and returned to the kitchen to prepare a green salad.

Soon after, she heard two vehicles pull up to the house. Hank had showered and looked his best. They both greeted guests at the door and Hank was introduced to Alice's friends. Hank helped Alice with drinks and had made a sumptuous fruit salad earlier. He was at ease with everyone and joked around, and complimented Pia on her appearance. Alice found his scripted charm sincere. Hank took the women's coats and purses into the master bedroom. While eating salad and sandwiches, guests remained in the dining room to discuss the shared novel. Meanwhile, Hank replenished their wine glasses and sliced chocolate cheese cake for dessert.

"Requests before I go on break?" Hank announced.

"Where do you think you're going?" teased Alice. "Trying to escape?"

"I need some fresh air, perhaps a stroll around the neighborhood. But I'll be back in a little while." He waved at the women engaged in animated discussion. Alice enjoyed the Merlot Hank had repeatedly poured and grew woozy.

"What's your last name, Hank?" asked Pia, who sipped a Martini.

"Why?" Hank scratched his chin and appeared surprised.

"Just curious. We want to know more about you."

Alice shushed her friend. "Let's not get too personal. He's entitled to a secret or two."

"It's Payne. I've got no middle initial, but I'm working on it." Hank smiled.

"Off you go then," Alice said. "We'll take it from here. Thanks."

Excusing himself, Hank slipped into the bedroom for a light jacket. A rustling sound came from the bedroom while Alice and company chatted and laughed nearby. Alice forgot that Hank was out walking and she lost track of time.

An hour later, Alice went into the bedroom to retrieve coats and purses and noticed rearranged items on the dresser. Then she screamed. Guests ran toward her, and into the room.

"What in hell!" shouted Alice. "Shit!" She lifted her purse and turned it upside down, dumping its contents over the bedspread. Alice sifted through the remains.

"Credit cards, cash, all gone. Can you believe this?" Next, Alice opened her top dresser drawer where she kept silver jewelry, rings, and emeralds. All gone, along with Hank.

Alice entered the walk in closet and saw her fire safe opened, and bent down to rifle through papers. Important financial documents were missing, such as bank account statements and insurance forms. She'd hidden the safe key and Hank had found it. Alice's friends had missing credit cards and cash. The room was a mess, and now a crime scene.

Alice collapsed, while Pia applied a cold washcloth to the back of her neck. She mumbled and cursed. Her body shook and she sobbed into a pillow. Alice ingested Hank's foul scent embedded in the pillowcase fabric. A toxic residue lingered like rotten eggs.

Friends consoled Alice and promised that everything would be okay. Pia suggested they drive the neighborhood and track him down as he wouldn't get far on foot. Unfortunately, he'd stolen Pia's vehicle. They decided not to pursue and contacted police to relay crime details. The police soon arrived to complete a report and sought help finding Hank by interviewing Alice.

Alice couldn't think straight. Friends offered to spend the night or help contact a nearby daughter. She thanked them, insisting she'd be fine, attempting to conceal her embarrassment and shame.

Later that evening and after everyone had left, she acknowledged what had happened. The next day, she'd contact credit agencies, her insurance company and an attorney. Hank was indeed gone. She was certain the conniving rascal had it all planned from inception. Alice sifted through subtle clues as to his intentions. She'd contact friends and promise restitution and apologize. She reprimanded herself for being naive and trusting, and unrealistic. The emotional cost of heartbreak stung.

Alice's attorney urged her to sue the retail store for fraud and misrepresentation. They both reviewed the purchase agreement and concluded they'd have to prove that Hank was intentionally designed to con and swindle. Or prove that a specific defect in the model caused Hank's criminal behavior. The store might argue that Hank acted by his own free will, and that their product was not a design malfunction. Alice wanted to hold the store responsible despite the initial contract.

She decided to return to the superstore and confront sales agent Larry Smith. She'd demand her money back in full and threaten a lawsuit. Her attorney had urged caution and patience as impulsive action could jeopardize her case. He needed time to review state consumer and liability law to determine if fraudulent cases were brought that would apply to this situation. If so, it would bolster Alice's claims. This would take additional time and resolve on Alice's part.

She felt impatient though, and wanted to grab agent Smith by the neck and shake him. She'd squeeze the false charm and sweet talk from him. The package of pure bliss that Smith had promised turned into a nightmare. Alice was far from violent, but fantasized inflicting harm. She knew she needed to calm down but felt too distraught to do so. Meanwhile, there were no promising leads locating Hank, who could've fled the region.

A week after the theft, Alice gathered her purchase documents and drove to the superstore against her attorney's advice. Pia offered to go, but Alice insisted on going alone. She drove there in a stupor and entered the lot. She parked and then grabbed the manila folder containing the sales agreement. Alice got out of the car and walked toward the entrance. A greeter, a silly looking male model dressed in polyester pants and plaid shirt bid hello. Alice demanded to see Larry Smith.

"Which Larry Smith?" asked the store Greeter. "We've got quite a few. Unfortunately, we had to recently let one go. He was selling defective models. But you didn't hear me say that."

Alice spoke up. "I want to see the store supervisor. Now, please."

The greeter reached for a phone and paged a Mr. Payne.

"You know," said the greeter, his tone shifting, "we're proud of our matchmaking track record. You're the first person who's returned looking dissatisfied."

"We'll see about that," Alice said.

A handsome well groomed model approached. He resembled Hank and shuffled his feet like him. Alice glared at the robot, and moved her face close to his. She imbibed a distinct scent and noted an inscribed code on his neck that read, 'TRS-80'. Alice recalled that Hank had a different code stamped there. She wanted to slap him but resisted. She'd sort this out in a civil manner without causing an embarrassing scene.

"Good morning. I'm the store supervisor. Is there a problem?"

"Yes. There's a big problem."

"Let's go to my office and we'll talk privately."

Alice blocked out the noise and commotion around her, a bad dream. They soon entered Mr. Payne's office, which stood a level above the merchandise floor. A glass partition separated this office from one directly next door, the room where Hank had been introduced and purchased. Alice sat down and removed documents from her purse. She turned and noticed an expectant woman in the office next door hurriedly signing papers. Alice stared.

Curious, Alice stood and pressed her nose against the adjoining glass partition. A male model was being preened and fussed over. He wore a nametag or pin on his dark sport jacket. Alice was convinced the robot was sales agent Larry Smith. A wad of cash was then stuffed in his coat pocket by another model performing a ritual grooming. She saw Smith staring at what could've been a script and watched his lips move as if memorizing lines from a play. Alice noticed a bottle of Bronner's liquid soap and a toothbrush on a stool. A familiar looking green duffel bag was unzipped, lying nearby.

"Is everything okay?" asked Mr. Payne. "Recognize someone?"

Alice saw Hank, *her* Hank, wipe down and spiff up Larry Smith. Hank pinned a red carnation to Smith's lapel and brushed dust off his jacket with a slender hand. Alice knew those hands. They had massaged her, hugged her, and robbed her blind. Her nose still pressed to the glass, she ignored Payne, store supervisor. Hank turned toward Alice and winked. To Alice, a sly smile flickered across his lips.

Payne placed a spiral portfolio on his desk and then removed photos of robot prototypes. He tried to engage Alice. "If your current model isn't satisfactory, we can transact a trade, an upgrade." He placed an air brushed photo in front of Alice. "This gem's been programmed for aerobic workouts, everything from Pilates to jazzercise. He was groomed in Madrid as a bullfighter and is swift and agile. Consider him a hybrid, part man, part robot." Payne tugged at his makeshift earlobes, trying to further engage Alice, who ignored him.

"Not interested," she mumbled. Alice focused her gaze toward the ongoing preparations next door.

Hank finished cleaning and polishing Larry Smith, and wheeled Smith out the office before closing the door behind him. Hank hoisted Smith by the waist, stepping down gingerly onto the main floor. A pleased female customer followed, her hand resting on Smith's shoulder. They approached the store entrance under bright lights. Hank ambled along and puckered his lips as if whistling, and then turned around. He glanced up at Alice and blinked, and then blew a long kiss. Hank waved bye-bye and mouthed 'see ya later, sweetie.'

Alice glared back and shook her fist, and almost ran down to confront the scoundrel. Instead, she held back and conjured up a better idea.

Alice would make Mr. Payne a fair and reasonable offer: Either agree in writing to full monetary restitution plus admission of guilt resulting in his and Hank's immediate arrest, or, agree to decommission Hank in front of her by slitting his wrists. Then she'd find out if he spilled human blood after all. She'd take a minute or two before pursuing her offer of forgiveness with an attached price.

Slaying the Green Monster

Slaying the Green Monster

When I describe Lonnie and his recent problems, it wouldn't evoke much sympathy. Lonnie's an opportunist and a lazy hedonist when pursuing women he desired and wanted to impress. His false flattery and sleazy track record was consistent.   He was now on his third marriage and barely hanging on to a kind, wonderful, supportive spouse. His swagger and compulsions blinded him from appreciating Susan, who radiated warmth and soul. What a fool. Lonnie told me that his father had acted the same way and was compelled to outdo Dad in blazing a self destructive trail.

The flip side: Lonnie's been a trusted friend since childhood and I value loyalty, probably to my own detriment. To cut to the chase, he screwed things up once again.

A month ago, Lonnie had phoned me at dinner time. My wife Julia was annoyed that I'd taken the call, but he sounded upset and confused. I got up and took the conversation to another room, having promised Julia to keep it brief. Then she rolled her eyes. Julia disliked Lonnie, but enjoyed the solitude whenever I ventured off on weekend fishing trips with him. This gave her full rein of the house.

I held the phone and listened to his subdued voice, which shook.

"You sound terrible. What's up?"

"I messed things up something awful," he said.

"How?"

"I had an affair. I cheated on Susan."

I glanced at the clock in the den and sat down, knowing

my dinner was cooling. I recoiled at his confession, think-ing, here we go again. Lonnie could be thoughtful, con-siderate, and generous with his time and money. I liked his silly humor and he'd put me in stitches retelling funny anecdotes of friends' mishaps. But I didn't think his ado-lescent urges of marital indiscretion were all that humor-ous.

"Why'd you do it?" I asked.

"Because," he stammered, "temptation and lust got the better of me."

"Is that your explanation?" I said.

"It's not bullshit. The primitive part of my brain takes control and I submit."

I could tell that he wasn't joking, and that he felt con-trolled by mid life hormones, or insecurities.

"Why don't you make an arrangement with Susan that allows for an open marriage? This way, you won't have to sneak around."

"That's not her style."

"Then why stay together if you're led astray, as you claim."

"I love Susan, but I act like an asshole sometimes."

I shook my head, unsure of what to say. I told Lonnie I'd meet him for coffee the following morning as I wouldn't have to be at work until later.

In the meantime, I'd keep Lonnie's confession from Julia. She'd dislike him even more, and I wouldn't defend or explain his actions, or I'd be in the doghouse as well. I was intrigued and amused by his rash impulses. He need-ed to be bold and reckless, but with Susan, and not with a stranger. Yep, I mumbled, the son of a bitch deserves what's coming to him.

"Be right back," I shouted. "Get started without me if you don't mind."

I went into the bathroom, and turned the sink faucet full blast while dunking my head under cold water. Damn, I *was* jealous of the philandering bastard! I let the icy water drench me, thinking that drowning would be a horrible way to go, but preferable to divorce.

The next morning, I left the house to meet Lonnie. I told Julia what he'd done, as I couldn't keep secrets from my wife. She surprised me by withholding comment on Lonnie's affair. Julia was no longer particularly close to Lonnie's wife Susan, and didn't feel compelled to disclose her husband's indiscretion to her. We both preferred to stay out of it. I'd soon listen again to Lonnie's woes, nod sympathetically, and offer trite condolences on his mid life calamity before offering to buy him another coffee with pastry. I kissed Julia and headed out. I was the devoted husband who played by the rules of civility.

Approaching the cafe, I saw Lonnie seated at a window counter and hunched over the newspaper. I walked inside the cafe and stood next to him, peering at the sports headline over his shoulder. He was unaware of my presence. He was a die-hard Yankees fan, and victory over the rival Red Sox lightened his mood. Lonnie buried his head further in the paper and I saw his lips moving. He was memorizing batting averages and game statistics. I tried not to startle him.

"What's goin' on? How 'bout those Yankees?"

Lonnie straightened up and folded the paper neatly. "Can you believe a sweep? Pretty cool, huh. They go at it again next weekend up at Fenway. Never been there, but I'd love to be at that old gem of a ballpark."

"You never know," I said. "We'll make it up there someday."

I sat down next to him, and then grabbed his empty

cup. I went for his refill and purchased a scone and a Mocha. He liked his coffee black and drank five or six cups a day. He was one juiced up fellow by dinner. I'd given him a birthday gift of a giant thermos, the kind that construction workers own. I'd vowed to find the heftiest thermos around so he wouldn't be without his stimulant.

"Tell me about your secret liaison," I said, acting detached and amused.

"I met her at a business convention and was smitten."

"Very conventional."

"Stop the bad puns. I'm serious."

"Sorry." I handed Lonnie a fork. "Dig in. Good pastries here."

Lonnie took a swig of his coffee, and then another. His cup was soon emptied. I started for his second refill, but felt a hand stop me.

"Sit down. There's not much to my indiscretion, other than we hit it off big time."

"Where does she live? Is it a one-time fling?"

"I thought so, at first. But then I got to know Rebecca over the convention weekend and grew to like her. You'll shit a brick at my impulsive actions."

"Yeah?"

"She's much younger, and quite spontaneous. Like a lightning bolt."

"Of course," I said. "I'd be shocked if she resembled Susan, who knows you well and tolerates your charming shortcomings."

"You're right. Susan lives with me and Rebecca doesn't. I suppose my quirkiness and highfalutin charm would grow stale pretty fast."

"Okay. You had a fun weekend. Forget it."

"It's hard to. I really like her, maybe love her."

"Get a grip and stop acting like a goofy teen on steroids.

Grow up. Get over it!"

Even though patrons were absorbed with laptops, I needed to lower my volume.

"I'd like to reveal my unusual pick up line," Lonnie offered.

"Sure, maybe I'll use it at my next out of town business convention." I pretended to remove a pad from my pocket and jot notes. "I'm ready, go ahead."

"Well, in the adjoining ballroom was a gathering for educators of the blind, and I poked my head in and learned a few things."

"Like what?"

"That blind people compensate by ratcheting up their other senses. And I thought I heard the speaker state that they make better lovers."

"Plausible, but not proven."

"No, it makes sense. They're more sensual without visual stimuli to distract from the task at hand."

"Profound," I said. I pretended I was scribbling notes for a Cosmo magazine expose.

"At break, I begin conversing with a teacher of the blind. Or do I say 'visually impaired'? I don't want to offend."

"You're a piece of work, Lonnie. Don't want to offend, my ass."

"I ask this very attractive teacher if it's true."

"If what's true?"

"If the blind are more sensual and romantic."

"And?"

"She pauses, then looks at me cross eyed and walks away."

"I don't blame her. You're being presumptuous, or arrogant. I suppose how you asked and your tone of voice turned her off."

"Long story short, we bump into each other later that evening, and we have tons in common: Same music and films, same sense of humor. We really hit it off at dinner. Things take off from there."

"Does Susan know? Did you tell your devoted wife about your liaison?"

Lonnie slumped down. "No, I didn't."

"Will you?"

"Probably not."

"Is Rebecca married?"

"No, she's recently divorced, and she knows I'm married. We live two thousand miles apart and won't see each other, despite my infatuation."

"Obsession."

"Same thing, I suppose."

"I agree that you won't see her again. That's good."

"Why, good?"

"Because you'll blow a good thing you've had going with Susan, who happens to adore you though I don't know why. You've taken her for granted. Easy for anyone to do."

"Including you?"

"What are you implying?"

"Do you take Julia for granted?"

"No comment."

I was becoming restless and checked my watch to see if I had to leave for work. Certified accountants have this reputation of being dull or boring, but it's untrue. I may crunch numbers for a living, but I *can* light up a dance floor. Just ask my wife. I make her look damn good when we're waltzing or doing the tango. Lonnie can't even dance, plus he's chunky and lazy. Why would someone much younger and attractive desire any part of his paunchy body, or enjoy his company. I'm not cocky and arrogant like Lonnie, and if I hadn't known him since first grade, I'd have nothing to do with the pretentious weasel.

"I see you're looking at your watch. Have to go?"

"Yep. But let's continue this intriguing conversation another time."

Lonnie stopped me. "Don't be sarcastic. I'm very conflicted."

"So go see a professional. Do you have insurance?"

"I've been to couples and individual therapy. And I'm still a wreck. Any suggestions?"

"Yeah. Cut it off completely with your weekend romance and come to your senses. That's my advice."

"Anything else?"

I don't know why this popped into my head, but I thought about a weekend retreat a friend had recommended some time back when Julia and I had marital troubles. She didn't want to go, but I vowed to check it out one day. Perhaps a men's retreat would be helpful to Lonnie and I'd be his chaperone. The grounds were supposedly beautiful and nestled in the woods. And I'd heard that the food was kick-ass fabulous.

"We're going on a men's retreat, Lonnie."

"We are?"

"Yep. I'll call you later with details."

"But real men go fishing to get away and renew. We've always done that."

"Not this time, pal. Besides, we're not real men anymore," I proclaimed.

Lonnie chuckled and we exchanged a playful fist bump. I don't enjoy watching an old friend self destruct, despite his desire to do so.

I spent part of the next week preparing for our getaway the following Saturday. We'd do an overnight at a retreat up in the Berkshires, a couple of hours from my home in central Connecticut. I put a deposit down for the one day gathering, hoping to clear my head as well.

I picked Lonnie up at his home early on Saturday. Both Julia and Susan were glad to be rid of us. I had urged Lonnie not to contact the woman he'd met on his recent business trip and he kept his word. I believed him. We drove toward Stockbridge and kept the conversation to a minimum. Lonnie drank his black coffee and stared out the window. We passed a couple of bicyclists and waved. It was a crisp autumn September day. Lonnie broke the silence with a confession.

"Did I mention that an old girlfriend recently died and generously left a portion of her inheritance?"

I turned toward Lonnie. Sometimes I wondered how many of his tales were completely fabricated. I'd insist that he stop concocting falsehoods even though I willingly played the straight man in his comic shtick.

"No kidding. How much did she leave you? And why would she?"

"Well, we were involved years ago, before I met Susan, and we got along. I liked her."

I decided not to ask questions even though I was curious. I didn't want to further feed his ego by lavishing more attention his way.

"I probably don't deserve it," said Lonnie.

"Deserve what?"

"The inheritance."

"You're right, you don't." If I agreed with him, I took the wind out of his sails.

"I don't deserve Susan either."

"That's right, you don't," I said.

Lonnie poured another cup of coffee from his gigantic thermos. The fall colors were captivating and I loved living here. I'd never leave New England despite the frigid winter, and I'd never give Julia any reason to mistrust me, despite occasional attraction to others. I prided myself on self control and didn't conceal my judgmental attitude toward Lonnie's whims and impulses.

"So you agree that I don't deserve Susan."

"Nope, you don't."

"Do I deserve your friendship and loyalty?"

"Nope, you don't." I playfully tapped his knee. "We're going to have one good time this weekend."

We arrived at the retreat and checked in. The grounds were spacious and rustic. We found our cabin and discussed the day's schedule. We'd have lunch at the main lodge and then begin our group session. Neither of us had ever participated in one.

Strolling back to the lodge, I noticed a small open meadow and thought of bocce or lawn bowling. The pristine grass field sparked memories of Lonnie and me sneaking off to Yankee Stadium by subway on opening day. We had skipped school without anyone knowing. After the game, we hid in the dank stadium tunnels under home plate which reeked of stale beer and nicotine fumes. The tunnels led to a path that connected the opposing player clubhouse to the team bus. We'd collect autographs and briefly chat with any player willing to oblige.

I yearned to be at Fenway Park for tonight's Yankee game, but also enjoyed this peaceful setting. I noticed a series of hot tubs lying alongside a stream below us and then glanced at Lonnie.

"Have you participated in a Men's group before?"

"I pitched on an intramural softball team a few years back," said Lonnie.

"I'm joking. I know what you mean."

"We'll be asked to disclose our fears and pain," I said. "And bond with others we've never met."

"What do you know about this particular retreat?" asked Lonnie.

"It's all in the brochure I handed you on the drive up. Still game?"

"Okay, let's do it," Lonnie said. "I'll try something new."

After lunch, we began our first session inside the main lodge. A fresh breeze came through an open window. Twelve of us, mostly middle-aged and graying, formed a circle. We waited for the group facilitator to arrive.

"Who's pitching tonight?" Lonnie whispered. "Few can pitch in Fenway without getting creamed. It's vicious up there on opposing players."

"I agree. Where is the person leading this session?"

"Probably at the ballgame," Lonnie snickered.

Then a stocky figure marched in. Chuck wore a large nametag pasted to his snug crew neck shirt. Barrel-chested, Chuck owned the strong jaw of a drill sergeant. His eyes were an intense blue. He spoke while we sat cross-legged on a carpet.

"Welcome. We'll begin by breathing gently and exhaling slowly."

Lonnie nudged me. "I don't know if this agrees with me."

"What'd you say?"

"We're not boy scouts at summer camp. Are we having a sing-along?"

"Stop being self conscious and do what he says, okay?"

Chuck looked our way. "Is there a problem, gentlemen?"

"No, we're just warming up," I said.

"Do you happen to know who's pitching for the Yankees tonight?" said Lonnie to no one in particular.

Chuck grimaced, his leathery skin tightening. "How the hell would I know? We're not here to talk baseball anyway. I don't want distractions or screw ups, you hear?"

The circle nodded in unison.

"We stick with the program," said Chuck. "We focus on our goals."

I squirmed and recalled our registration fee, and vowed to extract something to bolster my marriage despite the silly opening routine.

Chuck cleared his throat. "Now gentlemen, say 'um' and release that stale and toxic residue buried deep inside your soul. Ready, go!"

Lonnie elbowed me. "Who's this guy and what are his credentials?"

"Just do it, Lonnie. Start grunting."

We closed our eyes and chanted. I kept thinking that the recent stock market surge was only temporary and that it was primarily due to reduced labor costs, and not based on real growth.

Chuck glanced my way. "Got a problem, buddy? You stopped."

"No, I'm chanting."

"Good."

"This dude's really uptight," Lonnie whispered. "He's into control, big time."

Suddenly Chuck stood and walked over to Lonnie. His six-foot-two inch burly frame towered over my buddy. "Repeat that."

"You're into control, aren't you," said Lonnie.

"Yep. That's right. And when I'm through with you, you'll be a changed man. Now, man up and take your licks."

Chuck backpedaled and sat down. He placed a wad of chewing gum, perhaps Juicy Fruit, in his mouth. "I'm here to confront you. There's no crying on anyone's shoulder around here. Man up! None of you are forgiven."

"Shit," I muttered. I doubted if this approach was helpful for Lonnie and me. Lonnie needed forgiveness and understanding, not scorn.

"Okay. You in the corner wearing the green polo-shirt. What's your story? Tell the group." Chuck's gravelly voice echoed off the wall.

The slender man in the polo shirt appeared intimidated and began rubbing his hands and blinking.

Even though it wasn't Lonnie's turn, he broke the silence.

"I recently had an affair and cheated on my marriage. I'm sorry."

"Was it your turn?" Chuck barked. "Okay Sad Sack, let's discuss why you felt the need to act on your urge. What was going through your head at the time? Did you consider the impact on your wife?"

I grabbed Lonnie's arm and led him out the room. I wanted no part of this healing retreat despite the fee we paid. Chuck's brash demeanor was threatening. Chuck was my bullying father in a foul mood.

"Where do ya think you two rascals are going?"

"Away. Good luck, Chuck."

"Can't stand the heat, chicken shits? Good riddance."

We exited the unlocked door. I'd write a letter demanding an explanation. Who hired this charlatan on steroids to lead vulnerable men? I'd have this creepy asshole fired and decommissioned.

"Calm down. Where are we going?" asked Lonnie.

"Far from here."

"Why? I was loosening up and venting and liked his

probing questions.   Besides, we've got dinner and a pancake breakfast coming. Let's remain on the grounds and
skip the next session."

I didn't want to linger despite urging Lonnie to confront his demons and focus on his marriage. I'd soon inform the staff about our abusive and nasty group leader.
We paid to relax, and to meet someone new and interesting to commiserate with. There are gentler ways to share
personal horror tales.

Besides, I'd hoped to gain a little insight into improving
my relationship with Julia, which had become routine and
predictable.

When I entered the office to report Chuck, the manager
claimed that the original group facilitator cancelled due to
illness, and that they'd summoned Chuck at the last minute. A staff member had recommended him based on his
no nonsense, no excuses approach to conflict resolution;
and out of sympathy due to his recent bitter divorce,
which had rattled him. I was told that Chuck meant well
despite his blunt manner.

I proposed my new idea as we retrieved our luggage
from the cabin and began loading the trunk.

"Let's drive to Boston and see tonight's Yankees game.
Chuck can choke on his excess testosterone. We'll tell our
sweeties that we gleaned new insights at our session and
are now more receptive to their emotional needs." This
sounded like claptrap.

Lonnie arched his brow. "You're doing a piss poor version of impressing an attractive woman with approval
seeking pretentious crap. 'Oh, you're a Nazi sympathizer.
You don't say? Me too'!"

"Your shallow side is rubbing off. Bad influence."

Lonnie scratched his chin and nodded. "Let's go to the

game. I've never been to Fenway, enemy territory."

Boston was a two hour drive, and we'd arrive in the late afternoon. I hoped we could procure bleacher seats despite a capacity crowd. We'd use discretion cheering on our boys or the bleacher mob would attack, especially if drunk. I'd urge a rowdy fan to see Chuck for analysis and lock them both in a wire cage and let 'em go at it.

"Let's be cautious and not piss off diehards in the stands," I said.

"I agree," said Lonnie. "We'll practice restraint, which isn't my forte."

We got into the car and left the retreat. Perhaps I'd return someday with Julia and take the weekend offerings more seriously and with a sharper focus. Our marriage would benefit from a shot in the arm tune-up.

Fortunately, the turnpike wasn't congested, and made good time reaching the outskirts of Boston . Then as we approached the city, traffic picked up. We crawled along, and I hoped there were still game tickets. It was a heated pennant race. Lonnie had refilled his coffee thermos at the retreat and guzzled a few more cups. I felt drowsy and had him pour me caffeine stimulant to stay awake.

"We've known each other a *long* time," I said.

"Since first grade," said Lonnie. His head leaned against the window.

"I was best man at your wedding, and loved dancing with my Julia. We drank and got woozy and zany together. God, I miss that."

"You've been wound tight lately," said Lonnie.

I ignored his comment, though suspected it was true."

"You didn't elope this time like you'd done twice before. I caught you sneaking a slow flirtatious waltz with my Julia at the celebration." I elbowed him.

Lonnie fidgeted. "I was a nervous wreck a week before the wedding.

"I remember. You'd be awake all night and passed the time ordering by phone from the LL Bean catalog. Was that true?"

"I was anxious," said Lonnie, "and needed an anonymous stranger to converse with to distract me. The female customer reps were soothing and calming. 'Yes, the lamb's wool cardigan in midnight blue. We have that in stock. What size? Sure, I can tell you more about the fabric. No problem, sir'."

"You beefed up your wardrobe. Nice job!"

"Thanks for tolerating me that week. I'd already failed at two previous marriages. Maybe I'm not cut out for fidelity."

I was enjoying our conversation and then chuckled at another flashback. I needed a distraction from ensuing road congestion.

"About a month after your wedding, didn't the four of us devour a midnight meal at the 24 hour Greek diner? We poked fun at others from our corner booth by matching patrons with a famous figure. How 'bout the two counter guys who were dead ringers for Dick Nixon and Dwight Eisenhower? Ike and Tricky Dick in person."

"I remember," said Lonnie. "They were eating pancakes and slurping coffee. Mutt and Jeff."

"Donuts and coffee," I corrected.

"Okay, whatever. I laughed and lost control, and mistakenly struck Susan with an elbow. Her arm was bruised, but she forgave me."

I was on a roll. "And the time we double-dated at Johnnie's, the indoor skate rink. I was the lucky novice who crashed into the railing head first and then collapsed onto the wood floor in one fluid motion. I know I impressed Julia with that Olympic feat. I've wanted to return with her, but haven't gotten around to it."

"It's closed down. Nothing's there now," said Lonnie. "Sorry."

A blaring horn startled me and traffic began moving faster.

We soon meandered downtown, and almost crashed along a confusing roundabout before finding stadium parking. The massive garage appeared empty, but the game wouldn't start for another few hours. Outside the garage, we walked the Back Bay area and proceeded to the stadium box office. I approached the window and asked for tickets. The game sold out months ago and we were out of luck. Also, a popular former Red Sox player would be honored before the game and this had stoked fan interest.

I turned toward Lonnie. "What next? Buy from a scalper?"

"Nope, too expensive," he said.

"So, do we admit defeat and declare our getaway a disaster?"

Lonnie perked up. "Have faith, we'll get into the game somehow. Let's hang about and see what happens."

"Pray for a miracle?" I chuckled at my hopeful but naive suggestion.

Just then, the box office agent informed us that a special impromptu stadium tour would commence in five minutes. The forty minute tour would include the outfield scoreboard interior. I liked the idea of exploring what lay near the ancient Green Monster wall, site of towering home runs and wild player collisions near the warning track. Opposing outfielders were spooked by the Monster wall, and how it sent line drives off in crazy directions.

Like a tragic Poe character, perhaps a distraught Yankee fan resided in limbo within the concrete Monster wall. We paid for the unadvertised tour and were the only ones signed up, which was surprising.

Lonnie and I climbed stairs and crawled under rafters and squeezed between poles and beams and eventually emerged inside the outfield scoreboard. We brushed aside cobwebs and inhaled a stale mildew odor. Ventilation was poor. An invisible and lucky fellow once tracked balls, strikes, outs, and inning runs by changing and posting numbers manually. This was my calling. Numbers were tidy, unlike messy and ambiguous relationships. Next, the tour guide introduced us to a man in his seventies who sat upright on a wooden stool. The stranger stood and smiled.

"Welcome to the catacombs of Fenway," the guide said. "The ghosts and spirits of Fenway lie here. Please respect their privacy."

I enjoyed his affable manner and banter.

"You're in for a rare treat," said the guide. "Meet the former Sox player to be honored at our game tonight. His rookie season was fifty years ago, in 1959. Meet Elijah Jerry 'Pumpsie' Green."

I shook the hand of Boston's first Black ballplayer. I'd read that he once boarded a plane with a teammate to visit Israel, but concluded it was only unfounded rumor. Green remained popular with teammates and hometown fans for his hustle and spirit.

"Sit down gentlemen, and make yourselves at home." Pumpsie brought over two round stools and placed them next to his. Our dark fortress was clammy and chilly, and I zipped my jacket. I felt drowsy and needed a hot coffee to warm my insides. The tour guide told us that he'd soon return to escort us back, and that we'd be in good hands.

"So what brings you here?" said the former second baseman.

He wore a red cardigan and dark trousers and appeared scholarly. A Red Sox cap lay on top of salt and pepper hair. He reached into his jacket pocket and removed paper with scribbled notes.

"Mind if I practice my speech on you? I'm being honored tonight."

"Of course not," said Lonnie.

Pumpsie chuckled. "Just ribbing. I know it by heart."

"Why are you sequestered inside the scoreboard?" I asked. "This isn't the most comfy place."

Pumpsie rubbed his chin. "Used to play poker or blackjack up here during long rain delays, or before games with the statistician. Mostly for fun and camaraderie. Pete was a gentle and understanding soul, even when I took all his money." Pumpsie laughed and I assumed he was joking.

I noticed an old reel-to-reel projector and screen set up nearby. Our host stood, plugged in the cord and turned on the projector and shouted: "Action." The machine produced a whirring sound as Pumpsie narrated.

"Highlights from long ago. There's Ted Williams taking batting practice at Fenway with my teammates. Nice guy, and the greatest hitter of his time if not all time. If you watch closely, that's me crouching near second base. I only played five seasons and finished with the Mets. A short but fun career. My first game was in Chicago's Comiskey park, but that's on another reel."

Lonnie and I watched vintage highlights of Pumpsie fielding, hitting, and running the bases. It was grainy footage yet the images were fresh.

"I have another surprise for you gentlemen." Pumpsie reached for a brief case and opened the lock and retrieved another reel. He blew dust from it, and pried open the metal cover.

"More highlights from your playing days?" I asked.

"You'll see. Be patient. Sorry we're out of sodas, but please accept these bags of salted peanuts you can snack on." He tossed us each a small bag.

Pumpsie removed the first reel and put it away and then mounted a new one. He flipped the projector switch and sat back down. The screen showed a series of flashbacks of a younger Lonnie and Susan devouring wedding cake and then dancing inside a grand reception hall. I turned toward Lonnie and he shrugged.

"A charitable donation?" I asked. "From your personal archives?"

"No," whispered Lonnie.

The film continued, depicting scenes of Lonnie's evolving relationship with Susan: Clowning at an amusement park carousel, then a trip to an exotic wildlife preserve, and at a festive family Thanksgiving gathering. We watched Lonnie and Susan whooping it up, laughing together and hugging affectionately. I could even envision myself acting all goofy with Julia, at our favorite roller rink or at the local midnight diner.

We stared in a haze until the footage abruptly stopped. I yawned and shook my head while Lonnie rubbed his eyes as if awakening from prolonged slumber. We both must have conked out from the long day.

"How'd you obtain the film?" inquired Lonnie. "It's not possible."

"I have mysterious ways," said Pumpsie, "and better if kept secret."

Pumpsie laughed. "I noticed you guys dozing off during my career highlight footage. Bored? Or were your active imaginations working overtime?"

"Sorry," said Lonnie. "Didn't mean to."

"That's all right, I get it," said Pumpsie. "But don't take anyone for granted, you hear?"

I touched Lonnie's shoulder. "Our Men's retreat relocated to Fenway. We finally made it."

"Was I imagining a nostalgic highlight film?" asked Lonnie.

"You've been dreaming," affirmed Pumpsie. "Now wake up. You pass 'Go' for a second chance. Don't blow it this time or your remains will be entombed within these cement walls."

Famished, I reached for the peanuts bag and ripped it open and swallowed handfuls, almost choking. Lonnie pounded my shoulder blade and restored my breathing and rhythm before I spoke up.

"What's your next stop after tonight's game?"

"Back home to the Bay area."

"Thanks for the revealing tour and insights," said Lonnie. "Mind if I take my personal highlight film?"

"Pleasure's mine. Would you like it gift wrapped for no extra charge?" Pumpsie removed a small box from a shelf and pretended to cut ribbon and tie a bow.

"Good luck," said Pumpsie. He clasped our hands.

Our tour guide soon appeared and led us back to the front of the stadium. I don't remember retracing our steps. I can't vouch for Lonnie, but I was light on my feet and giddy. Then our guide reached into his pocket and handed us tickets to tonight's game.

"Compliments of the man upstairs being honored," he said. "Enjoy."

We enjoyed the game and savored the Yankees close victory. We watched from the bleachers with a muted cheer as the Yanks rallied in the ninth on a two out double that zigzagged off the Green Monster. After the game, we walked toward the parking garage outside Fenway. I tapped Lonnie's shoulder.

"I've got an accusation, and a confession."

"What's up," said Lonnie.

"I think you've been a lying, devious shit toward Susan when you pursue affairs. I also envy your spontaneity and recklessness. I wish I had cojones. Especially with Julia."

"Meaning what?"

"Passion. Mojo. Routine gets stale with us and I've got to shake things up but can't seem to. Julia deserves better, but I get bogged down with avoidance rituals I depend on. I still respect her and want it to work. We've been together a long time."

"What avoidance rituals? Like flossing your teeth for ten minutes when you should be on fire in bed?"

"Yeah, something like that."

Lonnie halted his stride and shook his head. "I play the compulsive jerk by pretending to seduce younger women. At my age it's pathetic. What do ya prove? It's a zero sum game, and frankly it sucks."

"Susan treats you well and she's a peach. And very sensual."

"It's a blind spot. Compulsions short circuit sanity, and I lose rational control for short term pleasure. That's my sorry addiction excuse."

Lonnie cleared his throat and continued venting, talking over the street noise. It was now dark and we had a long drive home.

"I admire your commitment with Julia, despite shortcomings. I envy your self control. Must be delayed gratification genes."

Then Lonnie dropped a bombshell as we entered the garage elevator. He looked down and blinked a few times. I hadn't noticed this nervous tick before.

"There's something I did a while back I'm ashamed of."

The elevator lights distorted Lonnie's coloring, giving him a washed out appearance. I'd become almost immune to his confessions.

"What'd you do?"

"About two months after your wedding I bumped into Julia at the outdoor weekend market. Susan was running errands and you were away that morning. Julia and I began conversing and laughing by the berry stand, and I started coming on to her."

"You what? You're kidding."

"Nope. I told her she looked fabulous and asked if she wanted to meet for coffee sometime. Just us two. Julia recoiled and backed away and I don't blame her. I'd do the same."

The elevator stopped, and we got out and walked to my car. I grew tense. My voice echoed in the near empty garage.

"You're really screwed up. Why the hell are you telling me this?"

I flashed on Julia vaguely mentioning this incident, but she'd clammed up when pressed for details. My neck stiffened as I clenched my teeth. I considered leaving the conniving weasel stranded in Boston.

"I betrayed you and violated your trust. And Julia's too."

"You did? Is this another contrived line you're throwing out for future practice? You wretched opportunist, Lonnie."

I didn't care if others heard my rare outburst. Maybe they'd figure I was drunk and pissed about the Red Sox losing.

I let Lonnie into my car and knew I'd soon calm down

and have to forgive him. And I wouldn't disclose my ongoing attraction and desire for his wife Susan, having done
a masterful job concealing this from everyone, including
myself on occasion. This wasn't fair to Julia. I valued marital fidelity and hated messes and drama.   If Lonnie
couldn't appreciate Susan, then he didn't deserve her and
could go to hell. I was also relieved that Susan wasn't
available. Lonnie took foolish risks, not me. Meanwhile,
barely a word was exchanged between us on the long
drive back home.

The Happy Hermit of Times Square

The Happy Hermit of Times Square

Harold decided to visit his estranged brother Morrie, who lived alone in the cellar of his building near Times Square. Harold had received a phone call from his brother who sounded desperate and troubled. He'd visit Morrie and lend him money so he could eat and survive. Manhattan rent was unaffordable for many but Morrie had luckily procured a rent stabilized apartment off of West 45th, not far from Hells Kitchen. Unfortunately, he'd been evicted after not paying rent for a year and ended up squatting in his building's cellar.

Harold lived in Woodside in a modest high rise studio overlooking busy Queens Boulevard. He subsisted on unemployment subsidies after leaving his position writing obituaries for a newspaper, one with declining circulation. He'd grown disenchanted and bored writing obits, and was recently let go after receiving lousy performance reviews from his editor, who also soon got laid off. Harold considered distracting his brother by reading a few of his recent obits, which had included splices of maudlin humor.

Harold rode the subway into Manhattan and had prearranged a brotherly rendezvous at a neighborhood coffee shop. Morrie had contacted Harold from a pay phone, and the ensuing garbled connection made it difficult for them to converse. They had lost touch over the past year. Morrie's finances and credit access dwindled along with his connection to external reality. There'd been a gradual falling out due to Morrie's situation, but with no lingering hostility. Harold cared about his only surviving sibling and family member and wanted the enveloping depressive fog to dissipate for them both.

Harold emerged from the subway and walked toward

the coffee shop on West 48th and Eighth Avenue. After raising his jacket collar against the wind, he hunched over, burying his cold hands in his coat pockets. Harold wasn't bad looking. A full head of grayish hair made him appear younger than sixty. Morrie had aged with hard times, though was only a year older and could soon apply for Social Security benefits.

Harold stood outside the coffee shop and glimpsed his brother hunched over the lunch counter. It'd been almost a year since they'd met up. He observed a wiry man behind the counter pour coffee into Morrie's cup. Harold walked inside and approached the counter. He didn't want to startle his brother so he made sure that Morrie saw him first before saying anything.

"Hey Morrie. Mind if I join you?"

Morrie straightened and managed a weak smile. He wore a faded plaid shirt, old jeans and worn sneakers.

"Nice to see ya, Harold. Have a seat."

Harold removed his coat and patted Morrie on the back. He placed his coat on the adjoining vacant stool.

"You chose a good spot. It's warm in here." Harold rubbed his hands and sat down.

"Would you prefer a booth? There's an open one by the window. It'll go fast."

"No, this is fine, Morrie."

The counter man placed a menu in front of Harold. He scanned the menu and ordered a chicken salad sandwich and fries with coffee.

"It's been a while," said Harold.

Morrie's eyes appeared bloodshot and his face somewhat puffy or swollen. "Yep. Been a while. You look good."

"You too," lied Harold.

"Thanks."

Morrie picked up the Times sports section. "Someone left this on the counter so I checked the basketball box scores while waiting for you."

"Think the Knicks will get far into the playoffs now that they've picked up a couple of veteran point guards?"

Morrie squinted or exhibited an eye twitch. Harold hadn't noticed this before.

"Suppose so. They're due for a good playoff run," said Morrie. "But it's been so damn long since their last championship. Was it in '72 or '73? I can't damn remember. Suppose it's not important."

"That Dave DeBusschere trade fortified their front line. The Knicks won in '70 and in '73. Didn't we attend a few games back then?"

Morrie hunched over and nodded. "It was wild at the old Garden. An organist named Eddie Layton got the crowd going. Maybe I got the name wrong. But I remember the organ and the beat and the energy."

"And post game we'd grab a hot dog at Snack Time," reminisced Harold. "We pumped poisonous nitrates into our digestive track and lived to tell about it. The indigestion was worth it."

Harold knew by waxing nostalgic he'd lure Morrie from his cocoon and loosen him up. He assumed he was Morrie's first prolonged personal interaction in a while. His brother had lost contact with former colleagues.

Harold's chicken salad sandwich arrived along with his hot coffee. He removed the toothpicks from the bread and bit into his lunch. It tasted good. He swallowed before continuing the conversation.

"Hey Morrie, wasn't your first summer job around here?"

"Yeah. I worked a summer in the Horn & Hardart Automat nearby and then another summer at a White Castle hamburger joint."

"What was it like working at the Automat? Did you procure free food on break?"

"All I remember were lots of clanging nickels and rows of vending machines. My job was to replace the bought sandwiches by sticking new ones on shelves inside glass cases. It was like a gigantic assembly line, a huge cafeteria."

"What was on the menu?" Harold poured ketchup over his fries and the counter man poured a refill.

"Let's see." Morrie scratched his chin and his eyeballs shot to the side. "There were no formal menus. Customers selected creamed corn, creamed spinach, mashed potatoes, mac & cheese and sandwiches. There was a separate hot food section and a cute girl named Linda or Belinda worked the register. She was a red head and had a nice smile." Morrie glanced down. "She never knew I was there."

"Can I buy you anything? A sandwich?" offered Harold.

"No thanks. I'm good. There was an old lady that came in every day around noon and sat down nearby at one of the concession machines I worked behind."

"At the Automat?"

"Yeah."

"A regular."

"Yeah. She wanted a cool place with fans to escape the suffocating summer humidity. She wore a sheriff's badge on her blouse and I overheard her talking aloud to no one in particular. She muttered or mumbled but I heard bits of her monologue."

"What did she say?"

"She described her morning to an imaginary friend named Abe. She'd say, 'I had a very busy morning Abe.

First, I blah blah blah. Then blah blah blah.   And so on'."

"Was she addressing Abe Lincoln?"

"Perhaps. That sheriff's badge was quite an ornamental addition, all shiny and silver. It fit her well."

"Did lonely folks frequent the Automat?"

"Probably. They had few friends or no place special to go. Maybe retirees on a flimsy pension or Social Security who needed a cheap place to eat and hang out."

Harold noticed Morrie squirm.

"Why didn't you work there other summers? You were putting yourself through college at the time I recall."

"I got fired in August, a week before school started back up. In fact, I recently had a bad dream about that incident."

"What happened?"

"I'd rather not go into it. But since you asked here goes: In the dream Mr. Horn and Mr. Hardart, the Automat founders, approach me. They're well groomed in dapper business suits and sporting droopy handlebar moustaches. Pocket watches dangle from their loose fitting trousers on gold chains. They scold and reprimand me for staring at the pretty cashier Linda and for neglecting my work. I replenish those damn sandwiches as fast as I can. Then I walk away from my station and begin biting into luscious desserts that revolve inside a case. I'm trying to catch Linda's attention by waving, but she ignores me. Then the bosses read me the riot act and order me to get lost."

"What desserts were you sampling? "

"Cheese cake, carrot cake, German chocolate cake and cream pies."

"Sounds like a good way to go out."

"Let's change the subject, Harold. I don't like bad dreams."

"No problem."

Harold finished his last fry and wiped crumbs from his chin.

The counter man took their plates. "Dessert buddy?"

Harold looked at his brother.

"No thanks," said Morrie. "We're done. Check please."

"Where to next?" said Harold, after paying the bill. "Your place?"

"Be prepared. I've been homeless for a month now since I've been evicted from my apartment."

"So you've been living in your building basement. That's what you told me on the phone."

"Yeah. It's not ideal. But I'm not excited about entering a homeless shelter, unless I'm kicked out of my current place."

"But you were kicked out for not paying rent."

"Hopefully, the landlord won't find me in the cellar."

"I'd like to see where you're living. Okay? I hope it's not too unsanitary and not inundated with mold. Winter will be a bitch. You've got to do something soon Morrie."

"I know. Okay. Let's go."

"If I may ask, what've you been doing for food?"

"My old tenant Rita has been very generous and leaves stuff outside her apartment door. She's the only one who knows that I'm squatting."

"I met her once. Wasn't she a high school English teacher?"

"Yep. Good memory. A very sweet and caring person."

"Is that your sole food source?"

"I frequent a bakery nearby that leaves unsold goods out in the back alley behind the shop. They've also been generous."

"No soup kitchens. Or food stamps?"

"Not yet. Too embarrassing."

"I see. Admitting to your situation is tough."

"Shall we leave," said Morrie. "You'll see my new temporary digs. I'm attached to my building and hate the thought of moving. I lived there for twenty five years!"

"I see." Harold tried not to be critical or judgmental. He had thousands of shortcomings himself. He knew of former friends and girlfriends that would have a field day deconstructing his failings and misdeeds. Harold mentally ran through a litany of shortcomings: selfish, critical, impulsive, emotionally removed, and narcissistic. Then he stopped himself and focused on his brother.

"Twenty five years, man. What a run. You loved living there."

They walked outside into the noisy street and chilly air and toward Morrie's current residence.

Morrie shouted to be heard above the construction jackhammer.

"Guess what I liked best about my old apartment?"

Harold cupped his hands. "What'd ya say? Repeat that."

Morrie leaned into Harold while horns blared. "Did you ask me to repeat what I said?"

"Yes!"

"I loved that my apartment was rent stabilized. I paid five hundred and fifty a month for a place that could rent for three or four times that."

Surrounding street noise prevented Harold from focusing and engaging in civil conversation. He'd wait until they arrived at his brother's new residence before finding out more about his struggles.

They approached the brick apartment building off of West 45th and Eighth Avenue. Morrie had lived on the fifth floor for twenty five years before being evicted for not paying rent. Harold had visited his brother more than a few times and recalled ascending a winding narrow staircase five floors and this had gotten his heart pumping. Harold recalled a tiny kitchen that overlooked a narrow alley. Morrie's living and bedroom windows also faced an alley. Another building, a factory or warehouse, could be seen across the way. The location was prime real estate for those desiring a converted condo or co op back in the late seventies.

"After getting evicted," Morrie explained, "I held onto a spare key and slept in my apartment for a week or so. I had stored my remaining furniture so I slept on the living room floor. Then they changed locks and I couldn't get in."

"Then you found an alternative."

"Right. I'll take you down to the cellar which my old key opens. I couldn't believe my luck."

They walked down a stairway from the side of the building. Morrie contorted his small frame trying to appear invisible and compact. He turned up his coat collar and resembled a secret agent caricature from a '50's spy thriller. Morrie motioned for Harold to stay close behind.

"No one has seen you? How long have you been doing this?"

"Sh. No problem. Only my upstairs tenant Rita knows, and she's sympathetic."

A metal door opened exposing a dark musty room with old furniture, including a sofa and chair. A hot plate sat on a table. A space heater leaned against a corner wall. There were no windows.

"Does the space heater work, or the hot plate?"

"There's usually no electricity. It's spotty. I wish I could boil water for tea or something warm. I've saved a few blankets from my apartment and sleep on the sofa."

"That musty thing?"

"It's not too uncomfortable. There's a protruding spring in one part but I avoid it."

Harold sat on the wooden chair and faced Morrie, who reclined on the sofa. Concrete walls blocked most outside noise, sealing them in.

"I came into the city," said Harold, "because you sounded desperate when you phoned yesterday."

"Yeah, thanks. I was having a bad day but I'm doing better now."

"What problem were you having?"

Morrie leaned forward. "I was broke, not a nickel to my name."

"I see. Have you entered and won the lottery between then and now?" Harold wanted to contain his anger and upset for the moment. How could his brother avoid paying rent and not expect this outcome. His disconnection with reality was much deeper than he originally surmised.

"I sold a few vintage rock albums earlier this morning and got a little cash. I hated to part with them."

Harold sneezed. His sinuses had become clogged from the dust in the room. It felt like an underground chamber where political prisoners are shipped off to and never heard from for years.

"What's your plan, Morrie? How much longer will you crash here?"

"Not to worry. I applied for senior subsidized housing a week ago and I'm expecting to move into a SRO in a few days."

"You were accepted? You occupy a single room?"

"Yeah. They convert old hotel rooms into small living spaces. I'll still need to pay some amount toward the rent."

"I'll lend you something until you get back on your

feet."

"Thanks!"

Morrie rose and walked over to a wood crate. He reached in and grabbed a donut from a box. Then he poured from an open carton of apple juice and offered Harold a drink.

"No thanks. I'm still full from lunch. But drink up."

It grew chilly and damp in the room. It was bleak and depressing, and Harold couldn't wait to leave.

Morrie picked up a matchbook and lit a candle. He placed it in a holder which lay on a crate. The flame distorted his face into a shadow puppet figure, and Harold suppressed a chuckle.

"How did this all happen, Morrie?"

"How did what happen?"

"How the fuck did you get into this mess?"

"Whatda ya mean? Be specific."

"Shit." Harold's sinuses grew irritated and he was tempted to plunk cash down and take off. His brother would have to proceed from there.

"Okay. I'll be specific." Harold modulated his tone so it wouldn't sound accusatory but this was tough to do.

"You were pulling four hundred a day as a computer consultant designing software programs. You put that MBA to good use."

"Three hundred fifty."

"Excuse me. Why did you quit doing this knowing you had bills, debts and rent. It's been three years since you've worked."

"Sounds about right. I lose track of time."

Morrie cleared his throat. The flame began to gutter and Morrie relit the candle. He bit into the remnants of his chocolate donut.

"You sure you don't want a swig of juice. I can tell

you're having trouble breathing. Sinuses acting up again?"

"Why did you leave a lucrative career that paid well?"

"If you must know, I wanted to go in a new direction. Develop ideas on my own."

"What ideas?"

"I was conjuring up innovative ways to access interactive programs on line. I can't go into specifics, but I'm still working on it."

"But you don't own a computer. How will you do this?"

"I'm working it out in my head. I'm optimistic that my efforts will pay off."

"Meanwhile, when you leave the tech field, it's tough to catch up on the latest applications and software. You're left in the dust."

"I know. But just wait and see. Something will develop."

"You're not feeling depressed about your situation?"

"Nope. Once I get a decent night's sleep I'll have the energy to pursue my goals. It's within reach. Just wait and see."

"What time do you get to sleep?"

"I'm up most of the night and don't turn in until four or five."

"What are you doing other than pacing the floor?"

"Thinking things through. Working out details of my life plan."

Harold had had enough. He stood and reached for his wallet. He was hurting financially but had to see this unfortunate situation through. Harold was pissed at Morrie but also knew he needed help. Hopefully, he'd soon move into the SRO and have a real roof over his head.

"You don't have to go, Harold. We don't have contact

that often."

"I should take off but please stay in touch. Okay?"

Harold placed cash on the crate. He knew that Morrie couldn't cash a check without paying exorbitant interest on the transaction.

"Wait. You said on the phone yesterday that you got into hot water at your recent news room job and no longer work there."

"That's right. I was asked to leave."

"What happened?"

"Why do you want to know?"

"Because we're all we got. No family left. All gone."

"I did something I shouldn't have and screwed up."

"I'm listening."

"I'd rather not unload, but since you're curious, I'll entertain you with one of my Pulitzer Prize pieces."

"Don't mock or underestimate yourself, Harold. You've got talent with the written word."

"Okay. If you cut the bullshit, I'll recite one of my recent obits. Hey, I just got a great idea Morrie!"

"What's that?"

"You could open up a poetry reading night down here in the cellar. Fuck your computer idea. Get a liquor license and conduct weekly poetry slams here in the dungeon."

"What the hell is a poetry slam? Are you smashing something?"

"Forget it. Sorry for the sarcasm. I'll tell you what I did that upset my editor and could've gotten my paper and me in hot legal water."

Morrie leaned forward some more. "What's it like writing obituaries. Isn't it depressing?"

"You know how a mortician makes the corpse look presentable on the outside. Well, I restore or embellish to make lives appear more interesting."

"Why not let someone's accomplishments tell a story. Why the need to change anything? Let the facts speak for themselves."

Harold grew perplexed as to how his brother's last hold on reality and clarity was overridden by irrational fantasies and lethargy. Harold thought it unfortunate that Morrie couldn't transform his dream world into something concrete and useful.

"I'd contact a family member or close friend of the deceased to gather details or highlights. I compiled info and summarized, and presented struggles in a positive light. Families often submitted their own remembrance."

"How's that bad or hurtful? A plumber fixes leaky pipes. You're like a handyman. You heal saddened hearts and help people grieve."

"That's overstating my effect, but thanks. I screwed up."

"How?"

"I did some good work, especially after the recent monster storm. I interacted with a few families after loved ones drowned in the Rockaways and Brooklyn. An electrician named Stan died about a month ago and he broke rules by crossing into the city to repair and restore power to folks' homes. He wasn't New York City certified but still came over from Jersey to fill a need. Not that old a guy. Congestive heart failure or diabetes killed him."

Morrie nodded. "I wish he'd restore power down here in the cellar."

Harold removed a piece of scrap paper from his pocket and held it close to the candle, the only light source. He recited aloud what he'd written.

A beloved fellow named Stan
Hung tough when crap hit the fan
He fought for the right
To turn on the light
When nasty storms killed power on land
Beloved Stan: You're dah Man!

"Thanks Harold. Not bad. Recite another one."
"In a minute."
"Your editor published that? It's quite unusual."
"No, he didn't publish that. I sent it separately to the family with a condolence card, in advance of the longer formal obit I'd written. They liked both remembrances."
Harold swallowed in an attempt to clear his parched throat.
"Pour me some apple juice. No beer in the fridge I guess."
"No fridge. But when I move into my new place I'll be better stocked."
"I also highlighted obsessive habits and compulsions of the deceased. I sometimes bypassed my editor's approval after final revision and occasionally upset a grieving family, but not with malicious intent."
"You're not a malicious fellow," said Morrie.
"This one widow out in Bensenhurst complained about her late husband's hoarding compulsion. He'd scour the neighborhood for remnants of anything not bolted down: Discarded bathtubs, sinks, wood scraps, scrap metal, all kinds of junk. It drove her nuts and she expected to drop dead before him from aggravation."
"Go ahead Harold." Morrie leaned forward and scratched his chin.
"The widow of the deceased found my poem slightly amusing. I placed it inside a condolence card which I'd

mailed. The formal obit appeared shortly after; and I highlighted her late husband's positive contributions, such as
his competency at fixing and restoring things that
would've gone to the landfill.

> Poor driven ol' Thomas K.
> Collected useless junk all the day
> His irate wife threw him out
> But soon developed a case of gout
> And his junk never strayed or decayed

"She claimed that the stress of living in floor to ceiling
stuff caused her painful gout. By the way Morrie, how
much are you paying to store your old stuff?"

"Too much. I can't afford to pay the storage facility a
dime."

"Anything of value?"

"Not really. An old bed and couch and assorted junk."

"Why did you stop paying rent for so long? Did you
think the landlord would just forget about your delin-
quency?"

"I was holding out hoping he'd offer me money to
move so he could rent out the apartment at a much higher
fee."

"And did he? What's his name?"

"George Test."

"Test?"

"He offered me ten thousand dollars and forgiveness on
unpaid back rent."

Harold stood and shook his head in disbelief.

"You turned down his offer?! Ten thousand and payment forgiveness. That's nuts!"

"I was hoping he'd consider more. I heard that he gave

thirty thousand to a previous tenant who moved out the year before."

"When you realized you had to vacate did you ask again about his generous proposal?"

Morrie sagged into the sofa and wiped his brow. "Yeah, I did but it was too late. He told me to move out immediately. I screwed up."

"That's an understatement."

"Recite another obit. You said over the phone that you'd distract me from my troubles. This is putting me in a better mood."

Harold silently prayed that Morrie's SRO approval would emerge soon. Being a senior, the chances of his landing something improved.

"Okay, last one. This did me in. It pissed off the family and they contacted my editor demanding my head. A woman was due a family inheritance and wanted it all to herself. She concealed the legal documents from her surviving sister, who'd been in declining health."

"Wasn't there an executor or someone to inform the ill sister of her rights?"

"I'd assume so, but I don't recall. Good question though." Harold paused and tried to recall where he'd left off.

"Continue. Sorry for interrupting."

"So she tries to poison her lone sibling and almost succeeds. This happens on the upper East Side. Then the schemer dies shortly after confessing to her adult son, who relays the incident to me."

"Why'd he tell you this and expose his late mom?"

"I assume he wanted to get the sordid details off his chest."

"Any other explanation?"

"Don't know, Morrie. Perhaps another family member

knew about it and would cause trouble. Just speculating."

"How'd she go about this?"

"She doctors up the dinner soup by placing moth balls in the broth alongside Matzo balls. She disguises it well, plus her intended victim had lost her sense of smell. Before she could bite into a phony Matzo ball, the schemer comes clean and tells her what she's done and begs forgiveness."

Harold reached into his trousers pocket for another paper, which was worn and ripped. He held the paper up and whispered.

> A scheming lassie named Ruth
> Planned to distort the truth
> She poisoned the Matzo ball soup
> Just to make off with the loot
> And confessed the foul plan as moot

"You sent that to the deceased's son? Risky I suppose."

"I got axed. Probably shouldn't have mailed this one but my impulsive nature took over. End of story. I submitted the formal obit for review, which wasn't published."

"Did you bring a copy? I'd like to hear it."

"I didn't," said Harold, who rummaged through his pockets. "But I recall pieces of it."

"Great. Go ahead."

Harold cleared his throat and stood. He fixated on a barren wall behind Morrie, preparing to address his captive audience.

"Ruth Tannenbaum died unexpectedly of natural causes on November 10, 2012 while strolling through Central Park. She leaves behind a loving sister Miriam and son Jonathan, both Manhattan natives. Her deceased husband

Phillip died in 2005, after sixty years of harmonious marriage. They'd met in college and became loyal lifelong companions."

"So far so good," said Morrie while Harold paused. "Nothing objectionable."

"Ruth exhibited qualities of tenacity and steadfastness which helped her transform into a successful marketing executive and small business owner. When she set her sights on an achievable goal, nothing or no one got in her way. She was lovingly referred to as a 'bulldog' by her surviving sister Miriam, who respected Ruth's inner focus and ability to control messy situations and difficult people. Ruth's softer and gentler side emerged through her generous contributions to charitable organizations such as the local Food Bank. She put her talented culinary skills to use by preparing and serving nutritious soups at homeless shelter kitchens throughout the city. She was known for her unique Matzo ball soup recipe, which was jokingly said to have revived the dead and listless. Her pungent culinary spices could rouse the comatose and liberate the downtrodden from lethargic slumber."

Harold needed a moment to remember the rest. He leaned back on his heels and looked directly at Morrie.

"Ruth took no prisoners according to former business colleagues. Her zestful energy and laser like focus boosted morale and inspired respectful admiration and distance from both friends and adversaries alike. Contributions can be made to the local Food Bank of your choice."

Harold sat back down and glanced at his brother hoping for feedback. "I guess it wasn't entirely flattering but I did my best to capture an honest portrayal. I don't like to airbrush prominent details."

"You showed this to your editor?"

"Yep. We never saw eye to eye anyway. Never got on well."

"Ya know, Ruth admitted to what she'd done to her sister's soup and sought forgiveness. No one got harmed. You could've given her a break."

"You're right. I was being judgmental. Don't know what triggers my cranky nature. I can be a grouch."

"Not always. Hang in there, Harold."

"I'll buck up. Let's initiate a support group for senior sad sacks who've been led astray or who've wandered off the chosen path. The disgruntled and condemned must band together."

"Focus on a *positive* plan. I'll soon introduce innovative software that will allow access to new on line games and entertainment. Just wait and..."

Harold cut Morrie off. "A plan: I'll arrange a hot date first. She'll be attractive and alluring. Then we'll go to a nice restaurant and I'll shed my sourpuss pose before the entree is served. But I won't expose myself as a fraud. I can fudge the truth and say I've been published and am accomplished."

"Too bad you lost your job, but I know you'll bounce back on your feet. You always do."

Harold flinched. "As the ultimate optimist, I see you've had your head buried in quicksand."

Silence ensued. Harold's mood darkened.

"Now that I'm done reciting, I'll take off. Please monitor how you spend the cash I'm leaving. I suggest supplanting your donut and Entenmann's Danish diet with something better. Where do you wash up and stay clean by the way."

"At the library nearby, or at the coffee shop where we had lunch."

As Harold was about to leave, they both heard shuffling

feet and a pounding on the door. Then a key turned the lock and before them stood George Test, building owner and landlord. Morrie rose and Harold noted his brother's pallor. For the first time that day Harold saw Morrie look scared.

George was tall and stocky and muscular. He towered over them both.

"Okay Morrie, the gig is up. I want you the hell outta here now. You're through. I'm returning in an hour and if I find you here, I'm contacting the police. I should've done this a while back but felt sorry for you. No longer. Gig is up. You hear?"

Morrie nodded.

George clutched a few pieces of mail and handed it over to Morrie.

"You still have mail coming to your old apartment. File for a change."

George turned and walked out, slamming the door shut. The brothers stared at each other. Then Morrie sorted through the mail, standing, and noticed an official looking envelope with a city seal on the front. He opened the letter and scanned its contents.

"A love letter?"

"I'm afraid not," said Morrie, who leaned forward while shaking his head. "It's from the city Marshal's office issuing a court summons."

"What'd ya do, try to poison someone?"

"Nope. I accrued fifteen hundred dollars of parking fines eons ago when I owned a car. I illegally parked in the neighborhood and never paid the fines. I managed to avoid getting towed."

"Fifteen hundred dollars in parking fines? You're kidding."

"It appears that they're coming after me. I thought I

eluded them for a while."

"It appears the Marshal's hot on your trail. George Test too. You'd better vacate before sundown or I'll be composing your obituary. And it won't be pretty."

Harold got Morrie's attention, who still clutched his court summons.

"But I'll make a generous offer because I'm a masochist. Join me for dinner and stay at my place for a few days, and we'll count on hearing about your new room. Stay on top of it."

Morrie sat back down and fixed his gaze on a brown bug that crawled along a wall. It got very chilly and dark.

"You need to respond to the summons and explain your situation and hope for the best."

Morrie snapped from his trance. "Thanks for the invite. I just need a few days at your place until I move into my new room. And sorry for the trouble."

"We'll make do, Morrie."

"It's all coming together for me. The Kaminsky brothers survive another round of adversity. We're tough cookies, ya know. Feisty and spunky!"

Harold helped his brother gather his few remaining things. He only had a couple of shirts, a spare pair of trousers, and other doodads. He'd leave the rest behind including the candle, which had burned out.

A Summer Night

A Summer Night

Mr. Levi lived next door to me in Queens. New York summers were sticky and humid, especially in August. Around six o'clock each evening Mr. Levi's 1960 black Ford Falcon pulled up the driveway. Then he turned off the engine. I peered through dining room Venetian blinds, my eyes fixed on his still form. No more than ten feet separated us.

Mr. Levi yawned while spreading his newspaper over the steering wheel. He slumped into the red bucket seat and read. And read some more. Soon he dozed off, his bald head rocking forward, tapping the horn.

Isn't he hungry? I wondered. Why doesn't he go inside and join his wife for dinner?

His dining room blinds were closed. What happened inside remained a mystery as I never saw any visitors. I envisioned mutilated rotting corpses, and pictured dark musty rooms of crowded furniture covered in stained bed sheets. On weekends, we'd exchange greetings by nodding and he appeared mild mannered and timid. I'd see him hand mow his tiny backyard on Sunday. His white sleeveless T-shirt exposed hairy shoulders and flabby arms. A folded newspaper lay on a rusted aluminum beach chair. When done mowing, he'd sit for hours while clutching a transistor radio in his lap, the ballgame blaring. Eventually he'd conk out.

Mrs. Levi had been locked out of her house a month earlier. She knocked on our door for the first time, seeking help. We invited her in and offered her a cool drink. She wore baggy shorts revealing hefty thighs. Purple varicose veins crisscrossed her lower thighs and calves. She sat with Mom and me in our cozy living room, making small talk. Instead of phoning a locksmith, she glanced at my skinny limbs and made an inquiry: Would I be willing to squeeze through an open space in her basement window, which she'd left ajar and unlock the back door. I agreed to help out. We left my house and walked across the driveway to Mrs. Levi's backyard gate and opened it. I stared at the basement window I'd slither through.

With Mom watching, I gingerly maneuvered my head, and then my torso and legs through the tiny cellar opening. Mrs. Levi clutched my ankles for support as I hung upside-down, peering at the floor below. She lowered me like a rope, and with palms extended, I plopped onto clammy basement tiles. It was a humid afternoon and sweat ran down my cheeks and neck. I stood, and somewhat dizzy, bumped into a post or beam. I was tempted to explore the dark cellar but quickly found the stairs leading to the kitchen. I soon opened the back door to my relieved neighbor. She entered and walked over to the counter where a cookie jar lay.

"For your trouble," she said. I took two oatmeal cookies from her freckled hand.

"Thank you," I replied.

I backpedaled out her door, pleased to be outside and proud of having done a good deed. My upper torso was sore from being dangled and dropped.

A week after Mrs. Levi's visit, on a sweltering July evening, Mr. and Mrs. Levi had fist fought in the gutter. I'd been playing an after supper game of driveway wiffleball with my brother. I heard shouting, and then they both scampered out the front door and stood under a street light. She was yelling bloody murder. Then Mrs. Levi pummeled her husband's face, which swelled. Crouching, he crossed his arms over his head. He occasionally glanced up and around him, his face flush with embarrassment or shame. Mrs. Levi's screams and taunts grew more intense. Her shrill sounds ricocheted off the hot asphalt.

"You flipping tightwad! Cheapskate! Do we ever go out to dinner or to a movie? Shopping? You know I can't goddamn drive, and hate the crowded bus."

She took a deep breath and continued.

"Screw you little man! I'm sick and tired of that goddamn house, that prison."

A jet flew overhead, drowning her out. Neighbors watched from open windows and blinds from across the way but stayed inside, not wanting to interfere.

Poor Mr. Levi, pale and staggering, morphed into a busted jack-in-the box, a disassembled Tin Man. My brother had tried to grab my arm and lead me away, but I stood my ground, mesmerized by her fury and physical strength. She glanced my way and ignored me, and soon the commotion ended. I heard voices ordering me back inside, which I ignored. I looked up at a bright full moon. Next, the antagonists staggered back onto the porch before disappearing.

Mrs. Levi had felt neglected and shut in and she let her husband have it. I watched for Mr. Levi's car every night after he returned from work, seeing how long he'd take before going inside his troubled home.

A 1960 Ford Falcon entombed Mr. Levi, who appeared groggy from his nap. It was almost an hour since he'd arrived home from the office. Carefully folding his newspaper, my neighbor sat up and grabbed a briefcase. Mr. Levi swiveled his round frame out the car door. He stepped onto the concrete driveway, landing on tiny shoots of weeds sprouting up between the cracks. Dragging his feet, the back of his bald head receded through the gate, the same one I'd entered before opening his basement window not long ago.

Sweet Sixteen

Sweet Sixteen

My neighbor Lenore invited me to her sweet sixteen birthday party. She lived next door to my buddy David, who'd moved onto the block two years before. They became friends and messed around a bit romantically. David told me that when Lenore babysat for a neighbor's kid, he'd sneak over and hang out. Lenore would signal him by flipping the porch light on and off after the child was fast asleep. They'd watch television on the couch and after a while, embrace and kiss and caress a little more.

"She's hot stuff!" David would say about Lenore.

"Just don't get caught," I advised. "You don't want Lenore's dad to find out that you two are foolin' around. He might think you're taking advantage of his teen daughter."

"I *love* Italian girls. They do something to me," said David.

"And her Daddy might do something to you, if you're not careful. By the way, does Lenore have any girlfriends?" I'd ask.

Lenore had lovely dark haired friends and eventually I met them: Donna, Fran, Candi, and The Queen, Debbie Leone. Debbie was pretty and wore strong lemon scent perfume. She lived a few blocks away and walked her dog Princess over to our street on Friday and Saturday evening. David and I attended the same public high school, and Lenore and her friends enrolled at the local Catholic girls' school. Occasionally, I saw them in school uniforms strolling. A green plaid skirt fell below the knee exposing pale flesh around the shin. They wore thick soled shoes with gray socks. Their plain cloth beanie looked odd and made the girls appear like scouts. A beret would've added elegance instead. Lenore's girlfriends would be at her sweet sixteen gathering and this excited me.

I'd never been to a sweet sixteen party. Some parents hired a band I was told, and stocked up on cold cuts, potato salad and sumptuous desserts. I purchased bell bottom pants for this occasion. They were brown with white pinstripes running down the sides with a crease or pleat. I'd slab on either Old Spice cologne or English Leather Lime my uncle had given me on my birthday. The cologne had come in a small wooden box with two compartments.

The neighborhood alpha males pretended that they were God's gift to girls: Smug, cocksure and making phony attempts at seducing. I'd plunge into an abyss rather than ask someone out and risk failure. This is why I befriended David, who acted confident but not cocky. He modeled that a bit of swagger couldn't hurt. He'd tell a silly joke, chuckle, and act tough when necessary. This toughness would soon come in handy at Lenore's party.

For Lenore's celebration, David said he'd go all out: Dark chino pants that hugged the hips, satin shirt, and tan sport coat with matching ascot. I'd seen photos of David in his butterscotch ascot, which he revealed on special occasions such as bar mitzvahs, weddings, and funerals. My dapper buddy liked his ascot.

We got ready for Lenore's party at David's house. His bedroom was in the basement. Except for a tiny window in his room, we inhabited an air raid shelter, isolated and way below ground. A pinup poster of a bosomy redhead named Sharon Fenster hung on the wall. On his chest of drawers lay a photo of a large white French poodle wearing a red ribbon or bandanna. In this family portrait, the pet poodle towered over a younger David and his sister. In this basement room we'd study for Earth Science midterms, conjugate French verbs and scrutinize family albums. We concocted tall tales about relatives living and deceased. His jokes could be sadistic and warped, which I loved. It was a warm humid summer evening as we discussed strategy for the party.

"Aren't you going to roast in that sport coat?" I asked.

"Nah, no problem. I can always remove it but I won't."

David straightened his ascot, splashed on Hai Karate after shave and then we left for the celebration. Lenore lived directly next door in a white house. A low front gate swiveled open to a small yard with lawn chairs. An iron railing led up to a tiny porch. Each house on the block looked the same from the outside. We stood on the porch and heard loud chatter and music coming from inside. Then we rang the doorbell and waited until Lenore's younger brother, Carl, opened the door.

"Hi guys," Carl said. "Come on in." Carl wore dark round glasses, nerd like, and appeared studious in his blue sport coat and red tie.

Lenore spotted David from the kitchen and sprinted up to us. She gave David a big bear hug and a kiss on the cheek. Lenore looked gorgeous. She wore a pink dress that resembled an evening gown. I also received a warm hug and beaming smile.

"Would you like a drink? Some cokes?"

Lenore led David by the arm toward the kitchen and I followed. We shook hands with Lenore's dad, Mr. Bonomo. He resembled Lenore's brother, round and stout and good natured. We met Lenore's mom and some aunts, uncles and cousins. The kitchen door opened to the backyard, exposing crammed tables of delicacies, appetizers, and cold cuts. Lenore's guests drifted out to the back porch as it grew warmer in the kitchen. I heard the shrill sound of cicadas and observed an emerging crescent moon. I was enjoying the calm surroundings and hadn't minded the heavy humidity.

Then it all changed unexpectedly. A car revved its noisy engine around front and doors slammed. We heard yelling and shouting from this direction. David and I stepped back into the kitchen. Next, we put down our food, and dashed through the living room, which led to the front porch. We opened the screen door and waited on the porch. A strange dude outside the front gate shouted at Lenore, who turned crimson. Two of his buddies stood behind him. Lenore opened the gate and confronted the intruder. She folded her arms and appeared tense. She began to argue as only a foot separated them. Their voices escalated and sounded shrill.

"Get *outta* here Joey!" Lenore screamed. "I don't want ya here! You weren't invited to my party, so go."

Lenore and Joey continued shouting, and then, she pushed him. Joey moved back a step, and grew more hostile. His black suede jacket made him appear lean and muscular. He had a pencil thin moustache and greasy slicked back hair. Who was this actor auditioning for the greaser role in a '50s movie? He'd drag race Corvettes and stir havoc for kicks. Where's your dangling cigarette, Mr. Tough Guy?

"I'm not your girl anymore. Remember, we broke up. Go away!"

Joey stood his ground, his dark eyes intense and resolute.

"I'm not going anywhere bitch, until you say you're sorry. Say it!"

"I had to be an imbecile to get involved with you. Now go away."

Meanwhile, Lenore's irate father saw that his daughter needed help. He raced down the hallway, and out the front door to the curb. Monte confronted Joey on the sidewalk. He jabbed a finger into Joey's chest, demanding he leave the premises. Joey pushed Monte. Monte pushed back, and the two got into a nasty brawl. Joey got Lenore's beefy dad into a headlock and their momentum spilled onto the porch, and through the open front door. Joey was younger and stronger. Lenore's dad tumbled across the living room, and then landed onto the kitchen linoleum. This happened in seconds.

Next, Monte sprang up and cursed at Joey. They exchanged wild blows to the torso and face. Adrenaline and pride kept them on their feet. Lenore screamed hysterically from nearby. She began to move toward her dad but her mom stopped her.

The combatants, including Joey's two buddies tumbled out back onto the lawn, and then began wrestling on the grass. Monte's relatives and neighbors joined the ugly melee, including my buddy David.

Lenore's uncles and neighbors hurled hard blows at Joey and his entourage and blood spilled onto the lawn. Meanwhile, Lenore and her mom, Estelle, stared in horror from the kitchen. Lenore began sobbing, and hyperventilated. Her girlfriends formed a protective circle, and tried shielding Lenore from the chaos. I remained next to Donna, Lenore's closest friend, certain of impending doom if I got involved. I'd get hammered and bloodied to a pulp, but needed to do something.

"Should we call the police?" I said. I wondered why no one called for help, but then saw Estelle dialing '911.' She put the receiver down in mid conversation, and appeared befuddled and pale.

Clumps of potato salad and coleslaw lay scattered about. David was now pinned, flailing his arms and legs like a trapped bug. His ascot was roughed up and torn. David's mom Ada, who watched from next door, leaned over the attached yard fence, and bellowed in a gravelly voice. She wore a terry cloth bathrobe over her night-gown. Her bloodshot eyes bulged. Mother and son never got along.

"What in hell do you think you're doing David! Get outta there *now*!"

Ada chain smoked. She puffed heavily on a cigarette with a long filter. David craned his neck, and glanced up at his mom from the pile. He yelled up at Ada in muffled groans while she continued her verbal lashing between coughing fits.

"You stupid fool, David. You're some hero. I said get outta there now!" Nicotine fumes from Ada's cigarette drifted toward David, as smoke permeated the humid air.

David wasn't going anywhere. He was still pinned under a mass of sweaty bodies. I knew I'd get my head bashed and bloodied if I joined in. My slender and tense body leaned against the kitchen table while clutching punch and pastries. I slipped and tumbled, and knocked over Lenore's sweet sixteen frosted cake. And unfortunately, I landed on top of the creamy frosting. I began removing green and white icing from the seat of my new bell bottoms and hoped no one noticed.

I sprang up and scooped cake remnants with a paper towel and spoon, and discreetly placed them into the sink. I'd be a pariah and an outcast in the eyes of Lenore and her friends for not defending them during the nasty brawl. They'd also ridicule me for destroying a portion of the cake. Most of the cake remained intact.

The fight was now going our way. Joey and his goons were getting pummeled. Somehow, David extracted himself from the body pile, and braced his sore arm. The intruders backed off, and then hobbled and limped along the side of the house. They cursed and vowed revenge. We heard car doors slamming and a revved up engine and screeching tires. Lenore, now far less hysterical, calmed down. Her face regained color.

David and I stood in the kitchen. "Are you okay?" I asked.

David straightened his trousers and shirt. His ascot was mangled and beyond repair. His cheeks were red and puffy.

"You're going to be sore and hurting tomorrow," I said.

"I'm all right. Just a few cuts and bruises, nothing serious. And you?" He began wiping grass stains from his trousers with a wet sponge.

"I fell on Lenore's cake," I said.

I know he wanted to laugh but he said nothing.

Lenore took turns hugging her family and girlfriends, and then David. She began sobbing joyful tears, now relieved that the ugly intrusion was over.

"I *love* every one of you! I love every one of you," she repeated.

Monte was shaken and pale. Estelle placed an ice pack on her husband's forehead, which was bruised and swollen. She placed another ice pack on his knee. Fortunately, no one needed serious medical attention. Joey absorbed the major beating and wouldn't return anytime soon. Lenore needed to avoid insecure hotheads like Joey. Perhaps, she and David wouldn't need to hide their occasional liaison if deeper feelings evolved between them.

My stomach was queasy, and more so when Lenore's mom invited everyone into the living room for coffee and sweet sixteen cake. I hoped no one witnessed my fiasco and prayed that other desserts would soon materialize. Lenore's friend Donna gently touched my shoulder.

"Don't worry," she whispered. "Fran and I brought some Italian pastries we'll share. They're over in the fridge in white boxes with red string and we'll retrieve them together."

I wanted to hug Donna for rescuing me.

"Thanks *so* much," I said. "You're unbelievable."

"You can show your gratitude by dancing with me later."

Her amber eyes sparkled and she looked enticing in her black gown.

"I'd like that," I replied.

David and I stayed and celebrated until midnight. On the way out the door Lenore whispered into David's ear and winked. He smiled back. We thanked our gracious hosts for a memorable time and stepped into a hazy summer night.

Neither of us had a strict time curfew. David would tell his mom that he survived the brawl, despite her reprimand for participating. Perhaps she was afraid that he'd get injured, and incur a costly medical bill.

Overall, we both enjoyed the party apart from the nasty brawl, and would thank Lenore's family again the next day. Perhaps I'd tell them about my accidental fall and we'd laugh. All would be forgotten, I hoped.

We walked the quiet streets and ingested the heavy stale air. David cracked silly jokes and rambled on, but I mentally rehearsed what I'd say to Donna when asking her out. Where'd we go, and what would we do? I changed the script and the words wishing and hoping I'd say the right thing when the moment came.

Getting It Down

Getting It Down

I keep lists. They serve as mileposts and reminders of important tasks I hope to accomplish. I value my list collection, which I record on small spiral notepads and store in plastic bins from Target.   These bins line my cellar and closet floors. List making keeps one stimulated and focused. I'd like to share some examples.

My home improvement list: Build a back deck and then retile the bathroom and kitchen floors. Unfortunately I don't get around to these projects, but it's nice to know they're here should I get the urge to pursue them. In a pinch, someone can come in and do the job.

Another favorite is a food list. When I was seven I helped Mom create her shopping list every Monday evening. We included red, brown, and black licorice in addition to Fig Newtons and Hydrox cookies. Afterwards we'd return home and lick rows of S&H Green Stamps into small booklets to be traded in for household goods. These days, vegetables sit in the refrigerator and spoil while I'm planning my next food list instead of dinner.

My health and well being list is useful. I record annoying aches and pains such as headaches, charley horses, bruises, scrapes, and the occasional toothache or upset stomach. It's not insulting to be called a hypochondriac by those too busy with life to notice their body parts wearing down. A caring friend suggests I visualize flowing beams of light, but this can become tedious. Instead, each morning I dissolve ginseng powder into green tea as an energy tonic. Then I mix a tablespoon of Brewer's yeast powder into my dry cereal, usually Shredded Wheat.

On weekend trips I pack fresh fruit and bring berries to

your standard breakfast diner, which never stocks fresh strawberries. As an experiment I tried cultivating my very own bean sprouts. I placed the seeds in a covered jar on the kitchen pantry shelf, but a week later they got moldy and died. Swiss dark chocolate and peanut butter sandwiches keep me fueled and fired up when feeling blue. My health list keeps evolving with each new food growing season.

Now my relationship list: I reflect on imagined hurts, slights, and rejections. Drawing columns, I note the person's name and date our friendship/relationship terminated. Naturally I record the reasons for the breakup and divide these into three subheadings: "my fault", "their fault", and "extenuating circumstances." I have amassed detailed flow charts depicting both independent and dependent variables affecting the demise and ruin of personal and work relationships.

To deal with life's confounding surprises, I keep a separate list called "Murky Zone." These are the contradictions and dilemmas only the wise Greek philosophers untangle. For example, if someone screws up and destroys an important relationship and no one is around to notice, did it really happen? Or if stranded on a deserted island with only a stale corned beef sandwich, and no other food source, do you offer a bite to a devout vegan? I keep this list locked in a closet safe as it's too precious and sacred to share with anyone.

There are mundane lists of housekeeping chores such as laundry, vacuuming, and changing the linen. Never underestimate the ordinary. No wild parties, no holiday eggnog for me, thank you. Cleaning a cat litter box elevates my spirits. I love to recycle each week and don't need to keep a list of what can be recycled. This list I have memorized: scrap paper, newspaper, metal, aluminum, plastic, colored glass, cardboard.   We can also recycle clothes, jokes, routines, body organs, bicycle parts, National Geographic, even the weather.   It's satisfying to use something again and again and reduce waste.

A full calendar keeps trouble and idleness at bay. At work meetings, I jot notes of upcoming meetings. I remind myself to look busy, act important, and by all means get results! My thoughts involuntarily drift to reducing tensions in trouble spots abroad.   My shirt pocket contains a special list of Middle East peace proposals or 'Talking Points.' I remove the list and review its salient points before concealing it from others' view.   Shall I fax it to an embassy and hope for a response?   Or would the acting CIA Director, a former school chum, take interest in my modest proposals. My lists might be used to resolve ancient disputes and promote peace on Earth.

Spring has arrived in my town. Daffodils and crocuses are sprouting. Cherry and plum trees bloom. I'm often distracted by other things to notice though. Truth be told, I'm adrift without lists. They are a reliable anchor. You won't find me playing hooky from routine or strolling down an unfamiliar lane. I don't want that mean Mr. McGregor spying me eating cabbage and snow peas from his off limits garden.

Then again, a recurring dream may be telling me something. In this odd dream I shred hundreds of my lists. I create papier-mache cranes from the scraps, gluing and pasting on layers for the head, beak and wings. The paper birds are fastened to a long sturdy string and released high into the sky on a clear blustery day, gone for good.

Brain Surgery

Brain Surgery

Family and friends are confused, but I'm not. Just three weeks ago I underwent successful brain surgery to remove 'fuzzy stuff', a clump of blood vessels that had been causing dizziness and seizures. Thankfully, no malignant tumor was found. I'm fine and grateful to be alive. Unfortunately, loved ones no longer recognize me. Janice says my personality has changed, or rather the pronouncements I utter. Here are some examples, though I suspect she's exaggerating.

I am now a confirmed die hard Republican, which I'm told is quite a change from pre brain surgery. My sweetie Janice soon confronted the surgeon and demanded to know why I've flipped. She swore that I'd been a loyal New Deal Democrat, committed to economic justice for working families. The specialist was confounded, claiming that the brain area targeted could not affect political party affiliation, and that she must be mistaken. Janice insisted I make a follow up visit and describe what I've been spouting off.

Two days later, my specialist agreed to meet over an informal lunch in the hospital cafeteria. The surgeon, Dr. Pepper, brought x-rays showing the targeted region and how I should be good as new, restored to my old self. Then I hoisted the local daily paper, which I now found stimulating, informative and well balanced in its coverage. I pointed to the headline and beamed.

"We've liberated the Iraqi people from tyranny. The war has cost billions, but is worth every million." Janice shook her head and recounted the peace marches we'd attended. She also claimed that pre-surgery, I valued the local daily for its obituaries and Doonesbury strip, but now found these features too depressing and threatening.

Meanwhile, I bit into a thick juicy burger.

"Dr. Pepper," said Janice. "Look at him go. Devout vegetarian before the operation, and now, all he craves is meat: sausage, bacon, beef, lamb, chicken. Is this a limited diet?"

I wiped with a napkin, preventing the dripping meat juice from soiling my cotton trousers. "Tax cuts will create jobs," I fired back, pointing to another article on the front page. "Keep faith, it will happen. *And,* we can beef up the military and homeland security too."

I was on a roll. "All this fuss about securing government entitlements. It's a dependent crutch! There's no free lunch I say. Cut, chop, ax! Traditional guaranteed pensions? Too damned expensive. We're being led down the road to bankruptcy and financial ruin. And don't get me started on excessive regulation." I watched Dr. Pepper arch his bushy eyebrows. He ran a hand through gray flecked hair while staring at me, taking notes.

"Tell me, Mr. Martin. Is this what you believed *before* surgery?"

"Probably, though the anesthesia knocked me out cold. The few details I recall from before I went under are a bit sketchy."

"What is your favorite ice cream flavor, Mr. Martin?"

I could tell that Dr. Pepper was probing. It seemed like a silly question.

"That's easy. Butter pecan, topped with syrup, whipped cream and nuts. And, add a maraschino cherry." I slapped the table with my palm. "Life is short, live a little."

Janice turned toward the doctor, shaking her head. "Dairy was off limits before the operation. He said it caused inflammation of the mucus membranes and made him sluggish. And he exercised, monitoring his saturated fat intake and cholesterol."

"And now?" Dr. Pepper munched on a crispy Caesar salad, and checked his watch. The crunching of the croutons was annoying.

"I want my *old* partner back," Janice demanded. "He may have been a hypochondriac, but a lovable one. I could deal with that."

Janice sipped iced coffee. It was air conditioned in the cafeteria, a good thing, as the mercury outside approached triple digits.

"Does he still exercise and explore nature?" Dr. Pepper looked at Janice, avoiding me. "In our intake interview, you shared previous mutual interests in hiking and bird watching."

I grew annoyed at being removed from the discussion. I weighed in with my thoughts. "Who has time to work out? I'm busy tracking stocks and financial reports online. Also, I'm conversing with friends and relatives by cell phone while driving to the mall. It's a hands free device so I'm not distracted. Except when I spot a pretty gal. Just joking. Then I do a morning mall workout by walking in and out of stores. I love air conditioning year round."

"You're rambling," said Janice.

"No, I'm sharing," I countered. "Just being friendly."

I bit into greasy fries while slurping a king sized coke. "They have to drag me from Home Depot these days. I'll spend hours in there and not get bored." I was proud of my new found interest in home improvement projects which I'd once shunned. I'd made project lists even though each endeavor lay on the back burner.

I touched Janice's shoulder, but she squirmed loose. The ongoing discussion and Janice's behavior were puzzling. I felt upbeat and positive. Things were crystal clear: I saw black and white, and not nuances of gray, my thought process direct and certain. Janice then informed the doctor that before surgery, I had feared my own internal demons, and now I saw demons lurking in the external world with our homeland's way of life and freedom threatened. She said I was no longer reflective or introspective, but this wasn't true.

I declined dessert, satiated from burger and fries. Dr. Pepper stood and apologized for ending our discussion. He appeared befuddled, and unsure of the alleged change in my perceptions and daily habits.

"We'll run additional tests, even set up an appointment with a psychiatrist, if both of you think it'll help."

Janice nodded and I grew antsy, knowing my favorite Fox talk show was on. I was missing stimulating call in AM radio; alarm warnings about our nation's plunge into dependency, due to welfare freeloaders and ungrateful pessimists unable to see the glass half full.

I shook Dr. Pepper's hand. "Thanks for saving my life and restoring complete health. I can't thank you enough!" I held onto his hand a bit longer. I'd read somewhere that the difference between life and death is a good surgeon and it's true. Janice had quoted from Consumer Reports magazine, or possibly from the Sunday Parade supplement. A voice broke my reverie.

"Take care Mr. Martin, and I'll let you know what follow up tests we can run. We'll try and make sense of this."

He removed his wallet, but I insisted on buying lunch. Janice and I walked out into brilliant sunshine, passing a sea of SUV's and minivans in the expansive lot. The sun's rays seeped into the concrete. A towering billboard advertised weekend getaways to Reno. I glanced up at the striking promotion, absorbed by the portrait of a smiling couple clutching golf clubs. They looked cozy together on the green fairway, not a care in the world. Now, that's an intimate moment.

I pondered how much fun it would be to take golf lessons, and whether Janice would be interested in a new weekend hobby. I considered purchasing a spanking new Humvee to take on leisure jaunts around town. I truly felt invigorated, eager and ready to seize the day, even if loved ones reluctantly tag along.

Reunion

Reunion

The invitation arrived in a plain brown envelope. It said: "Please attend thirty year reunion of Archer Messenger Service. Reception held at renovated Chelsea Hotel. Address: 222 W 23 St. in New York, July 15, from 1PM-5PM. Sumptuous lunch buffet provided. Get reacquainted with former colleagues. Your presence requested."

I put down the half eaten sandwich and examined the letter. I stared out the kitchen window, daydreaming. Are you kidding? Archer Messenger was my first job, when I was sixteen, a blurred and troubled time. Who'd found me? Had I contributed to a messenger endowment fund?

I pondered, and decided to attend the event out of sheer curiosity. Besides, I needed a reprieve from summer doldrums and daily routine. I craved diversion, no matter how silly, and had accumulated paid vacation time from the Postal service. I'd leave in a few days after requesting permission from my supervisor.

The next day, I booked a red-eye to New York and began packing for the trip. I'd been away for years, rarely visiting anymore. I lost contact with old friends and had begun a new life in Oregon. The invitation piqued my desire to see how my native home had changed.

I imagined, for a moment, moving back to Brooklyn, and renting a tiny studio overlooking a park or playground. A six hundred square foot flat for twelve hundred a month would come with a loud, hissing radiator that kicks in at the wrong time, keeping me awake all night. I'd apply for and get my old messenger job back as well.

Each morning, I'd sit in the cockroach infested kitchen and gnaw on a soggy buttered Kaiser roll. I'd scan the sports section of the paper and glance out the window, at pigeons scurrying across the playground chasing wind-blown bread crumbs. And cheer on smug, but sensitive older dads showing off their darling offspring, proving to pretty moms that it's cool to dote on Junior or Princess. I continued to daydream about moving back while packing for my East Coast reunion.

I take the D or F train under the East River to my old messenger job. Once settled, I meet someone attractive at a weekend party on the Upper West Side. A romantic rela-tionship soon develops, though we have little in common. She becomes bored with my flat demeanor and poverty, and has an affair with a dapper attorney (of course he's married!) I conjure up maudlin songs that remind me of her lustful and flirtatious ways while hiding in a dark al-ley, or luncheonette. Back on the subway, commuting to work, I gaze at station ads plastered on cream tiled walls. It's Miss Subway of the month admiring me. Her majestic wholesome portrait hangs from station poles. Would Miss Subway be interested in dating someone like me? And can I endure another frost bitten shivering winter in New York.

As foot messenger in the late sixties, I had delivered business letters, packages, and documents to companies throughout the city. Tony Alverez, my boss, gave me subway tokens if the destination was beyond a mile. I sometimes pocketed the token and walked instead. At day's end, I logged over seven miles of city walking. Summer was humid and sticky, but it didn't deplete my energy or resolve to be quick and efficient. I'd plug in my transistor radio earpiece and move to the rhythm of sum-mer pop tunes.

Sometimes I'd need a break and a chance to cool off. I'd enter air conditioned Nedicks or Chock Full O' Nuts for a soda and linger, noting attractive women walking by outside. I marveled that *everyone* had once emerged from *someone's* womb, a product of DNA. At evening rush hour commuting masses boarded the New Haven Line or the LIRR, perhaps to plush suburban homes, removed from the day's hustle and bustle. I hoped to someday secure a stable and comfy home environment without conflict or distress. I fantasized about a peaceful haven to retreat to.

Dinner smells great! I'll tell you about my busy day after I wash up. Whew sweetie, what a day!"

I'd repeat this greeting to my gorgeous, calm, devoted wife. Then she'd describe her harried day to me. Perhaps we'd chuckle and commiserate, or after a few years of this, stare in silence having little to share. We'd sit down to pot roast or chicken and wine while watching the evening news. This was both an alluring and unsettling future scenario. Routine and stability would have its benefits I had convinced myself. I'd worry about stifling rut and boredom at a later time.

Propped on a stool at the luncheon counter between messenger deliveries, I'd wonder which patrons were having affairs, or hiding pain. I had mentally blocked the blaring taxi horns and construction jackhammers. Soon I'd leave and deliver the next bill of lading receipt, or import-export document. Steamship freight forwarders like Maersk, 'K' Line, and Dart were clustered in lower Manhattan near Bowling Green and Wall Street, my territory.

Once, I was sent to LaGuardia Airport, which broke routine. When ordered to Queens, I'd take the E or F , which stopped at Ely Avenue in Long Island City. No one got on or off the train at Ely Avenue. The barren platform made me wonder about life above on 23rd Street. Was it dangerous or deserted?   I vowed to disembark one day and explore.   I envisioned potholed sidewalks and smoke belching factories and warehouses.   I believed the Ex-Lax factory was nearby, but discovered it was in Brooklyn, near my brother's apartment on Atlantic Avenue.   As the train emerged onto an elevated track above Long Island City, the Drakes Cupcake factory appeared.   The stench of Ring Dings, Ding Dongs, or sweet chocolate permeated the train window on sticky humid days.   Cause of death: Asphyxiation.   Factory soot belched, clogging your lungs, making you lightheaded.

Riding the subway could be hot and dirty.   Many trains weren't air conditioned and ceiling fans malfunctioned.   I once felt buried alive under a moist armpit when an F train suddenly stopped in a dark tunnel.   I affirmed the power of prayer. Thank goodness she was sultry and I hadn't minded.   She wore a red sleeveless dress and her delicate sweat rolled onto my pale cheek. I felt reenergized, reborn. It was an odd turn on, very primitive.

A close friend had taken the train from lower Manhattan out to Coney Island, the end of the line, every day.   It took over an hour to complete its round trip run.   He told me his house was chaotic, and that he'd found refuge on the subway.   He could relax, do homework and study for exams. Back and forth, back and forth he went all evening, munching on huge salted pretzels and grape Pez for nourishment while buried in texts.   I'd join him occasionally and also did my homework to escape a chaotic home.

There were subtle ways to secure a seat on a crowded train.   On the platform I'd position myself alongside the sliding doors and as riders exited, I'd dash, scan, and dive. Quick reflexes got a coveted seat.   It was a game of musical chairs.   I'd keep my documents and small packages balanced on my lap and not drop or crinkle them.

When standing, I clutched onto a leather strap or metal hook, tightening my grip as the train rocked. My palm slipped on the sweat saturated hook. The train rocked and when losing balance, I'd be supported by a comforting body. Sometimes a rider fell asleep and his head grazed a neighbor's shoulder. You avoided eye contact and never smiled while protecting what privacy remained.

I'd pass time by reading the subway maps, a mess of zigzagging colored lines with obscure patterns. Few cartographers could quickly untangle this confluence of lines, numbers, and letters. Tourists attempted to trace their route, but some grew befuddled and gave up.

A garbled intercom voice announced the stops and transfer points, but the voice crackled and slurred into oblivion. There were tales about homeless people who resided underground, beneath the subway itself. I was unaware of this reality but found it plausible. I didn't believe tales of alligators and serpents roaming the subway sewers. But perhaps it was true.

My midnight flight from Oregon to La Guardia was uneventful. I arrived in New York on a clear Friday morning, and soon checked into the Columbus Circle YMCA near Central Park. The accommodations were basic but affordable. I'd been awake during the entire flight and was exhausted. I took a mid morning nap in my room. Then I read The Times before showering and dressing for the reunion. I wore black jeans and a green polo shirt, nothing fancy. Needing exercise, I walked down the nine floors to the lobby. A cluster of young backpackers discussed their agenda, in French, while examining a city map. They stood next to a slumping couch near the entrance. The hostel displayed its maps, brochures, and message notes by a bulletin board. I couldn't decide if I was a tourist, or just a devotee returning to his sacred birthplace.

Outside in the bustling streets, I dodged traffic to hail a cab. Blaring horns vibrated. Thick wads of smoke or steam rose from a manhole. A few runners emerged from Central Park. People huddled around a newsstand next to a subway entrance reading magazines. The vendor was blind and customers either placed change into his palm, or into a cigar box. I finally caught a cab and rode downtown to the Chelsea (the gathering spot), and made small talk with the Russian driver. He maneuvered through Broadway traffic, pumping the gas pedal when spotting an opening. We avoided a few collisions with his lightning quick reflexes. The taxi was air conditioned and comfortable and I didn't want to leave.

The Chelsea hotel, a restored older building, had little balconies overlooking retail stores and pizzerias. It exuded European charm. Along the sidewalk, vendors sold watches, sunglasses, jewelry, and cell phones. Next, I entered a dimly lit lobby. I spotted a sign by the main desk, welcoming former Archer Messenger employees. Someone had sketched a cartoonish but cute pencil outline of a messenger carrying a package, his giant shoes turned upward in mid stride. It was the infamous Mr. Natural comic hero, striding down the avenue, one with the world.

The sign read: *"Reunion gathering moved to 110 E. 46th St.(between Madison and Fifth), former Archer Messenger site. Buffet held in basement. We apologize for the inconvenience."*

I tried to confirm the change with the desk clerk. He shook his head, stating he hadn't seen anyone post this message, but added that he'd been on duty for only an hour. I began to wonder if this reunion was a practical joke or hoax.

Outside, pizza aroma engulfed me, and I considered

skipping the reunion buffet.   Then a cab drove by and slowed down, and I got in. It proceeded to midtown, toward the new gathering site. I glanced out the window. A bicycle messenger whizzed by, almost knocking down a pedestrian.   These intrepid kamikazes on bikes swerved around obstacles like pedestrians and vehicles. Inside a fenced concrete schoolyard, a pick-up basketball game ensued. Handball players behind them whacked tiny black balls against a high cement wall. Some wore gloves but others didn't. The scene was familiar, as if I'd never left.

I paid the fare and tip, and stood at Madison and East 46th. Glass and steel office buildings hemmed me in. I never liked the stiff claustrophobia of midtown. Had fax machines made foot messengers obsolete? Bulky packages requiring same day delivery would still require a foot or bike messenger.

I approached a plain office building with a green awning and hoped I had the correct address. I scanned the directory on the outside lobby door, but didn't see Archer listed. I pressed a few buzzers, waited, and went through a glass door. I descended a staircase to the basement, as I'd done countless times for three consecutive summers, eons ago. At the bottom I turned right, and saw a typed note taped to a metal door: *"Welcome to Archer Messenger 30 Year Reunion. Please enter."*

I inhaled and paused, unsure of what to expect. I considered turning around and having lunch at the corner deli and then returning to my room for another nap. I opened the door and peeked inside before entering. An underground windowless room, like a dungeon, lay before me. It was like being submerged in a cavern or bomb shelter, stuffy as hell. The paint on the wall was peeling. The room was preserved exactly like it had been when I received my delivery assignments here. Hard wooden chairs lined the wall where messengers once sat, waiting to be summoned to the desk for a delivery.

My old boss, Tony Alverez, sat behind a long metal desk scribbling in pencil. He'd aged, but I recognized his bushy dark eyebrows and blood shot bulging eyes. Seated next to Tony was his assistant Sylvester, a lanky Jamaican with a winsome smile. An ancient radio emitted pop tunes, like before. Sylvester had had a favorite song by Ronnie Dyson: 'If you let me make love to you, then why oh why can't I *touch* you!" That silly tune had anesthetized me, turning my brain into mush. Tony and Sylvester now barked into phones while jotting notes on a yellow scratchpad. Were they still working for Archer, or requesting additional deli cold cuts for the buffet?

The walls were bare, except for party streamers and balloons that clung to dull green paint. I shook my head. Framed portraits of former messengers were mounted along a back wall. Each appeared as they looked thirty years ago, like phantoms. Beneath each photo was an engraved plaque listing name and years employed. I scanned the wall hoping my portrait wasn't mounted too.

A rectangular buffet table of cold cuts and salads filled the middle of the room. Fifteen to twenty men hovered over corned beef, pastrami, coleslaw and potato salad, and rhythmically loaded paper plates. An older gentleman motioned to me, while coleslaw covered his puffy cheek.

"Please join us and don't be shy. Grab a plate and dig in."

Each person wore a name tag. I hated name tags but reached for one anyway and slapped it onto my perspiring shirt.

"Don't you remember me?" said this jovial older man. He extended his free hand, and balanced a full plate with the other. His handshake was firm and welcoming. He looked tidy and dapper in his blue sport coat with brass buttons. A handkerchief was folded into his coat pocket.

"I'm Otto. Tony would send me to Beaver Street, near the stock exchange. I loved delivering there and knew the territory like the back of my mottled hand." Otto grinned, and patted me on the back.

He was almost seventy *then*, and it seemed miraculous the warrior was still around, and robust. "You look great, Otto, and you must be a hundred, right? Nice job." I hoped I contained his resolve.

Otto had fought for the German army in World War I. His bald freckled head shone bright, reflecting light from overhead. He wore thick framed glasses that covered deep blue eyes.

"Yes, my friend. I'm still here." Then he took a breath. "I've been resurrected from the dead, the undervorld. You see, Archer had a vonderful pension plan, which includes freezing and then resurrecting the body vhen you die. But you need thirty years of service to reap the benefit."

Otto let out a howl and a shriek, while jabbing me in the ribs.

"Seriously my friend, Archer has a vonderful pension plan."

A wiry ghost like figure emerged. I glanced up at the wall of portraits, and matched his face to someone we'd nicknamed Joe Beach. We called him this because he remained extremely pale and light skinned. He would've been harmed by excess daylight exposure. Joe Beach had always kept to himself, shy and wary of others. He limited his contact with both people and harsh summer heat. These precautions had made sense. He may've been teased or bullied at one time, his flight or avoidance response heightened.

No foot messenger was faster and more efficient. Joe Beach covered the pavement like a gazelle, his long strides soft and elegant. He glided and hustled to avoid toxic ultraviolet rays. He'd been prudent to avoid the sun, when feasible. Joe's pale skin had made him an excellent candidate for melanoma. As I sought Joe Beach out along the buffet table, to inquire about his well being and recent whereabouts, he vanished.

Clustered about the food table, munching and chit-chatting, were Big Al, a beefy man, always helpful with directions to new addresses; and Stan, a dull chunky wise guy who got promoted to a managerial position at Archer. Nearby, Dave Cantor or DC, had quit to drive a cab. It was better money and he got to vent pent up angst from behind the wheel. DC smacked his lips like a seal, devouring Coke after Coke at the buffet table. I'd known him since seventh grade, when he gulped milk from a carton seated across from me in the cafeteria. He loved tuna heroes, and had ordered the same goddamn thing for lunch every day. His slurping, wheezing, and wisecracking became an ongoing feature at our school.

Tony Alverez rose from his swivel chair, hoisting a champagne glass. He pointed a finger toward the ceiling to get everyone's attention, and then stuck two fingers in his mouth to release a shrill whistle. Suddenly the chatter stopped. He was still the Boss. A ceiling fan swirled above his head, blowing the only fresh air in the room.

"Here's a toast to the greatest foot messengers on Earth! May God bless you all." Then he crossed himself.

Was he grandstanding, a phony?

Tony's eyes welled with tears. He cleared his throat and spoke up. "As a treat, I thought we'd retrace Otto's steps, as he's Archer's senior messenger. We'll proceed down to Beaver Street, and Otto, if you don't mind (Tony winked at him), will reenact his final delivery and drop off before retiring. Otto my friend, you'll reenact your last pay phone call to me from outside 10 Beaver Street."

We raised our glasses and cheered hip hip hooray for Otto's retirement. His face blushed, but I could tell he felt proud and admired. The old warrior's thick eye lenses bounced light in diffused waves. As if on cue, the men grabbed sandwiches and drinks and marched out the room. They climbed the staircase and exited onto the sidewalk.

I was alone. I looked around the room and then spotted my portrait on the wall. I barely recognized the skinny, pale teen appearing somber and serious. Queasy, my hands shook and I needed to leave. I closed the door behind me and bounded up the stairs and exited the building.

I joined other former messengers by the sidewalk front entrance. Tony asked us to circle up and then distributed subway tokens as he'd once done. Then we strode down the block and descended into the 50th street subway entrance. I questioned the value of this ritual reenactment, but played along to honor Otto. Grown men replay famous Civil War battles after all.

Twenty of us rode an air conditioned subway car downtown to the financial district, site of many former deliveries. I discovered that tokens were no longer used to enter the turnstile, but Tony still treated us to the fare.

We surfaced from underground and dawdled, strolling past the Stock Exchange building, then Trinity Church with its grassy courtyard, and finally walked to Battery Park. People milled about, while others on lunch break bit into club sandwiches. Some read on benches facing the Liberty Statue. The Staten Island Ferry cruised out into the harbor. A row of sidewalk vendors greeted passersby. A new foot and bicycle path meandered along the waterfront past tall condos and shops. I wanted to rent a bike and explore the area after the reunion broke up.

A warm breeze skidded along the harbor, and slowed time down. We escorted Otto to his last delivery stop at 10 Beaver Street. We waited outside the twenty story office building overlooking the harbor. Tony handed Otto a plain brown envelope, an Olympic torch, to be taken inside the building lobby. Next, Otto pushed through revolving doors, completing a full circle. I thought he'd get stuck inside the narrow revolving doors. I envisioned hoisting him onto our shoulders while he made the mock phone call to Tony, checking out for the day as he'd done on a regular basis. But there were no pay phones or booths to make calls.

Soon the gathering dispersed, and we exchanged handshakes and addresses, promising to attend the next Archer reunion if planned. As we went our separate ways, my former boss Tony approached me. He looked puzzled, as if bumping into someone you never expected to see.

"You have a good time?" he said, scratching his chin.

"Sure. Why not?" I hesitated. "It was fun seeing the guys again."

We stood next to the Whitehall Street subway entrance, down by the ferry terminal. I thought he might invite me on a ferry ride to Staten Island, and almost laughed at the absurdity. Then Tony got serious.

"Didn't I fire your freakin' ass when you worked for Archer? I asked you to drop off and pick up somewhere in Queens and you wouldn't do it."

He remembered. I felt embarrassed, yet defiant at his gumption for resurrecting this. I may've been the only one fired at Archer for refusing to deliver somewhere.

"Yes, Tony. You got it right. You sent me to Bellrose or Bellmore or Bellsomething. Heard it was an unsafe area so I declined."

We stood toe to toe in silence until Tony broke the stalemate.

"Don't get me wrong. I'm glad you came today. But why?"

A pigeon landed near his foot, scavenging for scraps on the sidewalk. It almost dumped on his shoe. I noted gorgeous women strolling into the park, the weather perfect. I wanted to be clever or witty and muttered under my breath, but loud enough for Tony.

"Well Tony, I guess I'm here to make amends. To redeem myself from past transgressions."

Tony gripped my hand and squeezed. "You're forgiven, wise guy. Let bygones be bygones." He wrapped his hairy forearm around my back and whispered in my ear.

"Wanna go for a beer?" His hot breath reeked from champagne and corned beef.

"Thanks but gotta go," I said. "Thanks for a good time." I forced a smile and it came out crooked.

"No problem, pal. You're getting another invitation to our next reunion." He jabbed an index finger into my chest. Was that a mischievous smirk or was he squinting?

"Where do ya live now?"

"Oregon. I moved there years ago."

"Ah Oregon," he said, scratching his chin. "God's country. Must be beautiful with all the trees and forests."

I nodded while shifting away from him.

"Why'd ya move there? Avoiding child support?" Tony chuckled, and reached over to slap my back. "Just a joke."

"I needed to leave because I wanted change. I saw no higher calling as career foot messenger beyond summer work." Tony ignored my mild dig. Was he feigning interest for his own amusement? I didn't trust him.

"Finish college?"

"Dropped out, didn't finish. I took Sociology and Education courses, but wasn't interested in pursuing social work or teaching."

"So? What'd ya do?"

"I didn't want to drive a cab like others I knew. High burnout. Let those with useless philosophy degrees drive taxis. They can do the mental drudgery while stuck in insane traffic." I fidgeted with my shirt.

"Hmm. How'd you make a go of it? Rob a bank?"

"I took the postal test in Portland. Been delivering mail along the same route for years and it's steady and predictable without much stress." I sounded stiff.

"Better pay than messenger, much better," he said, wiping his brow.

I could tell he wanted to change the subject.

"Got a sweetheart? Married?"

"Nope. I've been working on it."

"What does that mean? Sounds like a job."

"Maybe I'll get lucky."

"Yeah, maybe you'll get lucky. You don't want to end up alone. *No* man should wind up alone. Remember that." Then he grabbed my hand.

"Good seeing ya, *Lenny*. Live a little!"

Tony swung his wide torso and walked toward the subway entrance, and then descended, the back of his head disappearing under the Whitehall station sign. Tony was gone, off to his next appointment or errand. He wasn't too unpleasant, but I was relieved to be rid of him, not quite knowing why.

A few days passed. Energized, I extended my stay and began contacting an old friend or two. I'd shaken summer blues and routine by vacationing here. I strolled across the Brooklyn Bridge on a radiant Wednesday morning, the city landscape behind me. It was dawn and the sky lit with brilliant color. A rush of cool air brushed my cheeks and hair. I loved taking this walk at this time of day, like I'd done before long ago.

Halfway across the bridge I stopped, and fell into a trance. Breathing was now easy, calm and easy. I felt light on my feet. Then transparent images, familiar ones, appeared in the river below and up in the clouds. Profiles of former romances and infatuations drifted above. I saw old girlfriends from broken relationships, ones I'd messed up without intending to. I began to mouth words of apology, vowing to do better if given another chance. I'd make it right this time.

A sensual sweetheart, Diana, hoisted a collection of love poems by Pablo Neruda, my favorite. She ripped pages at a time, releasing poems onto the bridge like confetti. She giggled and waved, urging me to lighten up and forget that I once behaved like a confused fool with a concealed heart. Her soothing voice beckoned, then another, reminding me that I was home now. Soon the enticing images and voices disappeared.

This startled me as I'd never hallucinated before. Sleep deprivation? My imagination ran amok with wild and silly but comforting distractions. I needed to focus on the real and concrete, fearing I was losing control. A crow or hawk circled overhead and squawked before diving toward the river.

The few bridge pedestrians jabbered and babbled into hand held gadgets. I closed my eyes. Next I began humming nostalgic folk tunes: *"If you need a friend, I will comfort you, like a bridge over troubled water."*

I sang louder while leaning against the steel railing. I

remained there as morning light wrapped around me from all directions.

A Very Brief Conversation on a Train

A Very Brief Conversation on a Train

Oscar and Charlotte rode the train from their Seattle home to the Canadian Rockies. They desired a simple but exotic adventure for a ten day vacation. They'd met back in college in a Physical Geography class and had enjoyed field trips to local wetlands near the university. Outside their compartment window lay an expansive meadow covered with early summer wildflowers. Sedimentary rock formations framed the landscape of eastern British Columbia.

Oscar bit into a stale bagel while onion flakes fell onto his lap. Charlotte put down her mystery novel and noticed a colorful bird resting near a glacial lake.

"I was thinking," Oscar said.

"Oh, you were?" Charlotte teased.

He did enough thinking for them both. His random ruminations lacked logic but Charlotte was a good sport and listened.

"Have you considered that some stories have an ambiguous ending and that's okay. A good story could be interpreted in many ways and go on indefinitely."

Oscar scratched his scalp.

"You're kidding," Charlotte replied, feigning surprise. "Is there something magical in that bagel? Your hands are gooey and disgusting." She handed him a tissue.

"Okay, what are *you* thinking about? I'm making a little conversation."

Charlotte pulled her auburn hair into a ponytail and secured it with a barrette. Oscar was enraptured when they'd first met, but questioned their compatibility on occasion. He suspected his desire for connection was a subtle need for approval. He knew this was an unhealthy pattern.

A Very Brief Conversation on a Train

"Thinking about? I'm fixated on bathroom shelves," said Charlotte.

Oscar knew she was planning their next home improvement project.

Charlotte smiled. "You see, we're a perfect match. One of us gets things done and the other, I'm not sure."

"Daydreaming keeps the mind from being dull and predictable."

"Keep dreaming, but meanwhile I suggest you turn and glance out the window."

Majestic glacial Rocky peaks hovered nearby. Cascading waterfalls dotted the landscape. Oscar would still be prisoner to circuitous thoughts if Charlotte hadn't roused him from inner slumber. She was concrete and got down to business and arguably did a better job living in the moment.

"Interesting cloud patterns on the horizon," said Oscar. "Note the interesting shapes. Is that an outline of a dragon or serpent?"

"Let's just watch," said Charlotte, placing a hand on his lap. "No talking, okay?"

Oscar nodded.

A few moments later, he rose and left his seat and walked to the lower deck. He stood between the cars to get a closer view of the rolling hills. The sun cast an orange streak along the horizon. The train's rocking motion and soft breeze soothed him. A half hour later, he returned to his seat. Charlotte now sat by the window.

"I love exploring new places," Oscar said. "Let's do this forever."

"Even when we're old and decrepit?" asked Charlotte.

"Yes."

Next, Oscar retrieved his backpack from the overhead

rack. Reaching inside, he removed Charlotte's surprise birthday card and also a poem he'd written earlier that morning. The poem described their two cats whooping it up on a cruise ship adventure in the South Pacific. In reality, the cats remained indoors and preferred that. A trusted friend was pet sitting while they were away.

"A present, sweetie." Oscar kissed her on the lips.

"Does having a birthday on a train meet your wildest expectations?"

"One day older and closer to death," Charlotte replied.

Then she kissed him and held his hand.

They rode on into the Rockies and approached Jasper, Alberta. Soon they'd disembark and look forward to stimulating conversation and reckless adventure together.

Fortunate Son

Fortunate Son

Ben Grossman heard his name called over the Portland airport intercom. Jarred from his funk, he liked the kind female voice paging him to go directly downstairs to meet his driver. Ben walked to the nearest courtesy phone and confirmed that he meet his driver by the main terminal exit. He hadn't requested a driver but craved any unexpected attention or surprises. Ben had flown to Denver from Portland to interview for a public relations position in a non profit agency. He'd been unemployed for months and had made it to the final round. Unfortunately, Ben didn't feel like he'd nailed the position. He'd been nervous about the interview and hadn't slept well the night before, and feared that he'd slurred or rambled on when responding.

Ben wheeled his luggage to the terminal exit while straightening his shoulders and posture pretending to be important. He knew the ride wasn't intended for him, but what the hell. He had nowhere to go but for a dull one bedroom place with no sweetheart or hot meal waiting. It could be a ride to somewhere important: A chance to meet interesting people, make new contacts, and charm impressionable women. Perhaps he'd find his future soulmate over wine and cheese and before long, they'd book a getaway adventure to a tropical island. They'd kiss and embrace under a full moon while leaning on a cruise ship railing at midnight. He'd take her in his arms, and invite his newfound sweetie below deck to a marathon session of Texas Hold'em with other passengers. The possibilities were endless if he pretended to be someone he wasn't.

It was late afternoon and Ben felt weary. His shoulders stiffened and he needed a nap to revive. Then he spotted a rotund figure holding a cardboard sign with his name printed in marker. Ben walked toward him and nodded. The limo driver, wearing a black sport jacket and cap, nodded back.

"Ben Grossman?"

"Yep."

"This way please."

The driver opened the back door of his limo, and as Ben was about to get inside a fellow about his age and height swooped in front and nudged him aside. He was slender and lean like Ben.

"Excuse me," Ben said. "I believe this is my ride."

"And who are you?" said the stranger.

"Ben Grossman. My name was paged over the airport intercom."

"How weird. I've got the same name and this is *my ride*. What're the odds this would happen Marvin?"

"You know the driver's name?"

"Of course. My dad arranged for my pick up. He told me to expect Marvin, though I've never met him before."

"Where you'd fly in from?" asked Ben.

"From Seattle. Up there on last minute business."

Ben's ride to somewhere else and beyond would not happen. He sized up the other dude and considered bribing or cajoling him to take a taxi instead. Ben wasn't sure how far he'd pursue this, knowing he was intruding.

"What an odd coincidence. Same name. Would you consider going to your destination another way, say, by taxi? And I'll ride with Marvin. I'll pay for your cab fare despite it straining my budget."

The other Ben Grossman laughed. "You're bullshitting of course. We'd end up at the same destination. I'm on my way to a family funeral and if I'm late, my dad will be upset."

"Conniptions? Just for being tardy to a funeral?"

The Second Ben glanced at his watch but was curious about this odd request.

"It's Dad's brother, my late Uncle David who suddenly died. I didn't get on with him, but David meant the world to my dad, his only sibling. And I won't disappoint family."

"I understand."

"Can't wait any longer," said the Second Ben. "Need to go now. Nice knowing you." Then he began coughing and wheezing.

"Pardon me for noticing this, but you appear pale. Are you okay?"

"No, I'm not okay," said Ben's double. "I really don't want to go to this service and would rather be home in bed resting. I feel like crap."

"Then I'll take your place," said Ben.

"That's insane. Why would you want to go? You didn't know my Uncle David or anyone in my family. Are you an odd thrill seeker or just bored?"

Ben considered admitting the real reason he wanted to go to a stranger's memorial service but settled on something else. Perhaps he'd disclose what really motivated him to his double later on.

"I've got no pressing need to return home."

The Second Ben wheezed and coughed, and bent over to catch his breath. He soon recovered and thought more about Ben's offer.

"Okay, you're on, but this is kooky. Nuts. I'll contact Dad and tell him I needed to get some medicine and that I'm running late. Meanwhile, I won't mention that you'll be filling in. I do need a little time to rest and recoup. I'm stressed delivering a eulogy praising my late Uncle, a dis-agreeable person I didn't care for."

"Your dad will know right away a stranger is delivering a eulogy about his dead brother."

"Let me think about that. Give me a minute to sort out the details. I hadn't planned on this."

"Will there be many people?" asked Ben. "I'll need to know what to say about Uncle...."

"David. No worries. I'll hand you some notes I made about his life. And being he had so few friends, hardly anyone will come."

"That's unfortunate."

"The rascal made his own bed. But I feel bad for my dad knowing that only a few will show up. I even thought of recruiting strangers to attend."

"That's bizarre, or shall we say 'unorthodox'. Why not contact your friends and invite them. Would your dad rec-ognize them?"

"Excuse me." Ben's double turned toward Marvin to apologize for the delay and promised that one or both would soon depart.

"Okay, listen up please. My Uncle David wasn't the most popular fellow around. He owed money and could be a control freak. Have you known anyone like that?"

Ben backpedaled. "Suppose I have."

"I'm only attending the funeral to please Father. Uncle had few friends and no other family."

"How sad. I'd like to help out." Ben desired to set off on a new adventure. Returning home would remind him that he was getting nowhere professionally.

"Go ahead," said the Second Ben after clearing his throat, "and attend the service pretending you're me. Stall for time. While you're doing this, I'll recruit strangers to attend the ceremony to make it look like my Uncle had personal and professional contacts. They'll pretend to be former associates or friends of my late Uncle."

Ben scratched under his chin. "You're joking. That's ridiculous."

"Dad won't be reminded that his brother was a no good philanderer and lout. He'll see that David was important, and block out the bad things and messes his brother had created."

"You shouldn't reference a family member in such negative terms, Ben. Family is all we've got sometimes. Besides, your dad must have surmised that his brother wasn't an angel."

"Family is all we've got? Is that a cliche you've dredged up?"

Ben moved toward his double and touched his shoulder. "I hope I can pull it off. What must I do?"

"Don't worry. Stand next to my dad and nod while he gives a tribute. Lower your head, blow your nose. Then give a short speech about Uncle David and highlight his benign traits and accomplishments."

"What accomplishments. For example?"

"I'll hand you notes that I've taken and embellished. I crossed out his failings and setbacks. Read these over during the ride to the funeral home and speak from your heart."

Second Ben handed a sheet of scribblings with dates, places, events and people's names. Ben took the paper and glanced at it.

"Where will you recruit others to attend the ceremony? I suggest you go home and rest instead. You look like crap to be honest."

"I'll have to bribe others to come, and promise sumptuous food after the service plus a small payment. I'll see if I actually attempt this. I know it's loony. What I really need is a breather and time to gather myself before taking over for you."

"Wouldn't your dad..."

"Hush. I said not to sweat it."

"Wouldn't Dad know these stand-ins aren't associated with his brother?"

"Dad didn't know Uncle David's business contacts or any of his few friends. Uncle was very private."

"And besides, how can I be You when Father knows I'm not you. I'm standing on the podium giving a eulogy three feet from your dad. He'll throw me out on my ass!"

Second Ben glanced at Marvin, who sat stoic behind the limo wheel. He held up a finger to signal that they'd both be hopping inside soon and on their way.

"Dad doesn't see very well anymore. Refused to undergo cataract surgery despite my urging. Wear my sport coat and trousers and he won't know the difference. Father never paid much attention to me anyway so he won't know you're not me. We look a lot alike, don't we?"

"Of course he'll know I'm not you. But what the hell. I've got nothing to return to at home."

"Good. That's the spirit."

"So, you'll contact your dad saying you'll be arriving late. And I fill in 'til you get there. Why not have someone else that your dad knows speak for you?"

"I'm under the weather and can't think straight. And frankly, no one else is prepared to speak. Are you up for this? I know it's disrespectful and odd, but as you say, 'what the hell'. I'll show up and pick up where you leave off."

"You sound hoarse. Dry throat?"

"Yeah. I may not have a voice by the time I get there."

"Where do we change clothes?" asked Ben.

"Oh, on the way to the funeral home."

"Then?"

"Marvin will drop me off along route. I'll taxi to a nice area and round up folks to attend the service. It'll make everything appear official and most important, that Uncle David was well liked."

"You need to rest up and forget about recruiting, and creating false impressions. Stop trying to protect your dad from your uncle's foibles, and besides, winning approval is an arduous and thankless task." Ben knew he was complicit to this deception, and considered bowing out.

"We'll see. You're probably right about trying to win over Father. And I'm growing weaker and feel downright lousy. Might be running a fever."

Ben clenched his teeth, knowing the outcome could turn embarrassing, but willing to risk public humiliation. He braced himself for the task, despite misgivings.

"Okay, let's do this before I change my mind." Ben handed his luggage to Marvin, who placed a suitcase in the trunk. The Grossman boys got into the back seat. Ben needed to study highlights from Uncle David's life. These were scribbled on lined note sheets written for the eulogy.

Ben changed into a black sport coat and pleated trousers. He retained his dark brown suede shoes which matched well with Second Ben's tie. He'd worn a tie for his job interview in Denver earlier that day, but preferred this one. The limo back seat was comfortable and Ben settled in as understudy for Uncle David's eulogy. Second Ben had left the limo and could be seen hailing a taxi on a main thoroughfare. Ben removed his reading glasses from his shirt pocket and studied the notes. Uncle David had torn through three stormy marriages and many jobs, having been fired often for his fiery temper and combative nature. Ben would sweeten these events into something positive, as there was no purpose denigrating a dead person at his memorial service.

Marvin, the limo driver, navigated the hills of Portland passing a spacious dog walking park and community center on Vermont Avenue. Ben needed a respite from studying his notes and decided to converse a little with Marvin.

"Been at this a while?"

"You mean driving for the company?"

"Yeah. Like it?"

"It's not bad. Good luck by the way." Marvin glanced through the rear view mirror and they locked eyes.

"I'll need it. If I'm discovered as a fraud I'll be run out of town and my already sullied reputation will take a further beating." Ben chuckled to relieve tension. Ben noted Marvin's fixed expression.

"I've worked for the Father a few times, and he's a serious man. Don't embarrass him. You better pull this off. I overheard your conversation while driving."

"No worries," said Ben with false bravado. "I'm up for this."

"Got family in the area?" asked Marvin.

"Nope. All gone. On my own for a while now."

"Finish college?"

"Finished grad school a year ago. I dropped out a while back, then traveled in Asia and eventually reenrolled."

"So no family around to attend your graduation. They'd be proud."

"No family around to attend. But that's okay. I'm relieved I muddled through my dissertation and finished."

The sun set over the West hills as the limo pulled into a circular driveway. The funeral home stood before them. There were only a few cars in the lot. Ben reached into his trousers for a tip, and handed five dollars to Marvin.

"May I assume that the fare has been paid for already?"

"Yep. Appreciate the gratuity though. Take care."

Ben shook his driver's hand and held onto it. "Thanks. But if you're not off to another job I may ask you to wait in case I need to make a quick escape. I don't want to be burned at the stake."

"I have to go. But you'll do fine. Keep the faith." Marvin tipped his cap.

"Thanks."

"By the way, I noticed a small stain on your pants. Take care of it."

Ben's bladder was bursting. He hurried from the limo clutching his notes while Marvin removed his luggage from the trunk. He'd store his suitcase in the lobby or in an adjoining room.

Ben walked to the entrance as Marvin drove away. He hoped that his namesake would soon appear and provide relief and backup.

Inside the funeral home, only a half dozen mourners faced the front while a rabbi delivered a solemn talk about life, death, and how our ethical choices impact others' lives. Candles lined the podium providing light. Ben rushed off to a bathroom and afterward, stored his luggage by the coatrack. Ben heard the rabbi discuss Uncle David's life in general terms and caught a few disjointed words of wisdom about hardship and suffering. Ben straightened the knot in his tie and brushed lint off his sport jacket with sweaty palms. His heart raced and his soaked armpits stained his dress shirt. He told himself to breathe deeply and exhale. He could see the Second Ben's dad seated next to the rabbi. Then the rabbi stepped down and Father moved behind the lectern. He was a short stout man, no taller than five foot five and had a pasty complexion. He had poor posture and appeared unsteady and weak. Ben held his rumpled notes and then was summoned to the lectern. Ben froze and couldn't move, paralyzed by an ugly flashback.

He'd been on his way to *his* father's funeral service driving alone. He decided not to attend and then turned around. He'd venture off to a Blazers playoff game instead. He'd been intent on seeing this important game against the Lakers. Besides, he hadn't written or composed anything of value to say at the ensuing service before burial. His mind drew a blank and he'd lost his voice, his feelings numb. No one would miss him if he didn't show.

Ben now felt *his* dad's presence nearby, overtaking his thoughts. *How could you have wasted that academic scholarship, Ben. All that free college money down the drain. We don't drop out or quit anything if you're a Real Grossman. Stay ahead of the curve and don't let your guard down! What's your plan? Clean up someone else's garbage as night janitor? Wax and polish the floors? You made a mess of your life, didn't you. It's a stain on our family pride and reputation.*

Ben snapped from his disturbing reverie. He heard himself summoned again to the lectern. This time, he didn't freeze, and straightened up and walked toward the stage. He was intent on making good. Ben heard Father address the scant gathering.

"Thank you for attending my late brother David's service. Before I continue, I'd like to have my son join me to honor my brother's life. Ben, you out there?"

Ben made a feeble attempt at shielding his face before stepping onto the podium. He stood next to Dad, who bowed as if praying or meditating. Ben didn't think he was recognized other than as the nephew of the deceased. He placed the notes in his coat pocket and put on bifocals to project credibility. He spotted an attractive woman in the third row who emitted a faint smile in his direction. Her stunning looks made him lose focus. Ben cleared his throat; it was his turn to address the sparse group. A large photo of Uncle David was mounted on a stand next to Ben. In the photo, David wore a tacky necktie and lavender sport coat. Uncle was bald with bushy eyebrows and wore thick lensed glasses. Ben turned toward the photo and nodded, while removing a handkerchief from his coat pocket. Meanwhile, Dad continued staring down and rocked back and forth. Ben rapped on the lectern with his knuckles to build momentum.

"I want to thank everyone who came to pay respect to David Grossman. We give tribute to his life and accomplishments. I also want to honor my father, who displayed continual dedication and loyalty to Uncle David, especially during Uncle's challenging moments. I consider myself fortunate to have a role model like my dad, a kind and compassionate person. Nonjudgmental and accepting. I'm sad that Mom could not be here with us today, but she is in spirit." Ben glanced at Dad, who now stared back. Ben's throat tightened but continued his tribute.

"Here are ways Uncle David enlightened others' lives: First,"

A coarse whisper cut Ben off. Dad craned his neck close to Ben nearly grazing his cheek.

"Who are you?"

Ben wanted to keep the flow unimpeded and continued, so he ignored the question. "First, David held a variety of positions to earn a decent living. His many employment stints show how adaptable and flexible he was at learning new trades and skills. For example,"

Again, Dad interrupted Ben, but in a louder octave.

"I said, who are you? You're not my son!"

Ben wished that his Second would magically appear with or without his coterie, and provide much needed support. Ben faced his faux father.

"I know, I know, please lower your voice and calm down. Others will hear you."

Father's pallor reflected the fluorescent stage lights from above.

"As I was saying. Where was I?" Ben stuttered and vowed to regain composure. He observed perplexed glances from the front rows. Ben focused on the attractive brunette in the third row and used her as a stationary marker to keep his equilibrium.

"We know that my uncle wasn't perfect. But who is? His three marriages prove that he wasn't afraid to commit to others and take the plunge when push comes to shove. He invested energy in work, relationships and hobbies."

"David had no hobbies other than skirt chasing." The raspy voice infiltrated Ben's consciousness. He was certain that everyone, including the rabbi, could hear Father's comment.

Ben froze again, and fixated on another chilling flashback. Ben's father's diseased heart had quit in the Intensive Care Unit. Ben leaned over his dad's shriveled lifeless torso. *You're cold and stiff, Dad. Rigid. I'll cover your whole body with this warm wool blanket, even your head. Stop? No, you're not being buried alive. Why think that? Feeling smothered? I want you comfortable, calm and serene. I do. Let's vis-*

ualize a pleasant time we've shared together. I know something
will emerge if we try hard enough.

Ben returned to reality. He stammered and opened his
mouth but nothing emerged. He removed the handkerchief from his pocket and wiped his moist brow. He
reached for a glass of water to hydrate, but there was none.
His parched throat needed fluids. Ben swallowed and
forged on. He wanted to honor someone, anyone, even a
stranger.

"As I look out, I see that we're overcome with emotion.
It is warm in here, isn't it? Would anyone else care to join
us up here and say something kind about my dear Uncle
David. Music would be nice. Can anyone lead us in
song?"

Ben saw Dad's hand ball up into a fist and prepared to
duck in case a left hook struck at his cheekbone. Then Dad
released tension in his fist and exhaled, producing a muffled sigh or whimper.

Ben spotted his double racing through the lobby and
into the small gathering hall. He was alone, and with no
entourage or following. Ben exhaled, his shift now concluded.

Second Ben dashed to the lectern, panting and out of
breath. He tried to hug Father, but dad stiffened and
withdrew.

"Sorry I'm late, but got stuck tying up loose ends. Also
got delayed in rush hour traffic."

"Where were you? Not even a phone call or message.
And who's this interloping stranger?"

"I'm Ben Grossman. Same name as your son. We
bumped into each other at the airport earlier today." Ben
removed his bifocals and began to apologize, while ex-
tending a free hand.

"That's right, Dad. We just met. And I'm late because I tried reaching Uncle David's old associates and contacts to remind them about the service. He was respected in the community."

"Hogwash, Ben. Don't give credit where none is due. You couldn't get anyone to come, could you!"

"No, Dad. Bribery and cajoling and monetary incentives didn't work. Everyone I approached thought I was nuts or that I'd exploit them. And with good reason I suppose."

"Tried bribing whom? And by the way, you don't look well. You're ashen. Got a nasty bug?"

"Sort of. Wish I'd napped and rested like I'd intended."

The attendees, including the rabbi, stepped onto the podium. Ben introduced himself to the alluring woman from the third row, and was drawn to her sweet smile and alluring eyes. He wanted to meet for coffee or lunch sometime.

Then Second Ben interceded and placed an arm around her shoulder, whispering 'sweetie.' She tensed, but smiled at Ben.

"I'm Amanda, and I must say I'm impressed with your speech and composure. You made me laugh without trying to."

"Thanks," said Ben. "Not my intention to amuse or entertain, but to fill in."

She pointed at her boyfriend, the Second Ben. "You're late. And no text, no message. I'm quite taken with this person's performance. He attempted a good deed under rough conditions."

Amanda turned toward Ben. "Care to join us for the dinner reception? I think we're heading out to a Chinese restaurant."

"Yes, I do. But I don't want to intrude any further."

Second Ben nodded. "Of course, join us. And thanks for filling in on a suicide mission. You look dapper and distinguished."

Ben smiled. "Some friendly advice I picked up: You missed the chance to take control and stay ahead of the curve. Don't let the train leave the station without being on board next time. You want your ticket punched."

"I get it."

"Oh, let it go for now." Ben patted his double on the shoulder.

Ben's cell rang and he took the call. It was from the public relations agency in Denver, the one that had interviewed Ben earlier that morning. He excused himself and took the call in the lobby. Ben wheeled his luggage while conversing long distance. Soon Ben halted and pumped his fist in the air.

After the call ended he returned to join Second Ben, his dad, and Amanda. Ben noticed Dad's facial expression softening and his demeanor more relaxed. He saw his double explain the concocted scheme and apologize for the ensuing confusion.

Dad addressed Our Ben.

"Why'd you do this? You knew I'd catch on. I was embarrassed up there."

"I'm sorry, Mr. Grossman. Instincts led me astray. I tried compensating for something left undone from before. My apologies."

"Okay, let's drop it. Still hungry?"

"Sure."

"Dinner's on me, Ben. Sorry I gave you such a hard time on the podium. I was startled, but you had good intentions. I'm not a cranky old geezer."

Ben loosened his tie and unbuttoned his soaked shirt. He'd have to swap clothes again, but not now.

"Just got good news. I begin my new PR position in a few days. My interview went better than I'd thought. A goddamn relief!"

"Why so surprised? You seem like a confident young fellow," said Dad, who patted Ben on the back.

"Get lucky on occasion. But did my homework about the organization and must have conveyed what value I could add or problems I'd solve. I was nervous as hell and thought I'd blown it. There was a question or two I didn't answer in detail."

Mr. Grossman turned toward his son and sighed. "I wish someone else showed this initiative and drive."

"Yep," said Ben. "You can't let your guard down these days. Gotta stay on top of things and be proactive. Can't rest on your laurels, gotta hustle!"

"You said you came here to compensate for something left undone? What might that be?"

"I'll tell you after a few drinks over dinner. It has something to do with someone who's no longer around. I wish we'd gotten to know each other a little more."

Mr. Grossman placed a hand on his son's shoulder, and then reached for Ben's hand.

"Congratulations. We'll go out and celebrate your good fortune, providing you stop pretending to be my son. One's already too many."